Prodigy

The Londo Chronicles, Volume 3

Patricia Simpson

Published by Patricia Simpson, 2020.

Prodigy

Patricia Simpson
Smashwords Edition
© 2020 Patricia Simpson
Lucky Publishing
United States of America

This is a work of fiction. Similarities to real people, places, or events are entirely coincidental.

PRODIGY

First edition. March 17, 2020.

Copyright © 2020 Patricia Simpson.

ISBN: 979-8215752975

Written by Patricia Simpson.

Table of Contents

Commensalism

COMMENSALISM: A relationship between two living organisms where one benefits and the other is not significantly harmed or helped. The word derives from the medieval Latin word, formed from *com-* and *mensa*, meaning "sharing a table."
—Wikipedia

Dedication

For F.F. Chopin
The poet of the piano
&
For my daughter, Camille

Chapter 1

LONDO CITY, THE ANGLO Territories—2515

Angela Beach returned from work on Wednesday to see two men dragging Citizen Dunn out of her flat. *Citizen Dunn.* Right. The alias hadn't fooled her. She had recognized the hoyden Joanna Wilder the moment she'd seen her, pale and feverish, struggling to carry a trunk into her flat. She also knew Joanna Wilder was wanted for crimes against the Overseers. And her. Gabriel Stone had turned away from Angela the day that woman had waltzed into their clinic.

And now, Joanna and a brat had moved in next door. She was most likely raising the bastard her sister had been carrying years ago, before the riot. Who knew where the real mother was. A family of sluts. That's what the Wilders were. Sluts.

Through the thin walls of the old townhouse, Angela had heard Joanna coughing all night. She was ill enough to be reported, taken away to the Central Compound and disposed of. What a stroke of luck that had been.

Angela hurried down the street. It was about time her fortunes changed. Since Gabriel had fired her, the only job she could find was washing coal, filling a position vacated by the hoyden's sister, Eva. She hated every minute of the job. But even more, she hated being forced out of Gabriel Stone's world.

And who was to blame for her fall from grace?

Joanna Wilder.

The moment Angela had recognized the woman, she had turned her in—doing her civic duty, getting her own back and qualifying for a hefty reward in one strategic move. And today was payday.

She skittered across the cobblestones to Joanna's flat.

"Citizen!" she called. "It's Angela Beach."

A slight man in a top hat ducked out of the flat. He held up a small dress. "You didn't tell us she had a kid."

For a moment, all Angela could do was gape at the agent's face. He had ugly pink scars on both sides of his mouth and blotches on his face and neck, where he had suffered other wounds that were still healing.

"Cat got your tongue, woman?"

"No, citizen, no. I'm sorry, what did you say?"

"I said, you never mentioned a kid."

"I thought the illness was enough. Is the child important?"

"Everything about a criminal is important."

Angela's heart skipped a beat. She didn't want to displease an agent of the Overseers. Her reward hung in the balance. Overseers used the slightest transgression to withhold food and favor. To ingratiate herself with the agent, she offered the only other tidbits of information she knew.

"She's probably at school, citizen. She looked old enough. She should be home any minute."

The agent peered down the street. "Well, that's good news." He glanced at Angela. "What's the kid's name?"

"I don't know. Verna or something. They just moved in."

"Hmm. Have you ever seen Gabriel Stone hanging around here?"

"The doctor?" Angela shook her head. "Of course not."

She would never betray Gabriel, even if she had seen him. Never. She loved him.

The short man shouted directions to his henchmen, ordering them to tie Joanna's hands and feet, take her to the coach and then drive the vehicle around the corner, out of sight. He ducked back into the apartment. Angela followed, worried that he was going to postpone her compensation.

"About the reward, citizen?"

The agent glanced down his broken nose at her. "What reward?"

"I was promised a reward for supplying information about the criminal."

He gave a curt laugh. "I don't handle rewards, citizen. Send an invoice to the Central Compound."

"But, citizen..."

"Out. You are interfering with a government operation." He held open the door and nodded at her to leave.

"But citizen!" she sputtered. "Might I have a receipt or something? To prove my claim?"

"I don't have time for that now." The agent slammed the door in her face.

For a moment, Angela stood on the stoop, mute with indignation. She raised her fist to pound on the door but thought better of it and let her arm drop.

She knew if she sent an invoice, the paperwork would be misplaced. She knew a reward would never arrive. That's just the way the Central Compound worked. She would have to be satisfied with the arrest of the hoyden and leave it at that.

Next time, she would insist on credits up front. And when and if she ever saw the man with the scars again, she would refuse to tell him anything.

EIGHT-YEAR-OLD VERONIQUE Dunn paused at the corner of her block, immobilized by the warning sign on her doorstep. A chill shot down the backs of her legs as she stared at the Londo City flat she shared with her mother. A black scarf lay on the doorstep of her home.

The sign of trouble.

Her mother's stern voice echoed in her head. "If you see my scarf on the doorstep, Veronique, hide. Don't come back until the scarf is gone."

A gust of wind blew Veronique's dress against her legs. The October afternoon was cold and damp and had seeped into her bones during her long walk home from school. Her toes and fingers were blocks of ice. She had looked forward to a warm fire and cup of tea.

But now this scarf.

Veronique would never dream of disobeying her mother. She and her mother lived a nomadic life full of secrets and worry. From a very young age, she had been taught not to trust anyone, not to tell anyone where she lived or what her mother did for a living. She knew she had a father, but he worked on the northern borders, doing something her mother refused to talk about. Her mother put foul-smelling paste on her hair to dye it to a mousey brown, so she looked like every other girl in Londo City. She hated that paste. And she hated looking ordinary. But her mother had insisted that she never draw attention to herself.

Worried and cold, Veronique ducked out of the street and into a nearby alley. Maybe if she waited a few minutes, the danger would pass, and she could go home. All would be well. Her mother would not explain anything, as usual. But she would hug Veronique and tell her that she was so glad she was safe and that she was a good girl. The best. Her mother's hugs and praise were wonderful. All she needed.

She would have to wait for hugs and praise, though.

If Veronique and her mother been living in their old apartment, she would have gone to her friend Jane Ulrich's house to wait out the danger. But she and her mother had recently moved, and Veronique wasn't sure where Jane lived in relation to their new flat. It would be dark soon, and she could not take the chance of being found wandering the streets after curfew. Her mother would get in trouble if that happened.

Veronique would have to bide her time alone in this unfamiliar neighborhood until the danger passed or her mother whistled for her. Her mother's whistle could carry for blocks, and was an effective, anonymous method of communication.

After an hour, the scarf was still there. Rain began to fall. Veronique hurried back to the alley, found a pile of cardboard boxes and made a tiny enclosure to huddle in. She clutched her legs and sank her chin on her knees, waiting for her mother's whistle.

The whistle never came.

IN THE MORNING WHEN she checked her street again, she saw the black scarf still there, like a dead crow lying on the doorstep. Fog rolled around Veronique's boots, as she stood at the end of her street, distraught.

"Mother, what has happened?" Veronique whispered. A sob caught in her throat. What if her mother had been taken away because of her illness? She had been sick for a week, barely able to get out of bed. People who got that sick often disappeared. Dread washed over Veronique. "What should I do, Mother?"

Cold and hungry and worried, Veronique trudged back to school. At least she would get a morning and midday meal there. Maybe her mother would come and get her at school. That had occurred a few times in the past, when they had moved to a new place without warning.

But after school, her mother was not waiting for her. And when Veronique returned to her new address, she saw the scarf still on the doorstep. A man in a greatcoat and top hat now stood at the door, tapping a cane in his hands and glaring up and down the street. He looked mean. And he was waiting for her. She could sense it.

Veronique's heart skipped a beat. She raced back to the alley and leaned against a brick building, trying not to cry. Her mother had always told her that crying never got a person anywhere. Thinking did.

She would force herself to think instead of succumbing to the panic flaring inside her.

It was clear that she would have to come back another time to search for her mother. The mean man would never let her into the flat. He might even abduct her. But she also knew that she couldn't face another freezing night in a cardboard box. Her only recourse was to try to find Jane's house. Jane would help her.

Veronique trotted down the alley and prayed she would find Jane's house before nightfall.

Chapter 2

TEN YEARS LATER—OCTOBER 2525

Veronique Dunn sensed something was wrong the instant she unlocked the gate of the churchyard.

She paused, one hand on the ancient latch and the other reaching for the knife sheathed in her boot. As she straightened, she held her breath and focused on the Pre-Reformation graveyard to her right. A strange panting sound drifted over the hush of evening and then broke off. In all the times she'd slipped through the rear door of the church, she'd never seen or heard anything out of the ordinary in the old burial ground. The place was so decrepit that even the dead had left it.

She leaned forward, trying to see through the ever-present mist that rolled along the ground, but all she could make out were vague forms of headstones and crypts. Perhaps what she'd heard was vermin scuttling through the weeds. Nothing more.

Then she heard the sound again: the odd breathing, and finally a sigh, as if someone had just relinquished a precious dream. The hairs on the back of Veronique's neck stood up and her ears began to ring.

Fog and darkness closed in on Veronique as she stood at the gate, wondering what she should do. She could run. She was good at that. Running had served her well for the past ten years. Or she could steal closer and investigate.

At this time of night, the only person who might be at the church was Citizen Carson, the rector. No one else but she and the rector had a key to get into the high-walled yard. If he were in some kind of trouble, she had no choice but to help him. She owed him. Even more, he was her friend.

Like a shadow, Veronique slipped through the gate. Her leather boots made no sound on the pavers. Her velvet cloak brushed against her thighs in silent caresses. She forced her rapid breathing to dwindle to nothingness as she crept forward, until she had gained the edge of the old graveyard. She ducked behind a crypt and peered around the corner.

There, between two tall headstones, Veronique saw a flutter of movement. She pressed against the side of the crypt and drew her cloak around her just as a kneeling figure turned to glance her way. She flattened against the stone, praying that he could not see her. Evil pulsed from the man while he scanned the darkness behind him. He had unusual reflective eyes like those of a cat, but with a gaze that glowed red instead of green. When his disturbing regard swept over the crypt, Veronique froze. Her heart thudded so violently, she worried that it would batter through her ribcage.

You do not see me. You do not see me.

Sometimes when she concentrated hard enough, she willed herself to disappear—or at least she had managed to vanish from some people's sight. Then again, maybe it had been just lucky coincidence that she had escaped notice. She could use such luck right about now.

The glowing eyes raked past her. Then the man jumped to his feet, as if startled. His face lost all color. Veronique blinked in surprise. Had she been seen after all? And if so, what was so frightening about a young woman dressed in cast-off trousers and boots? Yet the man was definitely terrified. He stood transfixed by fright, with his arms outstretched and his mouth hanging open.

Something swept past Veronique—more shadow than shape. She realized she had not been the one to frighten the intruder. Someone who had been standing directly behind her had terrified him. The shape took form and substance in front of her as a tall man in a Brandenburg coat materialized out of the swirling shadows. Veronique stared at the man, but in the darkness and with his back to her, all she could make out was the glint of his shining shoes and the flash of his gold-tipped cane.

"You!" the intruder gasped.

"Yes." The tall man strode forward.

The intruder raised his hands. "Have mercy!"

"Why."

"I was only doing my job."

"At whose bidding?"

"Moray's. Agent Neal Moray."

"Did he tell you to kill for pleasure?"

The intruder stumbled backward, tripping over a grave marked only by a hillock of weeds. "I didn't mean to!"

"A lie."

"It's the truth!" The intruder scuttled backward as the tall man pressed forward. Veronique could see a rumpled body lying on the ground nearby. "He was weaker than I guessed!"

"Stupidity as well as a lie."

"He was old. Older than allowed!" The intruder backed into a headstone, which blocked his retreat. Desperate and afraid, he hugged his arms around his scrawny chest. "Have mercy, Colonel!"

"What were you doing for Moray?" the tall man demanded.

"Looking for someone."

"Who?"

"If I tell you, will you let me go?"

"I don't bargain with murderers."

"Come on, Colonel," the intruder pleaded. "Favor for favor."

The tall man twisted his cane between his hands, and Veronique heard a clicking sound. "I repeat: who is Moray looking for?"

Terrified, the intruder eyed the cane. "A girl," he blubbered.

"Why?"

"He didn't tell me. I swear. All I know is that she might live at this address."

"At a church? I hardly think that's the case."

A chill raced down Veronique's spine. Someone was looking for a girl living in a church. It could only be her. The Overseers must have finally found her. After ten years of dodging their agents and spies, she had been found out—and just three days before her eighteenth birthday when she could no longer be arrested for being an orphan. She would have smiled at the irony if she wasn't so afraid.

"You're lying," the tall man barked.

"No! I swear! I'm telling you the truth! Everything I know!" The intruder held out his hands again. "Please—have mercy, Colonel."

"Very well."

Veronique watched in horror as the man swept up his cane and with a powerful downward thrust, plunged it into the chest of the intruder. She heard the smaller man cry out, make a queer gurgling sound, and then go silent.

"There's your mercy," the tall man declared. Then he turned.

Veronique froze a second time. She pressed against the crypt, her arm holding the cape around her head, and didn't move a muscle. Through a crack in the cloak, she watched the tall man stride back to the body on the ground and lean over it. Veronique saw two booted feet twitching as if the person on the ground was riding an imaginary bicycle. Then the boots touched at the tips and went still.

Before Veronique could make sense of what she was witnessing, she saw the tall man straighten, twist-click his cane in both hands again, and turn for the flagstone path—and her.

You do not see me. You do not see me. Dear Bob Eleven, you do not see me.

The man swept toward her. He was much taller than she was, with pale skin and dark hair cut long over his ears. But the rest of his face was lost to the darkness. As he came abreast of her, he paused. A soft scent of sage laced with pine wafted around him. Veronique didn't dare take a deep breath, even though the fragrance was more seductive than anything she had ever smelled. He turned his head to study her.

Veronique flushed. It was obvious she had not made herself invisible to this man. But she didn't lower her arm to reveal herself, afraid that he might notice that under the male clothing she wore, she was the very young lady the intruder had been looking for. Instead, she tightened her grip on her knife, in case the man with the cane decided to attack her. If she caught him by surprise and nicked him, she might have a chance to get away.

"See to your fellow citizen." His crisp baritone voice rang with authority, like that of a man accustomed to being obeyed. He had a slight accent as well, as if he had been raised outside Londo City, which was peculiar. "He is not long for this world."

To her immense relief, he resumed his forward progress and passed into the shadow cast by the crypt. And then, without so much as the slightest sound, he vanished.

Very peculiar.

Veronique's knees shook as she lowered her arm and let her cloak fall around her shoulders. The last few minutes had frightened her to the core, more than all the times she had faced danger in the streets. Clutching her knife in a trembling hand, she rushed toward the figure on the ground. The closer she got, the more certain she became that it was indeed the rector who had been attacked.

She dropped to her knees in the damp grass beside him. "Citizen Carson," she whispered. Sick with worry, she inspected his body. The rector lay on the ground as if asleep. His face was deathly white, and his lips were a strange gray color. While she was still staring at him, she saw his eyelids flutter. Hope soared in her chest.

"You're going to be all right!" she urged, reaching for his hand. She was shocked at how cold he was. His fingers were as cool and clammy as the claws of a bird. "Hold on!"

"After you," he gasped, without opening his eyes.

She clutched his lifeless hand to her breast. "What?"

"Someone. Monsters."

He validated what she had already surmised—that someone nasty named Neal Moray was after her.

"Don't speak," she urged. She could tell that the effort to talk had sapped what little energy he had left. "Save your strength!" She scrambled to her feet. "I'm going to get some help."

"Letter, Vee," he added. "Symphony."

She had received a letter from the symphony? Joy tangled with dismay streaked through her. Citizen Carson was close to death, and yet he was talking about a piece of mail. Surely, he wouldn't mention such a thing at a time like this unless the letter had something to do with the attack. The letter must have led the murderer to the church, and to the old man who had endangered his life to protect her.

But why were people after her?

She had no time to think about that, much less the Symphony Committee and her audition and what it all meant. She had to get help for Citizen Carson. Veronique yanked off her cloak and draped it over him.

"I'll be right back!" she promised. She hated to leave him, but she had no choice. He needed a doctor.

Veronique dashed across the churchyard, burst through the back door of the church, and took the stairs leading to the sanctuary two at a time. She skittered past the altar where food was distributed every Sunday, and then ran into a nearby corridor. At the end of the hallway, she spotted the gleaming glass and brass PneumoTube fastened to the wall. Next to the tube was a collection of short yellow pencils in a cup and a stack of note paper on a shelf. She'd never had occasion to send a message, but she'd seen others use a PT, so she was pretty sure she could master it.

Her hand shook as she scrawled a plea to send an emergency team as soon as possible. Then she stuffed the paper into the awaiting canister, pressed the button to create a seal, and the paper flew off to the operator at the other end. With any luck, a medical team would arrive within the hour.

Veronique dashed back out to the graveyard, hoping the rector had regained some of his body heat while draped in the warmth of her cloak. But as she hurried to his side, she couldn't help but notice that he hadn't moved. In fact, he looked eerily still. She knelt beside him again and saw that he wasn't breathing.

"Citizen Carson?" She reached out to touch his cheek and was shocked to discover his flesh was already cool with death. Desperate to find signs of life, she slid her fingers down his neck, searching for a pulse. His throat was flaccid. She pushed down the cloak, laid her hand on his chest and bent to his nose. He wasn't breathing. His chest remained still.

"No!" she cried, her heart breaking. Why would anyone want to hurt Citizen Carson? He was a harmless soul. A kind soul.

Tears welled in Veronique's eyes as she smoothed back the old man's white hair and gazed down at him. She knew it was useless to try to rouse him. He was gone. The only father figure she had ever known was gone. For a moment, she sat beside the old man in stunned disbelief.

Veronique and Citizen Carson had shared a strange table. As a child, she had spent many nights at the church listening to him play a piano. He had hidden away the instrument in a subterranean chamber made soundproof with layers of cardboard and wadded newspaper fastened to the walls. The room not only suppressed sound,, it was also the warmest chamber in the cellar. For over a year, Citizen Carson had not suspected a young girl lay against the wall in her own roll of cardboard, lulled to sleep by the music of Chopin, Mozart, and Schubert. She had listened well, and easily memorized the passages the old man played.

One night, the rector had come upon her sitting at the keyboard and picking out the melodies she had heard. Instead of chastising her for trespassing, he had sat down beside her and shown her the rudiments of music. On that evening, her life had changed forever. In three short years of evening instruction, she surpassed the old man in both technique and interpretation. And when his hands began to tremble with the onset of age, making him unable to play the pipe organ during the Distribution and endangering his livelihood, Veronique took his place at the keyboard. No one had been the wiser. No one could tell that a tall young woman in a hat had replaced the bent old man in a hat. In return, Citizen Carson paid her a small salary, enough to fool the authorities that she had parents to feed and clothe her, and that he was still capable of doing his job. No one knew that for the most part, Veronique lived in a church.

Citizen Carson had been father, teacher, and mentor to her. She would never forget him. But she would have to grieve for him later.

Veronique wiped away her tears and scrambled to her feet. Her immediate concern was for her own safety. She must gather her meager possessions and clear out. She couldn't take the chance at being discovered in the church when the emergency team arrived. She was underage, illegal, and—now more than ever because of the rector's murder and some person named Moray—on the run from the law.

Veronique left the church by a side door and headed for the nearest train station, where she wouldn't look out of place with a bag. She sat on a bench in a pool of light from a gas lamp and by habit placed the small satchel that contained her entire wardrobe between her feet, safely out of reach of thieves. Even though she was the only person on the platform, she tilted her hat to keep the pale light from illuminating her face and betraying her age. No decent young person would be out at such a late hour. For a moment, she sat in silence, struggling to marshal her senses after the harrowing events of the evening. Then she pulled the letter from inside her vest and held it in her hands for a moment before she opened it.

She had found the letter propped upon the keyboard of the hidden piano, where Citizen Carson had been certain she would find it. She turned over the envelope and looked at her name and address typed on the front.

This was the first piece of mail she had ever received. This was the first official recognition of her as a living, breathing member of Londo City. After ten years on the run since the disappearance of her mother, she had taken the chance to announce her existence by entering a musical contest. Her eighteenth birthday would arrive in just three days, and once she was eighteen, she could no longer be picked up as an orphan and spirited away by agents of the Overseers. In a matter of hours, she would become a certified adult and could finally come out of the shadows.

Still, she couldn't help but damn the arrival of the letter for causing the death of her beloved friend. Citizen Carson must have taken the envelope to the soundproof room and had been accosted by his assailant on his way back home. His last words still haunted her. He had spoken of monsters and someone pursuing her. The only monsters in Londo City that she knew of were hunger and poverty—and maybe that man with the cane who had slaughtered the killer in the garden.

Who would send someone to track her down? No one in his right mind would pursue a penniless orphan. There was nothing to gain.

Filled with grief and worry, Veronique flipped over the envelope and tore open the flap.

Chapter 3

VERONIQUE PULLED OUT a piece of cardstock and held it to the light. The uneven strokes of an overused typewriter spelled out her name, the address of the church and then a message.

CONGRATULATIONS

Your application has been accepted by the Symphony Committee. Music for your audition is enclosed. Memorization is required. Once the audition times have been determined, you will be notified by post. Please use the enclosed envelope to verify the receipt of this notice and to confirm that you are still eligible to compete in the contest. Again, you must be between the ages of eighteen and twenty-six, born in Londo City and female.

VERONIQUE REREAD THE message and then pulled out the sheet music that had been folded and tucked in the envelope. It was a Souza march. Predictable. The only tunes permitted in Londo City were marches. She scanned the score, saw nothing that was overly challenging, and then put the music in the pocket of her vest. She slumped against the back of her seat and wondered how she would respond to the Overseers without giving herself away again. She tapped a finger on her lower lip as she considered her options.

Now that the rector had been killed, she had only two choices: give up her dream of becoming a member of the Londo City Symphony or find a new mailing address. She would never give up her dream. Music was going to be her way out of poverty. She would do anything to get to the symphony audition. But the only other mailing address she could think of was the home of her friend, Jane Ulrich. Would sending mail there put Jane's family in danger? She couldn't risk it.

Before she could come up with a less threatening alternative, she saw the last train of the evening puff into the station in a cloud of steam and a screech of brakes. Quickly, Veronique returned the cardstock to its envelope and then pushed it back into the safety of her inner vest pocket. She grabbed her valise and rose. She would ride the train to the end of the line, find a place to hide for the night, and then ride back into the city at first light. She didn't have a ticket, but she didn't care. The worst that could happen was to be roused by the conductor, discovered to be a vagrant, and thrown off the train. She was accustomed to being tossed off trains.

Veronique settled into a hard seat at the back of the car, pulled her cloak around her, and used her valise as a pillow. If she didn't waste any time, she could catch a few hours of sleep before a conductor walked through the train. Sometimes at night, the conductors didn't bother to check the handful of passengers at all. Maybe tonight, she'd get lucky and remain unmolested until they arrived at the end of the line. She tucked her hands under her armpits to keep them warm and closed her eyes as the train chugged out of the station.

As she drifted into sleep, her thoughts turned back to the church and poor Citizen Carson.

With a pang, she remembered the way he had looked during his final moments of life—so white and still. Grief constricted her heart and unshed tears burned her throat, but she took a deep breath and fought off the heartbreak. She couldn't allow herself to blubber. She had to block this evening from her mind and concentrate on the future.

In the morning, as Veronique rose stiffly from her resting place behind a rubbish bin, she thought of Jane again, and she suddenly recalled the vacant apartment next to the Ulrich's. She could use that location as her temporary address, at least until the postman caught on to the error. Veronique brushed off her cloak and smoothed back her hair. Today she would go to Jane Ulrich's house and ask her to keep track of any mail delivered to the place next door. Even better, if Veronique could find a way to break into the abandoned flat, she could stay there until she was selected to be part of the symphony.

If she were as good a pianist as the rector had claimed she was, her cold, dreary nights spent huddled in corners of basements and alleyways might soon be over. The plan included a lot of "ifs" to be sure, but it was time her luck changed. She trotted back to the train station to catch the first run to the heart of Londo City.

While the crowded train chugged toward the city center, Veronique's thoughts filled with memories of her only female friend.

Jane was the one person in Londo besides Citizen Carson who knew Veronique was an orphan living on the streets. They had met in school, a place that Veronique had utilized more as a source of food and shelter than as a fount of education. Breakfast, lunch and afternoon snacks were served at school, as the majority of parents worked in the fields far from town and did not arrive to pick up their children until late in the day.

For most of the children, after school care was just another dreary part of their daily schedule. For Veronique, after school care had been a lifesaver. During her first years alone, there were many days when she had nothing to eat besides the skimpy food provided by the government. But it had been enough to survive on.

For the last ten years she had kept her unusual social status a secret, except from Citizen Carson and Jane, who had been not only perceptive but also amazingly kind to her. She had slipped her sweet treats, hand-me-downs, and even a birthday gift last year. Jane claimed Veronique was the sister she would never have, but the two girls could not have been more dissimilar.

Jane was tiny where Veronique was tall. She was mousey where Veronique was a contrast of milky skin and vibrant—although hidden—russet hair. Jane was a dutiful citizen and outstanding student, while Veronique received honorable marks only in her physical education classes. Her teachers thought Veronique was just another dull street urchin, doomed to work the land for the rest of her life, never to be chosen for marriage, never to have children or a career or a future. None of the teachers suspected that Veronique possessed a brilliant talent for music. She had to hide that part of herself from the world, just as she had to hide everything else about herself. Playing music, other than condoned governmental marches and ditties, was frowned upon as a frivolous waste of time.

Veronique sighed and leaned her head against the grimy windowpane of the train car. She didn't care how many people thought music was frivolous. It wasn't frivolous to her. And it never would be. Music was all she had. All she had *ever* had.

That afternoon, Veronique rapped on the door of the Ulrich's flat, anxious to share her good news and hoping she could keep from telling Jane about Citizen Carson. The less the Ulrich's knew about the crime, the better it would be for them should they ever be questioned by the officers of detention.

It would be difficult to keep from confiding in Jane, however. She needed to confide in someone. But she knew it would be selfish if she sought solace for herself at the expense of her friend's safety.

Jane was ecstatic about her symphony news and urged her to mail back her reply immediately. She dragged Veronique out the door, down the walk, and headed for the nearest mailbox.

"But Veronique, you also need to tell my folks," Jane grabbed the worn cambric of Veronique's sleeve and pulled her to a stop outside her townhouse. "You just have to!"

"Not in a million years." The less Jane's parents knew about her, the better. That had been her theory for the last ten years, and it had kept them safe.

"But it's such an honor. They will be so happy for you."

"I'm not telling a soul unless I get selected." Veronique walked to the wrought iron mailbox at the side of the street and placed her hand on the flat top of the cylindrical box.

Thousands of hands had done the same over the centuries. Wars had been fought, bombs had been dropped—*the* bomb had been dropped—but the mailbox had survived to stand as a testament that some things could survive the violence and stupidity of man. It was reassuring to look down at the squat mailbox and still be able to read the embossed metal letters that spelled out "Royal Mail."

Royal Mail. If all went as planned, Veronique soon might meet a royal male—or as close to royalty as her society got. The Anglo Territories no longer supported a king and queen as they had in the old days. Londo City and the outlying areas were ruled by a mysterious group called the Overseers, who had come to power after the last drop of British blue blood had been spilled during the Second Reformation five hundred years ago. That much she knew. But Veronique had no idea what the First Reformation entailed. History was no longer taught in school. History was considered useless information that no one benefited from. The Overseers were all about the cost to benefit ratio.

Now that survival was not so difficult, the Overseers had eased up a bit. The curfew had been extended. Ration tickets for meat were easier to get. Colored fabric had been introduced, as long as the color was practical—which meant dark. A weekly newspaper had even been allowed to be published.

But more importantly to Veronique, the Overseers had announced a talent search to establish a new Citizen Symphony. For the first time in hundreds of years, Londo City would host public concerts.

Veronique had jumped at the chance to apply for a symphony position. She had made the first cut, which involved the sifting through of thousands of applications and essays. She would do anything it took to get to the next step.

She slipped the gray envelope from the pocket of her violet and black striped vest and held up the letter in the late afternoon fog. A hush settled over her, as if the fog were wrapping itself around her, whispering in her ear, urging her take the future into her hands and show the world what she was made of, no matter how much her mother had told her to keep in the background and never make waves.

Her mother's warnings and worries, as well as her face, were only vague whispers now.

Veronique said a silent prayer, pressed the envelope to her full lips, and then slipped the paper through the slot. The heavy envelope slid away into darkness. Veronique watched it disappear and heard the soft plop as it landed. Then all went still and final. A thrill laced with dread washed over her.

Lately, she had become accustomed to such unsettling sensations. Ever since her seventeenth birthday a year ago, Veronique had become aware of a transformation inside her. She was losing what little patience she possessed. She couldn't concentrate and couldn't sleep. The urge to run—to physically tear through the streets—came upon her so strong sometimes that she thought she would burst. The night air seemed more piquant and the moon more seductive. Inside her roiled a wild restlessness, driving her to break away and leave her tattered childhood far behind.

Sometimes she wondered if the hunger she felt was simple sexual desire. She was of the age to want to lay with men. But she knew better than to give in to such desires. Extramarital sex was illegal and punishable by death. Unlicensed pregnancies, though rare, were ruinous—and the infants were quickly whisked away by the authorities, never to be spoken of again. Proper young ladies never spoke of sex either, even though they all wanted to experience it. Especially Veronique. But sex for the most part was something only the elite enjoyed. Most people were too malnourished and too tired to pursue such exotic pleasure.

Veronique patted the top of the mailbox and turned.

"It's done, Jane." She glanced at the row of townhouses behind her, which were dingy even in the failing light. "So that's Plan A." She brushed her hands together. "Now for Plan B." She adjusted the moth-eaten velvet cape at her shoulders.

Jane stared at her. "What's Plan B?"

"I need a dress and shoes for Plan A, so I'm applying for a job at Whites."

"You aren't serious! That's a gentleman's club!"

"So?"

"Well, it's no place for a girl!" Jane sputtered. "Not a decent one, that is. You aren't planning to turn illegal—"

"Of course not." Veronique marched down the weed-choked sidewalk. "I intend to take the piano player's job. I saw an advertisement in the paper."

"But isn't that a night job?"

"It is."

Jane caught Veronique's elbow again, and Veronique tried to ignore the flash of fear in her friend's eyes. "Do you think it's wise taking a night job? How will you get there and back?"

"I'll manage somehow."

"But it's dangerous at night in the city. Everyone says so. The curfew—"

"I know how to keep my wits about me." Veronique waved her arms wide. "Besides, look at me. I'm very tall for a female. No one ever bullies me. No one ever has." She shrugged. "So I don't think it will be a problem."

"But do you think you could do it—the job, that is?"

Veronique didn't grace the question with an answer.

"Not that you aren't a *wonderful* musician, Vee." Jane struggled to keep pace with her. "It's just what kind of music do men like that listen to?"

"I don't think they care." Veronique replied. "I'll just make it interesting. Men are visual creatures, Jane. Looking good is ninety-eight percent of the battle. Dress me up. Put some lipstick on this mug," she waved a hand near her mouth, "And I'm pretty sure I'll be fine."

"More than fine. But it could be very dangerous, Vee."

"I'm aware of that. But I will just have to take the chance. I'm not working in the fields like our parents. I'm not going down the same road as everyone else around here."

"So does that mean there's no Plan C?" Jane asked.

"If you are referring to the field work application, no. I'm never sending that in."

"But you'll miss the window! I've sent in mine. I hoped we might work together. It would make it more bearable."

"No offense, Jane, but field work isn't for me." Veronique patted her friend's shoulder as a wave of claustrophobia swept over her. The thought of toiling in the fields was like being sentenced to prison for life. "It's music or nothing."

She stopped at the gate of a townhome with a drab wreath hanging on the door. Jane's mother brought home low-grade vegetables from the fields, which she dried and wove into wreaths and wall hangings. Her pieces were the only domestic adornments most of their neighbors could afford.

Jane touched her arm. "Do you want to come in for a while? There's some porridge left."

"Thanks, but I need to head out. I'm not sure how long it will take to get to Whites. And I want to be there the moment they open." Veronique placed her hand around a spike of the fence that bordered the neglected garden at the front of the house. "Do you want to tag along?"

"My parents would kill me if I went that far from home!" Jane opened the gate beside her. The ancient hinge complained with a wail.

"Well, I have no choice." Veronique threw back her shoulders. "Wish me luck?"

"Oh, Vee!" Jane hugged her. "Be careful."

"I will." Veronique hugged her back, but stiffly. She wasn't accustomed to physical displays of affection. When people touched her, it always felt as if they were sucking something vital out of her. She preferred to keep her distance.

"I have to go." Veronique stepped out of the embrace. "I'll be back in a few days, if not sooner, to see if the Overseers have mailed the schedule. Will you be sure to check the mail next door for me?"

"Of course." Jane took a step toward the house behind her. Her troubled thoughts were plain to see on her face. "But I worry about you, Vee. It's not good to want so much. What if you don't get the position?"

"I don't know. But I'm not going to think about that. Not until I have to."

"Just remember what we were taught, Vee. '*Self-involvement and greed for fame are evils all should strive to tame.*'"

"I'm not looking for fame." As if to accuse her of lying, wind from the Thames wafted past, adding to the autumn chill. Veronique pulled her cloak around her as the cold threatened to settle into her bones. "I'm just trying to survive. On my own terms."

A second thrill raced through her, but she wasn't sure if it was in anticipation of the interview to come, her defiance of the teachings of her childhood, or just out-and-out terror at having to walk the streets alone that night.

Veronique waved good-bye to her friend and set off for the long trek to Whites.

Chapter 4

VERONIQUE BREATHED a sigh of relief when she finally arrived at the block on St. James Street where Whites was located. But she wasn't so relieved to discover her journey had ended at a high stone wall and simple black door. There was no sign of a gentleman's club on the deserted street—not that she was certain what a gentleman's club looked like. Hoping for the best, she lifted the heavy ring and rapped it against its brass plate.

As Veronique waited for a response, she checked the time on a man's pocket watch that she carried on a chain around her neck. She was shocked to discover it was seven o'clock. It had taken her two hours to walk the distance from her shabby neighborhood to this more fashionable side of town. If she got the job—*when* she got the job—she would definitely not be able to make the trip on foot every night. Precious money would have to be spent on public transportation—if there was such a thing to be had in the middle of the night.

The door opened, and a man dressed in a black suit and white shirt and tie looked her up and down as if she had fallen from the sky. "Yes?" he demanded.

"I'm looking for Whites."

"Sorry, young lady, but Whites is for gentlemen only."

"I've come about the advertisement." Nervous, she thrust the scrap of paper in front of his face. He arched backward, as if disgusted by the proximity of her hand.

"Tradesmen around back, citizen." He nodded to the left and slammed the door before she could ask anything more.

"Well! Good evening to you, too!" she said under her breath while she gave her striped vest a sharp yank. Though her feet complained, she set out down the pavement, hurrying to the end of the block and around the corner. There she found a service alley. Though the narrow passageway was dark and littered with garbage, she plunged down it until she came to a small break in the wall, spanned by an iron gate and bordered by a sandstone guardhouse.

A sour old man wearing a cap leaned out the window and glared at her.

"I'm here about a job?" Veronique held up the paper.

"Stand back," the man waved her to the side as a chugger rumbled up. The bed of the vehicle was stacked with wooden barrels. He bent to turn a crank, swearing the entire time. The gate squealed open and was pulled aside by two heavy chains. For a moment, Veronique watched the van roll forward, and then she realized this was her chance to get into Whites—perhaps her only chance. She grabbed a wooden rail of the truck bed and hung on as the chugger rolled through the gate.

"Hey!" the gatekeeper yelled, rushing out of his small enclosure. "Come back here, you!"

Veronique ignored him, dropped from the truck and dashed toward the lighted door by the open freight bay. She knew if she could just get into the building, she would have won half the battle.

She scampered down the stone stairs and slipped into the club, surprised by the cacophony of the place. She had entered a hallway near the kitchen. Dinner service was in full swing, with food frying, chefs shouting, and wait staff rushing back and forth with trays piled high with glassware and roasted meat. Veronique's stomach growled. She hadn't eaten meat for days. In fact, she hadn't eaten anything at all the entire day.

The smell of food made her feel sick, and she sank against the wall as waiters brushed past, glaring at her for being underfoot. She stumbled forward, hoping she would find the manager at the front of the house before someone threw her out the back.

Leaving the noisy kitchen behind, she hurried down a corridor and spotted a set of stairs. She climbed them, dodging waiters galloping back down with empty trays and dark looks.

"Where is that bastard!" a man growled at the top of the stairs. As Veronique gained the top step, she saw a short man with a florid complexion marching toward her at such a pace she thought he would plow right through her.

"Sir, could please direct me to the manager?" She held up the paper again.

"I *am* the manager." He pushed by her. "Rotten musicians. An untrustworthy bunch—the lot of them! This is all I need tonight!"

"Sir, I've come about the job—the piano one—"

He turned and narrowed his eyes as if he had taken notice of her for the first time. "Eh?"

"I've come about the job. I play piano, sir. If you would just give me a chance to—"

"You say you play?"

"Yes."

"You're just a girl."

She raised her chin. "I'm a young woman, sir."

He glanced down her figure as if searching for proof. "How old?"

"I'm twenty-five, sir."

"You don't look it."

She flushed, hoping he wouldn't catch her in a lie. "Okay, I'm twenty-one. Just last month."

"I thought as much." He looked down the stairs and then back at her. She didn't blink or take a breath.

"The guy that is supposed to be playing here is late again. Probably drunk again. And the owner of the club is due any minute."

"It doesn't have to be a problem, sir. I'm here, sir."

He regarded her, and she could tell he was considering her. Her heart flip-flopped.

"I don't normally employ females."

"That also won't be a problem, citizen. I play as well as any man I know." She wasn't lying, but she wasn't saying much either. Other than Citizen Carson, no one in her small circle of acquaintances owned a piano, much less played one.

"You're dressed like a bag of rags."

"In the dark, no one will notice." She had to sell herself now that she had the chance and sell herself hard. "And once they hear me play—"

"Don't flatter yourself. No one really listens. Just stay in the background. That's all that is required." The man hurried back up the stairs and waved her forward. "Do an adequate job tonight, and I might consider you. But I'm not making any promises. I prefer hiring men at Whites."

Her heart surged with joy.

"You won't be sorry, sir!"

She followed close at his heels, her lungs tight with trepidation. She had never played for a crowd before, and worried about performing for a discriminating audience. She had no way to judge her skill level, other than the praise of the old rector. Perhaps if what the manager said were true, no one would care how she played. Still, she would do her best and hope someone might appreciate her talent.

"Stick to the classics," the manager remarked over his shoulder. "I assume you know the classics. I'm talking about the old classics, not the crap that we hear from the Overseers."

"If you mean pre-Reformation composers, of course."

"Where's your music?" He glanced at her hands.

"Up here." She tapped a finger on her right temple.

He rolled his eyes and plowed forward, snaking through the crowded bar and over to a dim alcove between the bar and the dining room.

Veronique had never seen such splendor. The floor was a vast expanse of marble overlaid with lush carpets. The walls were hung with flocked wallpaper that looked like damask, and the windows were draped in heavy velvet the color of a rich red wine. Crystal chandeliers sparkled from the ceiling and reflected in the mirror behind the bar. Men in suits and shining shoes drank from expensive glassware, smoked cigars, and played at dice. Where had such men come from? She'd never seen people so finely dressed.

She guessed they were agents of the Overseers. Commissioners. She'd heard of such citizens but had never seen a member of the upper strata of society. The Anglo Territories were supposed to be a socialist republic with none of the parasitic royal overhead of the past. But obviously there was a layer of society that existed beyond her imagining.

None of the men turned to watch as she walked by. Apparently, the pianist at Whites was just another piece of furniture. Or perhaps she was too drab to be noticed in her castoff clothing and scuffed boots.

"All right. You are to play for an hour. Take a fifteen-minute break afterward, then do another hour. And so on until midnight. Got that?"

Veronique nodded, but his voice dissolved into a faint hum the moment she set eyes on the instrument she was supposed to play.

The piano at Whites was the most beautiful thing she had ever seen. Even in the darkness, she could tell that it was a work of art. It was a square grand piano, with legs carved from rosewood in a motif of vines and flowers cascading down to the claws of a lion. Above the keys was a panel decorated with dyed wood and mother-of-pearl inlaid in the shapes of hummingbirds and morning glory. The music rack was a filigree of vines surrounding a lyre that looked more like a screen of lace than a functional object. Veronique had never seen wood carved with more skillful delicacy. Every edge of the piano undulated in curves that begged to be touched.

Awestruck, Veronique sank to the bench, unable to speak.

She swept her fingertips over the top of the piano in the lightest of caresses, and then hovered her hands above the keys, almost afraid to touch the ivories but dying to hear the sound such a remarkable piece of art would make. She was no longer conscious of the portly club manager standing behind her or the cutlery clattering in the vast dining room. Nothing else existed for her but the piano and her desire to play it.

She touched the keys with her right hand, playing the first tantalizing notes of Nocturne Number 1 in B Flat, Opus 9 by Chopin. The melody flowed like honey from the piano, and Veronique felt tears scald her eyes. The sound was so exquisite and pure, she could hardly bear the sweetness. Joy blossomed inside her, sweeping her away. Closing her eyes, she succumbed to the spirit of the song, adding her left hand, then the pedals, and finally the soul inside her.

When she finished the nocturne, she breathed in and looked down at the keyboard. It took a few moments for her to realize the dining room had fallen silent. Worried, she glanced up to see a hundred white faces staring back at her. No one said a word. No one clapped. But the moment was the most empowering interlude she had ever experienced. She had brought the room to a complete standstill. Then one gentleman raised his wine goblet in salute. She gave a slight nod to him and began to play another song from her endless repertoire, born of a lonely childhood and countless hours spent in solitude in the bowels of a church.

Soon drinks began to appear, and coins were dropped in a jar on the dais. By the time midnight arrived, Veronique had slipped into a trance brought on by rapture, hunger, and too much red wine.

When she played the final notes of her last song, she slumped into silence to savor the sigh of the perfectly tuned strings. To her surprise, she heard a soft clapping behind her. Startled, Veronique swiveled on her seat to see a gentleman sitting at a table quite close to the raised platform on which she played.

He was dressed in crisp eveningwear, his collar starched to a brilliant white at his throat, his tie held in place by a diamond pin that winked in the candlelight. Veronique had never seen a diamond before. Wearing jewelry was against the law, but apparently the Adornment Code was not enforced in this establishment, or this gentleman was far too important to observe such restrictions.

The man's face was bathed in shadows, but even in the darkness she could tell that no amount of finery could offset the rough cut of his features. The candlelight jagged across his deep-set eyes, his hawked nose—which looked as if it had been broken at one time—and then disappeared at the feline rise of muscle above his mouth. He appeared to be both gentleman and barely suppressed beast, and she wasn't sure which was his true nature. Dark brown hair swept over his ears and fell across his high forehead. But all else faded to insignificance when she noticed his eyes. They were light-colored eyes—the color of rain, of ice on a river—made even more startling by the downward strokes of his sooty lashes.

"You make the piano sing," the man said. "And beautifully."

"Thank you." She took one last look at the piano, knowing the night's work was over and she would have to go back to the darkness outside. Where she would go that night was anyone's guess. The last train had run long ago.

The gentleman rose as well. Veronique glanced at him, hoping he did not intend to waylay her. She was exhausted and lightheaded, and had a long walk ahead of her.

"Allow me to introduce myself," he said, sweeping a shallow bow. "I am Brandt. Roman Brandt."

"Veronique," she answered, nodding her head. "Veronique Bishop." After the incident in the churchyard, she wasn't about to reveal her real name to anyone, especially a strange man.

"Bishop, did you say?" His gaze flashed over her again.

"Yes."

"Miss Bishop, you do my beauty justice."

She glanced at his face. It was difficult to judge his age. His eyes were an engaging blend of alertness and melancholy that hinted at a life far advanced in years. His manners spoke of years of practice as well. But his face showed no signs of aging. The line of his jaw was as taut as that of a twenty-year old, his skin as smooth, and his figure as fit as that of a young man.

As soon as he noticed her regard, he looked away, as if he didn't like being evaluated.

"This piano is yours?" she asked.

"Yes. I come here sometimes to listen to her."

"It is the most wonderful piano I have ever played!" She didn't usually gush, but she couldn't help it.

He smiled, and his pale face came alive around his glinting, hooded eyes. Before she knew it, he had stepped up to the dais with the help of a gold-tipped cane.

Veronique stared. Many men carried canes in Londo City, even gold-tipped canes. She took in the man's height and the breadth of his shoulders, as she compared him to the man in the churchyard. The dark hair was the same color and cut, but she couldn't be sure about the figure. The Brandenburg coat the Colonel had worn had been topped by a series of capes around the shoulders, which had made him appear much bulkier than the man dressed in evening clothes in front of her. But as he brushed past her, she caught the unmistakable scent of the previous night—sage mixed with pine. The hairs on the back of her neck raised, and it took all of her self-control to hide her alarm.

Brandt didn't seem to notice her reaction. He limped the few steps to the piano. "It is a G&H Barmore. Very old." He ran the fingertips of his gloved left hand along the edge in an adoring caress, much like she had done. His fingers were long and slender, and she wondered if he were a pianist, too. "Built in 1850."

"The sound it makes is unbelievable. Perhaps wood was of better quality back then. Or the craftsmanship was better."

"Everything was better then," he murmured. "But tonight, you have brought it all back to me. And I thank you for it." He turned to face her. "May I buy you a drink, Citizen Bishop?"

"Thanks, but I must be going." She gave him a quick smile and stooped for the tip jar just as the club manager bustled up behind her.

"Well, that was all right for a girl," he said, taking her elbow before she could grab the money. "I'll think it over and get back to you." He turned her toward the bar.

"That was just all right, Milton?" Brandt's voice stopped him. "It was incredible. Hire her. Hire her this instant."

Milton glanced at the man with the cane. "You can't be serious."

"Do I not look serious?"

"But she's just a girl!" Milton retorted. "Whites is not the place for females."

"There did not seem to be a problem tonight."

"That doesn't mean there won't be a problem in the future. You were here tonight. People behave when you're here." Milton reached for the jar full of coins. He poured the money into his hand and much to Veronique's dismay, slipped the tips she had earned into his trouser pocket.

"As there were no problems with the last hire for the position?" chided the man with the cane. "Where is that fellow? Passed out in an alley somewhere?"

Veronique tried to follow the conversation. Her immediate future depended upon the outcome of the conversation. But seeing her hard-won tips being denied her sapped the last of her energy. A dark wave rolled over her, narrowing her vision. The room swirled and the voices of the two men buzzed in her ears. She swayed to one side but couldn't muster the strength to right herself.

"Good Lord!" Roman exclaimed, catching her as she fell. "She's ill!"

Chapter 5

JOANNA WILDER WOKE from a nightmare, drenched in sweat. In her dream, she had forgotten something—something incredibly, terribly important. But like most of her dreams lately, she couldn't remember much detail once she gained consciousness.

The few times she had mentally surfaced, she never remained conscious for more than a few seconds.

She glanced around. She had been moved from the basement prison in Londo City to a spacious bedroom in what appeared to be a large house. It was a better prison, but a prison all the same. Sunlight poured through metal bars that covered the windowpanes, making a grid on the opposite wall.

Sunlight? She must not be in Londo City.

Where was she? How long had she been asleep?

She tried to sit up, but her body would not obey her. She tried to move her head to see the other side of the room. Her head would not move. Frightened now, she used her eyes to see as much as she could of her condition.

She lay in a bed, stuck with tubes in her arms and abdomen. Her wrists were clamped with manacles, chained to the sides of the metal bedframe. Her legs looked like they had wasted away.

A large woman with enormous breasts and a soiled apron bent over her.

"Ah, Citizen Wilder, look at you. You're awake. At last."

Where am I? Joanna demanded. But her tongue stuck to the roof of her mouth, withered and useless.

What has happened to me? She yelled with her eyes.

The large woman didn't seem to notice her distress. She smiled and stuck a thermometer into her mouth. Joanna would have spit it out if she could have. But at the moment, she could control only her eyeballs.

"Well, look at that. No fever!" the woman crowed. She stood up and shook the thermometer at her. "You'll be your old self in no time, mark my words."

Joanna wondered who that old self might be. She had no idea. Her memory was as paralyzed as her limbs.

"Time for your blood test." The nurse drew blood from Joanna's arm and stuffed the vial in a pocket of her apron. Joanna had not even felt the prick of the needle. Was her flesh dying? Terror washed over her.

"Now, let's do your exercises." The nurse picked up her left foot.

As quickly as Joanna had awakened from the nightmare, she slipped back into it.

She felt nothing. Heard nothing. There was only blackness overlaid with endless dreams.

Chapter 6

WHEN VERONIQUE CAME to at Whites, she was sitting in a chair at the table near the dais, with the florid manager glaring down at her and the man with the cane holding a cool napkin to her forehead.

"Sorry," Veronique gasped. Nausea washed over her again.

"How much have you drunk?" Brandt demanded.

"I don't know. Some."

"You should know better than to drink when more than one gentleman buys."

She closed her eyes. The man's tardy advice might be annoying but his ministrations with the cool cloth felt wonderful. "I'll keep that in mind."

"Good. If you are to survive here, Miss Bishop, you must be careful."

Before she could retort that she wasn't a complete idiot, he turned to address the manager.

"She needs food, Milton," Roman barked. "Fried food. Greasy food."

"Whites does not serve *greasy* food, sir."

"Make her eggs and bacon, then. Wheat toast. A nice big glass of milk. Whole milk. And coffee. Quickly, man."

Veronique sensed the exit of Milton and relaxed into the chair. Had someone mentioned *bacon*—that nirvana of meat she had tasted only once in her life?

"How are you faring?" the man with the cane asked. His breath puffed near her ear and his cologne wafted over her. Under normal circumstances she might have found his scent provocative and would have breathed him in with appreciation. But smells right now just made her dizzy.

"I'll be all right," she answered. "Thank you, citizen."

"Roman. I insist."

The name was more rumble than anything, especially when pronounced in his rich baritone voice.

"Roman," she murmured. His name tumbled easily through her lips, more easily than she would have liked. She didn't want to have anything to do with this man. She wanted no familiarity to spring up between them. She had seen the other side of this man—his darker side—a side that could kill someone without blinking.

She tried to pull away but was too weak.

"Am I making a scene?" She fought to bring the dining room into focus but couldn't make out anything in the gloom. "I can't afford to make a scene."

"No worries. The club has cleared for the evening."

She struggled to sit up. "I really have to go."

"You aren't going anywhere." He pressed her back down with a gentle hand. "Not until you have a decent meal. How long has it been since you've eaten?"

"Why does that matter?" she retorted. "I'm fine."

"You don't seem fine to me."

She glanced up to find his glittering gaze sweeping over her. His survey was far different than the probing gaze of Citizen Milton. Roman's regard was brisk and impersonal, as if he was assessing the state of her health, not the size of her breasts, and was not overly pleased with the results of his assessment.

Still, having the man stare at her made her uncomfortable. She pulled herself upright. "I'm fine. I really am." She laid her right forearm on the table, hoping to keep her body from slumping back to its helpless state.

"What you are is a very bad liar." He chuckled softly and sank to the chair beside her, flipping out the tails of his coat in a practiced gesture. Again, she wondered if he played the piano.

The next thing she knew, a waiter swept in with a tray of steaming food. Saliva flooded Veronique's mouth. A plate of scrambled eggs and toast swimming with butter was placed before her. Then the waiter set a rasher of bacon down, and Veronique pounced on it.

Veronique was amazed at how swiftly the food restored her, especially the crisp caramelized bacon. She would have saved half of it to savor later but didn't want Citizen Brandt to think she was a complete rube by wrapping the meat in a napkin and stuffing it in her vest. Instead, she ate every piece—all six succulent ribbons. Within minutes, her head cleared. Within a few minutes more, she was confident she could walk the two hours back to her neighborhood—maybe even run most of the distance. The strange urge to dart through the night swept over her again, pulling at her.

When she had finished every morsel on the plate, she sat back in her chair, dabbed her mouth with a napkin, and raised her glance to the gentleman's face.

He smiled. "Better?"

She nodded. "I owe you."

"Not at all. It is I who owe you for the pleasure you provided me tonight." He tipped his head with easy elegance and glanced away. The man's every move was a study in elegant restraint. She wondered if, when he kissed a woman, he would hold back as he was holding back now. She could feel a kind of humming inside him that he was obviously struggling against, as if he were bound by an invisible but finely wrought chain.

Then again, she shouldn't be wondering what it was like when such a man kissed a woman. Brandt's carnal inclinations were none of her business. She stood up and glanced around the room for Milton. He had disappeared.

"So, do I come back tomorrow?" she asked. "I am not sure where things stand."

"Yes. Come back." He pushed against the cane and got to his feet. "Six o'clock, I believe, is the time the music generally starts."

"And what about payment? Do you know if I speak to Citizen Milton about that?"

"I am certain he will have paperwork for you tomorrow."

"Then nothing tonight." She struggled to hide her disappointment, but she must not have been successful, because he chuckled again.

"You could be given an advance if you so desire. I know the owner of Whites. I'm sure he would advance you money."

"I'm not a charity case." She drew herself up. Citizens who couldn't handle their lives or finances often disappeared under mysterious circumstances. "It's just that I have no change on me for a cab. I was counting on using the tips."

"And they were well deserved. Milton was out of order." Brandt slipped his hand beneath his expertly tailored evening coat and pulled out a wallet. He slipped three bills from the leather slot, bent them between two of his long fingers and thumb, and held them out.

"But I didn't mean from you, sir."

He smiled again. "Why not?"

"It isn't right. That's your money."

"My dear young lady." He laughed, and the sound rumbled all the way into her bones. "I used to spend more on a single bottle of wine."

She stared at him and wondered how life could be so unbalanced. She had no idea where her next meal was coming from, while this gentleman could spend a fortune on drink without a second thought. Obviously, he could spare a few units. She took the money he held out, afraid that it might disappear as quickly as the coins in the tip jar.

"Thank you. I'll repay you as soon as I get paid myself."

"No need." He bowed and rose in an easy gesture. "As I said, it is I who am in your debt."

"Mine?"

"For your artistry." A shadow passed over his features. He closed his eyes, tipped his face to the ceiling and sighed, as if remembering something sweet and sad. "It is so difficult to come by. So rare these days. And so powerful."

She stared at him, finding it hard to believe a man would say such a thing, especially a man who could kill someone in a split second and then just walk away. Still, he had just verbalized what she believed herself but had never admitted to a living soul. To her, there was no greater power than music.

In fact, there were times when music could sweep her away to a magical world completely different than her dreary Londo City existence. But the ability to travel to that far-flung place was ephemeral, and sometimes she couldn't get there.

She didn't know who the master of her music was—her or a spirit much more powerful than she was. But she knew one thing for certain. She had never met another human being who understood what music meant to her. Not until this moment.

Her ears began to ring. *Danger.* This man was dangerous. With all his talk of music, his elegant manners and beautiful clothes, there was still the beast inside him. She had seen him in action. And she could feel the beast studying her.

"I must go," she blurted.

His expression shifted from melancholy to concern. "And you have no method of conveyance?"

She held up the money. "Like I said. I'm going to take a cab. Thank you for everything. And goodnight." She headed for the bar.

"It is no small feat to find a cab at this hour," he commented behind her.

She paused and slowly turned to face him.

"Allow me to have my driver take you home."

Before she could protest, he held up a hand. "I insist, Miss Bishop. It is far too dangerous for you to be out alone."

"Thanks, Citizen Brandt, but I prefer to take a cab."

She hurried out of the club, down the alley, and out to St. James Street. The road was deserted and lighted only every other block. Not a cab was in sight. Veronique hugged her arms and peered left and right as she prayed for a vehicle to appear. None showed. The abandoned streets stretched out around her, and the hush of the silent shop fronts made her feel vulnerable.

After ten long minutes, Veronique spotted a coach coming around the corner. She wondered if it might be Roman Brandt. She knew better than to take a ride with a stranger, but she also knew that waiting on the street like this was just as dangerous. The two horses clip-clopped toward her, until the vehicle rolled to a stop in front of her.

"Citizen Bishop?" The driver tipped his hat. "Citizen Brandt said you might be needing a ride," he said.

Veronique scanned the coach for occupants, but the curtains were drawn across the windows.

"Thank you, but no."

"Sure?" The driver plopped his hat back on. "He'll have my hide if I go back without doing his bidding."

"He's not in the coach?" Veronique asked. The threat of abduction and assault was certainly lessened if Roman was not waiting for her in the carriage.

"No, he's playing cards for the rest of the night." The driver slipped to the ground. "It won't be any trouble, citizen. He won't need his coach until the early hours. He told me to tell you that."

She couldn't trust anyone, least of all Roman Brandt.

"Thank you, citizen, but I think I'll walk."

Veronique turned and headed down the deserted pavement. To her dismay, the coach followed, rolling slowly behind her. For a good mile the driver dogged her heels, with the clip clop of the horses echoing behind her. She couldn't allow anyone to know where she lived or—to be more precise—where she *didn't* live. She had only one recourse. Though she didn't relish traveling the dark closes alone at night, she had to take her chances. She dashed through the first passageway she came to.

Veronique ran through the silent maze of corridors she had used hundreds of times when eluding agents of the Overseers. She could still hear their voices shouting at her to stop where she was. She had never obeyed them. She had never stopped. And she had never been caught.

An hour later, Veronique jogged up to the vacant house next to Jane's townhome. Fog hung in the air like gauze, muting all shapes and sounds. Veronique glanced around at the familiar surrounds, made unfamiliar by mist and silence. She had never been outside this late, and never would have guessed the world could be so quiet. She should have been frightened to be outside alone, but she wasn't. There was something potent about the stillness, as if the darkness held an undiscovered secret sighing behind the calm. Even so, she knew she should seek shelter as soon as possible.

Veronique retrieved her satchel from its hiding place in a window well behind a shrub. Then she walked to an all-night café a few blocks away to wait for dawn to arrive. She huddled in a stall, close to the back door and easy escape should the authorities march through, looking for people without a curfew pass and rounding up vagrants and orphans, or anyone else who wasn't a productive member of society.

She drank weak tea and searched for a place to rent in the advertisements of a cast-off newspaper. With the money Brandt had given her, she could afford to rent a room. She could finally have a place of her own. Maybe even a real bed—at least until the audition. The one thing missing was a piano to practice upon.

She had to find some way to practice or she would lose the competition. But she couldn't take the chance of returning to the basement of the church. Agents of the Overseers would be posted at the scene of the crime until the rector's death was investigated and the murderer caught. There would be no practicing in the soundproof room. She would have to use her time at Whites to perfect the audition piece. She pulled the sheet music out of her vest and played through the notes with her fingertips tapping the wooden table in front of her.

Chapter 7

NOW THAT ROMAN BRANDT felt healed enough to make social calls, he decided to stop at the medical clinic and see his old friend Gabriel Stone. While in prison, he'd heard rumors that Gabriel had disappeared and was presumed dead. Surely the rumors weren't true. A being like Gabriel was difficult to annihilate. Even Neal Moray had returned from the dead, scarred and broken, but on the mend. Most Overseers had the grace to remain in seclusion until perfectly restored. But not Moray. He'd come back after a mere eight years.

The coach turned the corner onto Chesterfield Lane. Roman spotted the clinic where he had spent countless hours working on the Commensalist Project with Gabriel. As the coach rolled to a stop at the door, Roman's hope of seeing Gabriel alive plummeted.

The once busy clinic was deserted. The lights that had been permitted to burn all night as a beacon to the ill and injured were dark and draped in cobwebs. Boards covered the windows of the cellar and ground floor. A loose shutter flapped in the breeze, banging a forlorn cadence to the thud of Roman's heart.

Gabriel would never abandon his practice like this unless he had been detained against his will or was dead. The rumors had been true.

Roman eased out of the coach, favoring his injured leg, and limped to the door. A sign was posted next to the bell.

Clinic closed until further notice.
If you have a serious illness or injury,

*contact the Health Commissioner
at the Central Compound.*

Clinic closed. Roman stared at the door in front of him, awash in disbelief. Never in all the years he'd known Gabriel had the clinic been closed. An assistant had manned the desk during the day, and another had manned it at night. Gabriel had been on call twenty-four hours a day since Roman had met him. The good doctor was definitely dead. But why? How?

Perhaps he could find a clue in Gabriel's office.

Roman slipped his clinic key into the lock and turned it. He stepped into the reception hall and glanced around. Nothing had changed in the last ten years. The same velvet and walnut furniture sat against the walls. The same receptionist's desk loomed at the end of the room. The corridor leading to the examination rooms and research lab still hung with medical education posters for patients.

Then Roman noticed something odd. Not a single surface was dusty.

He limped down the corridor. He could smell the presence of a human. A female. Middle-aged. Familiar. The odor grew stronger the closer he got to Gabriel's office. Careful not to make a sound, he approached the door and eased it open.

Roman's acute sense of hearing picked up the thunder of a racing heartbeat. Someone was hiding behind Gabriel's desk.

"You there," Roman commanded. "Come out."

Nothing.

"Come out. You are in no danger."

Nothing.

He evaluated the smell of the being, trying to recall where he had encountered it before. Then a memory came rushing back.

"Citizen Beach," he said. "It's Roman Brandt."

The heartbeat steadied.

"Come out, woman."

In a rustle of clothing and a slight grunt, Gabriel's assistant stood up from behind his desk.

"Colonel Brandt!"

"I'm back."

"I see." The woman smoothed back her hair with fluttering hands. "Sorry. I thought you were an intruder."

Roman stared at her. He couldn't believe how much Angela Beach had aged in the past ten years. She looked pinched and frail. Her wiry brown hair was streaked with gray at the temples. Her hands were red and chapped, as if she performed hard labor in the cold instead of doing office work.

"Why are you here?" Roman asked. "Isn't the clinic closed?"

She flushed and pushed up her spectacles. "I come here to clean. To keep it just the way Dr. Stone liked it."

"Isn't he dead?"

"Not to me. I won't believe he's dead until his body is found. I refused to go to his funeral, too."

"There was a funeral?"

"You should have seen the people crying in the streets." Her eyes shone with pride and her own unshed tears. "He was a wonderful man. Wonderful."

"He was."

"And if he comes back, I want him to know that I kept everything in order. Pristine as always. For him."

Roman glanced around the man's office. Not a paper was out of place, not a folder left open. Not a book unshelved. Not like Gabriel at all.

"So tell me, Citizen Beach. What happened?"

She shrugged. "Apparently, Dr. Stone told his...the other...uh... assistant that he was going to Port Pennwood."

"Why?"

"We don't know." The woman shrugged again. "You know how Dr. Stone is. So busy. Never an extra word for anyone. Never sharing his personal goings on. I would have helped him. Gone with him. He needed only to ask."

The earnest look in her eyes blazed too brightly. There was something not quite right about the woman. Actually, now that he recalled, there had always been an air of fanaticism about her. Her gaze had trailed after Gabriel as if glued to the man. He wouldn't have been able to abide such adoration.

"Had he been there before? To Port Pennwood?"

"Yes. To quell an uprising there. That's what I heard."

"Uprising?"

"Someone freed the prisoners headed to the Norsea work camps. Rumor has it, that it was that woman again." Her mouth ticked. She pressed a fist to her lips, trying to conceal the tick from him.

"Joanna Wilder?"

"The very one. Dr. Stone's life was never the same after that hoyden started interfering."

"I see." Roman walked to the desk and pulled out the chair, forcing Angela Beach to skitter out of the way. "I am going to have a look through Dr. Stone's things. You may show yourself out."

"Colonel?"

"If I locate Dr. Stone, I will be sure to mention your efforts here."

"I would be grateful, Colonel. I really would."

"Until then, you should look for another place to clean in your spare time. I doubt you are being compensated."

"I don't mind doing it for free. I really don't. Not for Dr. Stone."

"It isn't safe. And it isn't a proper use of your time. Goodnight, citizen."

At the dismissal, a shadow passed through her eyes. Roman turned away from her stony expression, hoping if he ignored her that she would leave.

He pulled open the top desk drawer.

NEAL MORAY TUCKED THE newly published newspaper under his arm and opened the door to his apartment at the Central Compound. The paper was a horrific rag sheet, someone's feeble attempt at local news, but at least it was a bona fide newspaper. The Overseers were finally allowing the printed word to be published—mainly due to his arguments that a newspaper could be a great propaganda tool. For once, the council had listened to him.

That was real progress. He kissed the newspaper and set it aside for later. *Progress.* He sucked in a deep breath of satisfaction. For the first time since he'd come back to Port Pennwood ten years ago—almost dead but still breathing—he felt hopeful. He was not only healing and would soon become his former glorious self, he would also triumph politically, once he healed Silas. Londo City would finally learn that he wasn't to be ignored—ever.

Gabriel and those Wilder sisters hadn't been able to kill him. Too bad the same wasn't true for them. Gabriel had been turned to dust at the base of a cliff. Eva had left the Anglo Territories. And Joanna was in a living hell, a prisoner of an illness that had ravaged her body and mind.

He could leave her a prisoner forever, he supposed. She deserved what she got. But he wasn't a *monster.* In fact, she should be grateful to him.

The only reason Joanna was still alive was because of him. Neal Moray. Well, that and electricity—which was forbidden, but who was to know? He had tucked Joanna away in the middle of nowhere with a solar-powered generator and bank of batteries to keep her alive. And no one the wiser.

It was amazing what machinery a person could find in derelict warehouses on the wharves. His men had discovered boxes full of brand-new medical devices in perfect condition. And he knew how to operate them. Such equipment had been his specialty in the old days. All they needed was to be plugged in. That's where the generator came in.

Neal smiled and turned to unlock the mailbox next to his door. The monthly shipment was due, and he was anxious to see if any progress had been made on that front.

Ah, there was the familiar package, done up in brown paper and string, waiting for him. How many boxes had there been? Twelve per year for ten years, minus the time Joanna had languished in his cellar. That would make it around one hundred packages.

Maybe the one-hundredth time would be the charm?

He unwrapped the box, put aside the note and lifted the vial from its jar of melting ice. Maybe this time, Joanna's blood would be back to normal, able to heal his lesions, and in turn, Silas' disease. Maybe his fortunes were on an upward swing at last.

He would give Joanna one more year to improve or to tell him where to find her daughter. If she failed to deliver, he would kill her. And that day was going to be like Christmas. Not the crappy C-Day they celebrated around here. A real celebration. Trinkets. Rich food. Wine. The works. His newly evolving physical body could actually digest small amounts of food these days. He appreciated his new varied diet.

The downside was not having decent toilet paper. All they produced in Londo City was something called Gayetty's Medicated Paper. Terrible stuff. But that's what newspapers were for. Shitting and newspapers had always gone hand in hand, so to speak.

Chuckling at his own humor, he carried the vial of blood to his bathroom and unbuttoned his shirt, enough to expose his right shoulder. Holding his breath so he wouldn't have to smell the stench of Joanna Wilder, he spread some of her blood over the red lesion on his back. In Port Pennwood, he had discovered the amazing healing properties of Joanna's blood. But since her bout of fever, her blood had become ineffective.

Still, with each shipment of her blood, he applied some to the rash on his back, to see if her special trait had returned. So far, it hadn't.

While he waited for the blood to dry, he returned to the box and picked up the progress report that accompanied the shipment.

He scanned the message. Joanna Wilder had awakened. Finally. Her blood still showed a high white blood cell count, too high to use probably. Dammit.

Neal crumpled the note in his hand. There was always the child. If and when he ever located her. Or if and when he could squeeze the information out of Joanna as to the child's whereabouts.

He had all the time in the world to dally with Joanna, except for the pernicious rash that had bloomed on his back and could be healed only by Joanna's special blood.

But he didn't wish to wait. He'd always been an impatient kind of guy. He liked that about himself, actually.

No one would ever accuse Neal Moray of laziness or of wasting time. Nicola Tesla and Edison were well known for the limited amount of sleep they survived on and for their unswerving dedication to work. One day, he, too, would be celebrated for his genius and focus. Just like them. Famous.

He smiled as he scribbled a reply to the private nurse that he had employed to take care of his long-term prisoner.

When she wakes up again, show her the items in the box I gave you. Make her look at them.

Do anything you can to stir her memory. I will visit as soon as I can.

—NM

Without waiting until morning, he addressed the message and popped it into the PneumoTube at the top of the stairs. Then he returned to his rooms to get ready to go out for the evening. The goon he had sent to the church to look for the girl had never come back with a report of his findings. That meant he was probably dead.

Neal would make some inquiries tonight. The rabble horde might know what had happened at the church. And then on to Whites to rub shoulders with the cream of Londo City society.

Of which, he was soon to be. He smiled again.

Oh, happy day.

Chapter 8

AT A FEW MINUTES TO six that evening, Veronique rushed to the bathroom near the kitchen at Whites, hoping to make herself presentable after her long walk. She yanked a dingy white blouse out of her satchel and slipped it over her head. Then she brushed through her long tresses, hoping no one would notice that she was in dire need of a bath or that the red roots of her hair were showing along her hairline. She pulled back her hair, knotted it at the nape of her neck, and glanced at the mirror to get a better look.

Her appearance took a turn for the worse when the real color of her hair, a rich mahogany, began to show through the mousy brown dye. She would just have to pray that no one would notice the roots. Her mother had insisted on disguising the true color of her hair to match the drab appearance of the rest of the populace, always adamant that Veronique blend in with her surrounds. She'd been so insistent about it, that Veronique had continued the practice long after her mother had died.

Veronique turned her head right and left and inspected the knot of hair that bobbed above her collar. The severe style made her appear older. But the dyed hair surrounding her ivory face accentuated her haggard features. She grimaced at her reflection. It was important that she conceal not only her youth, but also her fatigue. No gentleman would want to look at a worn-out drab. She dug in the depths of her purse for the pot of rouge Jane had given to her on her birthday. She rubbed some on her cheeks and dabbed more on her lips. Still, she looked wan and worn out.

She'd had quite a day, running all over Londo searching for a room to rent. The task hadn't been as easy as she had assumed. Added to the challenge was the limited amount of money she had available to bargain with. She'd ended up renting a furnished garret on the third floor of a dilapidated Edwardian next to an abandoned church. The graveyard was as close to a garden as she was going to get, and the stairs would be a challenge on the days when she was bone-tired from walking the streets of Londo City. But at least the room wasn't in a dark and gloomy basement, and the view of the crumbling spire and stained-glass windows of the church was a welcome change of pace as far as Veronique was concerned. Plus, it was hers. A thrill of accomplishment spiked through her.

Thanks to Roman Brandt, she had a place to go back to, a place where no one could prod her with a night stick and tell her to move on—a place where she wouldn't wake up covered by dew, with her joints aching and her toes numb. Her heart caught in her throat. She had her own space. From this moment on, her life could only get better.

At one minute to six, Veronique took a deep breath, threw back her shoulders and marched out of the toilet, carrying her satchel. The bar was mostly empty as she walked toward the piano. But by seven, the bar and the restaurant had filled to capacity. Veronique played Chopin all evening, interspersed with Mozart and Liszt. Throughout the night, she looked for Roman Brandt, but did not see him. The dining room, however, was nearly as dark as the bar, so he could have been there, sitting in the crowd, unseen.

As the night wore on, she felt more and more disappointed when Brandt did not show. But it was for the best. Even though he was a fellow music lover, he was dangerous. She had to remember that.

Veronique waited until her last set was over, emptied the tip jar, and then searched out Citizen Milton. He hadn't spoken to her the entire night. Either he was careless with paperwork or was merely using her to fill in the gap of male musicians. She had to know if she had a job or not, and how and when she would be paid. She found Milton in the bar, sitting in the corner in the shadows, tallying receipts. A glass of frothy beer sat near his hand. When she walked up to him, he looked at up her without so much as a smile.

"Excuse me," she began. "Citizen Milton?"

"Yes?"

"Do you have a moment?"

"Only a moment, Citizen Bishop."

She held out a hand toward the hallway that led to the rear of the house. "May I speak to you privately?"

He managed to look down his nose at her, even though he was sitting and she was standing. "This is as good as any place."

The bartender leaned over the gleaming wooden bar. "May I get you a drink, miss?" he asked. He was middle-aged, with curly brown hair and a sad but friendly face.

Veronique hadn't forgotten the events of the previous evening and hadn't drunk more than one glass of wine. She smiled at the bartender. "Do you have tea, sir?"

"Coming right up."

"Your problem?" Milton put in, briskly. "I don't have all night, Bishop."

Milton had a talent for making her feel insignificant and unwanted. Still, she guessed that he wouldn't like being confronted about the job any more than she looked forward to asking him about it.

She put a hand on the bar and faced him, with her back to the dwindling crowd. "I would like to know if I have the job, sir."

"The job?" He stopped going through the receipts and looked up at her. His little eyes flared.

"Yes. The job. It's been two nights, citizen. I have commitments."

"You think two nights is enough to prove that you're dependable?" His glare burned her, and then he stared out at the men still enjoying their cigars and cognac. "Or that my patrons have any interest in watching you play? You're rag-tag, Citizen Bishop. Nothing but a cur."

She flushed at his derisive comment. "I may not be the height of fashion, but I am dependable. You can count on me."

"I'm not interested in doing all the paperwork unless I consider you a sure thing. In fact, I'm still not certain you are right for Whites. Look at the state of you."

Veronique froze, worried that Citizen Milton might use a legal technicality to withhold the tiny salary she had coming to her. She raised her chin.

"I can improve my appearance. Especially if I am paid what is rightfully mine."

He threw a sharp glance at her. "I don't like your tone much either. That's got to improve if you think you're going to work for me." He held out his hand. "The tips this evening?"

Her heart sank. "But I—"

"All tips are communal at Whites, Citizen Bishop." He shook his hand. "Hand them over."

She had no choice but to fish out the coins and deposit them on the table next to the receipts. She kept two slugs back, which was money she had brought with her to pay for a ride back to her flat.

Milton jabbed the air with his hand. "All of it, girl."

"But this money is mine."

He stared up at her with his cruel watery eyes. "Do you think me a fool?"

"It's my taxi fare!"

"I don't care what it is. It's tips. You got it from the tip jar. I know you did. So, hand it over."

Flushing with outrage, she slapped the two coins on the table.

"But what about last night?" she countered. "Am I to have a share in the tips from yesterday?"

"You're not an employee. Last night was an audition."

"A six-hour audition? I hardly think that's the case, sir."

Milton's face grew more florid the more she contradicted him. He planted both his fists on the table. "Citizen Bishop, do not presume to tell me my business!"

She stood her ground. "But sir, I deserve to be compensated for my work."

"And as an employer, I deserve to be afforded respect! If you cannot abide by the rules of employ at Whites, Citizen Bishop, then you should not expect to be paid at all! Get out! And don't come back!"

"You aren't paying me?" she gasped. She needed money to get home, now that he had taken everything, even her last couple of coins.

"Pay you?" he retorted. "I should report you to the Overseers!" He scraped the coins into his hand. "You have played fast and loose with a cornerstone of Londo!"

"But—"

"Count yourself lucky that I am letting you go and keeping my mouth shut," he added. "You could be fined for not observing the rules of employment."

"But, sir, you never employed me. You can't threaten me with that!"

"Off with you, girl, before I change my mind!"

She stared at him, outraged that he was not only denying her a share of the tips she had earned, but was throwing her out without paying her for two nights of work. Worse, she had rent to think about now. She had counted on keeping this job at Whites, in case she didn't win a seat in the Citizen Symphony. She couldn't believe he was throwing her out.

He stuffed the coins in his vest pocket and snatched up the larger stack of receipts. Then he shot a glare at her. "What are you waiting for?" he barked. "Want me to call the officers of detention?"

"Oh!" she cried. Anger tangled all rebuttals in her throat. "You are a terrible man!" was the only thing she managed to blurt.

He sneered at her and returned to his work. His dismissal and her helplessness in the situation seared through her. But other than jumping on top of the man and tearing at his hair, which was what she wanted to do, she had no recourse but to leave.

Shattered, Veronique hurried down the stairs, past the kitchen and out the back of Whites. Not until she felt the first rush of wind, did she realize she had left her cloak and satchel stashed beside the piano. She glanced at the lights of the building behind her but knew she couldn't return for her things. Milton would never let her back into the bar.

Veronique clutched her arms to her chest and strode toward the gatehouse. She would have to run toward the new flat until she could no longer feel the cold. Though she hated to admit it, Jane had been right. She never should have considered working at Whites.

Once she made it through the gate and out to the street, she calmed herself by stuffing down her emotions with practical concerns, just as she always did. She would have to concentrate on remembering how to get to the new address and get there safely. She would also need to keep her mind on her surroundings, and not allow her thoughts to dwell on the last frustrating minutes at Whites.

Veronique jogged down the littered alley, scanning the shadowed doorways and rubbish bins. Ahead of her, a gas lamp lit up the fog rolling between the buildings on the main street. It was as if she were running toward a gray, slow-moving river. Just as she turned the corner to walk along the high wall surrounding Whites, she saw two men push away from the sandstone blocks and turn toward her, their long coats flapping in the breeze and their pale faces glowing in the fog. It appeared they had been waiting for her.

Veronique's breath caught in her chest as a new and more frightening chill raced over her skin. Fog lent objects and people more mystery than they actually possessed. She was accustomed to the tricks played by the ever-present Londo mist. But this was different. She could sense danger in the two men. In fact, she could feel evil emanating from them, just as she had sensed evil pulsing from the man who had killed Citizen Carson. She paused, bracing her muscles for a dash back to Whites.

"Citizen!" one of the men called. His voice echoed in the mist.

Veronique took a step backward. Her heart thumped in her chest.

"A moment!" the other called, chuckling. They ambled toward her, their canes and the heels of their evening slippers clicking on the pavement. Their coats flapped around their slender frames, and she could see the crisp lines of their clothing. These dandies were not ruffians off the street. They had probably been smoking cigars at Whites only moments ago. They had probably been watching her play.

A sixth sense told Veronique to run. She plunged back toward the alley, praying for speed to outrun the two men. She would rather take her chances with Milton than these two.

Fear and adrenaline roared through her, thundering in her ears as she dashed for the gatehouse. She could hear the men clatter after her down the dark hallway. But all too soon, she heard the puff of their breath behind her. She couldn't believe how quickly they had closed the distance between them. Gasping in fright, Veronique splashed through a puddle and stumbled forward, just as one of them caught her by the arm.

"Veronique!" he called. "Why do you run from us, sweet?" His voice was warm and musical, but the sound sent terror spiking through her.

She yanked backward, trying to break free, but he only laughed.

"Let me go!" she demanded. She hit him in the chest with a fist. "This instant!"

"Careful now!" the second gentleman commented. "Don't ruin those hands of yours."

"You play divinely, Miss Bishop," her captor purred as he inspected her face. "Almost preternaturally divinely."

She stared up at him. The man was pale in the dim light, and his eyes glittered at her with unfriendly humor. But what caught her attention most was his full mouth. His lips were plump and crimson, as if the bulk of his life force centered on his mouth, lending him a most provocative expression. She felt the seductive pull of that expression, which was almost as strong as her fear of him.

"Who was your tutor, eh, Miss Bishop?" his companion asked. Before she knew it, he reached down and grabbed her free hand. She had not even noticed the movement. The more the gentlemen spoke, the slower her reactions and thought processes became, as if honey had been poured over her mind. She tried to pull her hand away, but the man held her fast. She watched in disgusted fascination as he raised her hand to his mouth and kissed the back of it. His lips felt odd—as cool as the marble features of a statue—but sensual at the same time. She felt a flutter of sexual desire twist inside her. The reaction confounded her. Still, she had lost the power to draw away.

"Let me go!" she gasped. The effort of speaking was almost more than she could muster.

The man smiled, squeezed her fingers and slowly released her hand. "We know someone who would love to meet you, Veronique. Come with us."

She shook her head. Something told her that she would never be the same if she went anywhere with these two gentlemen.

Nica. Nica. Nica.

The breeze seemed to whisper her name—the name someone had called her long ago in a life that was now just a fragment of a memory. The fog seeped into her thoughts and clouded her judgment. She took a step toward the man who had kissed her hand.

"Come. We insist." The man with the provocative mouth bent close to her face. His breath fanned over her throat. Odd, but she had ceased to feel the chill of the autumn night. It was if the two men had numbed her to all but their enchanting voices. She felt her will slipping, drifting up and away, and into the rolling fog.

Then, out of the darkness came the clatter of hooves and the crack of a whip. Somewhere in the distance of her muddled thoughts, she heard a third man shout her name. An instant later, she felt the sigh of a breeze lifting the tendrils of her hair. Something fluttered at her ears, brushing the sides of her face, releasing her.

Suddenly she was standing alone in the alley, blinking back to consciousness, while a familiar figure in a top hat and cloak jumped from a coach and limped toward her.

Chapter 9

"MISS BISHOP!" ROMAN Brandt called. "Are you all right?"

She nodded. She had never been happier to see another human being in her entire life. Her first thought was to rush forward, fling her arms around him, and hold on until her heart stopped thumping. But her second thought was to stay where she was. Roman Brandt was not the type of man she should fling herself upon.

She hugged her arms instead.

He looked down his broken nose at her and gave her a slow and critical survey as she rubbed the backs of her arms.

"They did no harm?" he asked.

"Just scared me." She glanced around the alley, amazed that two men could vanish so quickly.

"Did they touch you in any way?"

"One grabbed my arm. And kissed my hand. That's all."

"Good." He slipped out of his greatcoat. Then, without asking permission, he draped it over her shoulders. A cloud of his savory cologne settled around her, and this time she breathed it in with appreciation. She grabbed the lapels of the huge coat to gather it more closely around her and glanced up at him.

He was dressed in evening wear again, with a top hat banded by black satin that glinted in the dim light, a bowtie at his starched color, and an ivory waistcoat whose low curve set off the slenderness of his torso. His coat and trousers were a soft black color, his shoes impeccably polished. But his expensive wardrobe could not disguise the coiled threat he presented.

His shoulders were much wider than the dandies he had frightened away, his frame much more imposing. He looked like a man who appreciated being clean but didn't mind getting dirty. He looked like a man who could kill with his bare hands. No wonder her assailants had scattered.

Veronique was glad to have a man like Brandt on her side. She'd never had a man stick up for her like this. She had never met her father. Because of her height and her secret social status, she never had a boyfriend either. Citizen Milton had been a great teacher, but in all other ways he had been a meek personality.

She couldn't recall a single incident when a man had fussed over her. That Brandt worried about her safety warmed her even more than his heavy woolen coat.

Still, she couldn't trust him.

"Miss Bishop, you must not walk the streets alone at night. No exceptions."

"I didn't have a choice."

"It is far too dangerous. Anything would have been preferable."

"I couldn't help it. I didn't have money for a cab."

"What happened to the advance I gave to you?"

"I used it for rent."

"And the tips from tonight?"

"Milton took them again."

"Unacceptable," he said, taking her elbow. His hold on her arm both alarmed and aroused Veronique and sent a sharp thrill spiking through her. She should have pulled away, but she didn't break the connection. His grip spoke plainly to her: he was there to support her and protect her but would release her immediately if she wished. Though he concerned her on many levels, she chose to remain connected to him.

"The man needs to be taught a lesson in decency," Roman added. He wore black gloves that made his slender fingers appear even longer than she remembered. "Come with me."

He led her to the coach, where the driver waited at the door to help her inside.

Veronique paused, torn by her distrust of Roman and the fatigue that dragged her down. She knew the most prudent recourse would be to thank Roman for saving her and then face the two-hour walk back to her garret. But she was bone tired. Her late night, busy day, lack of sleep and the frightening run-in with the two dandies had sapped the final dregs of her strength. The last thing she wanted to do was trudge two hours to her new address and then climb three flights of stairs.

As she mulled over her options, she spotted a woman sitting in the coach. Her fears ratcheted down a notch. Perhaps Roman wasn't the man from the graveyard after all. Perhaps she had misjudged him. He might simply be a wealthy man out for the evening with his lady friend. Not dangerous at all. Not a murderer. Maybe even a gentleman. He had certainly proved his gallantry by coming to her rescue.

For once in her life, Veronique decided to put her distrust aside. She allowed the driver to guide her up the step and into the coach. There she settled into the nearest corner and glanced at the lady across from her as Roman sat down beside her.

The woman was dressed entirely in red-violet—from her tiny high-button boots to the satin dress pressed tight against her torso by a beaded bustier, all the way up to the dotted netting draped from a hat slanted over her brown hair.

The woman's wine-colored splendor made Veronique feel more drab than ever. She pulled the coat close, hoping the woman couldn't see the frayed velvet trim of her skirt and the scuffs on her shoes.

"What have we here?" the woman asked. Her husky voice was round with amusement.

"The newest employee at Whites," Roman sat down beside the woman. "And a very talented one at that."

"Talented?" the woman drawled. She propped one elbow in a gloved hand and drew on the longest cigarette Veronique had ever seen.

Veronique struggled not to gape at her. A woman was smoking. And inside a coach. She had never heard of such a breach of manners.

A plume of smoke streamed out of the woman's red lips as her gaze darted over Veronique's face and figure, assessing her mercilessly. "In what capacity, pray tell?"

"Piano player," Veronique put in before the woman could make too many assumptions. "But—"

"Ruby, this is Veronique Bishop." Roman tapped his cane on the roof of the coach to signal their departure. "Miss Bishop, Ruby Valentine."

Ruby Valentine? He had to be joking. The name sounded as if it belonged to a prostitute, not a well-bred woman. But as usual, Veronique held her tongue. She leaned forward and shook the hand of the other woman.

"I am pleased to meet you," she said.

"Enchanté as well," Ruby purred. Her painted mouth lifted without displaying any teeth. The expression was more tick than smile. Then she laid claim to Brandt by lowering her hand to his thigh while she stared through her cigarette smoke at Veronique.

Veronique got the message. She sat back against the cushions of the coach, disappointed that Brandt had a female companion, especially one so flamboyant. Then again, she should have known such a man would have no shortage of women. She had assumed, however, that his taste in females would have been more refined.

"I am trying to impress upon Veronique the fact that she should not be walking the streets alone," Roman commented.

"As well she should not. Streetwalking should be left to professionals." The woman laughed and took another long drag on the cigarette.

Veronique had never met such a person. Her clothing, behavior, and choice of words all seemed selected for shock value. But the strangest aspect of her appearance was the way the woman looked at her. Her gaze was predatory, flat, and under all the laughing, humorless. She shifted the coat even closer.

The woman continued the interview. "You aren't a *professional* piano-player, are you?"

Before Veronique could reply—or perhaps because she looked taken aback—the woman laughed again.

"Roman prefers amateurs, you know. He can't resist a fledgling piano-player, can you, darling?"

Roman appeared to be put off by the question. He frowned and glanced at Veronique. "What is your address, Miss Bishop?"

"I'm not sure," Veronique fumbled with the edge of the coat, enough to find the pocket of her vest. She pulled out the shred of newspaper and handed it to Roman. "Can you read the address? It's for the new place I just rented today."

Roman nodded and held the scrap of paper to the lamp set between the windows of the coach. Then he gave it back to her.

"I'm taking you home. And tomorrow, you will take a cab, Miss Bishop."

"There won't be a tomorrow, sir."

"And why not?" His stare drilled into her.

"Milton fired me."

"He fired you?"

"Yes. Without paying me anything for my time."

"Outrageous." Roman's frown deepened. Then he glanced up. "But for the best."

"Not for me."

"Playing your beautiful music in public will only lead to trouble."

His compliment made her flush, which prompted a chuckle from the lady in red.

"You see?" She took a drag on her cigarette. "My parents never liked my line of work either, Miss Bishop. But a girl has to do what a girl has to do. It's in the blood, wouldn't you say, Roman?"

He ignored her prattle and turned to bark their new destination into the speaking tube. The coach lurched to a start. Roman directed his attention back to Veronique. "You are aware of the opinion of musicians these days, are you not, Miss Bishop?"

"Of course," Veronique replied. "We're the lowest of the low. Chopin and me?" She tilted her head. "We will drag you into the gutter with our decadent music—without exception."

Ruby laughed. Roman smiled and shook his head.

Veronique didn't find anything amusing about the laws regarding music. Because of the Overseers, music was a dying art form. Popular music was prohibited. Only a few places with special dispensation, such as Whites, were allowed to offer music to their clientele, and only certain classics could be played. Children were punished for humming. A person couldn't even stand on a street corner and play for coins. Songs were no longer recorded and sold. She wondered if anyone even *wrote* new music anymore.

To prohibit human beings from expressing themselves in melody was like her teachers not allowing her to think for herself. It was senseless and limiting. Veronique remembered a scrap of dogma from her school days that still made her angry.

Words in song can steer you wrong.

Words in song could start revolutions—that's what they could do. The Overseers must be worried about the people rising up against them again if they had to prohibit simple songs from being sung.

One thing gave her hope, however: the formation of the Citizen Symphony. Perhaps she would see the dawn of a new day for the citizens of Londo City and with it, forge a career for herself. If she were chosen, she would dedicate her life to using music to open up the hearts and souls of people, and fight for the right to play the classics in public again. But she wasn't about to tell anyone of her secret dream, not until she had aced her audition.

As if Roman had read her mind, he said, "I've heard rumors that the Overseers are forming a Citizen Symphony. I've been out of town for a while, though. Out of touch."

"It isn't a rumor," Veronique replied.

"Really? It seems an odd move."

"Maybe they are finally coming to their senses."

Roman sat back, and the movement cast his expressive face in shadow. "I would not trust in that sentiment, Miss Bishop. I'm not sure what the Overseers are up to. Not just yet. But I can't believe it's in the best interests of the public."

His comment chilled her. She was glad she hadn't mentioned her audition, for she was certain he would have something negative to say about it. The last thing she needed was more negativity.

"I don't see a downside to a symphony," she countered.

"Even so, please take my advice, Miss Bishop, and keep your talent to yourself."

"That's easy for you to say." Veronique rolled her eyes. "I bet you make a decent living and have a warm house and plenty to eat."

Ruby took a long drag on her cigarette and gazed at Roman with smoldering eyes.

"If you need a job so badly, I could help you procure one." Roman switched his cane to his right hand. "Something that isn't so dangerous. And if you wish to continue your musical education, I would be honored to pay for a tutor for you. In fact, I am willing to speak to your mother or father, if you think it would help."

She flushed at the offer, and then realized what his plans entailed—taking her home and speaking to parents that didn't exist. Until her birthday tomorrow, she could still be rounded up as an orphan. She didn't know what was worse: admitting to Brandt that she was underage or allowing him to see the deprived conditions in which she lived. She could imagine Ruby Valentine would take one look at the new room and laugh in disbelief that anyone would put up with such shabby surrounds. Veronique didn't want Ruby Valentine coming anywhere near her living space.

Or near Roman Brandt, if she were honest.

"Thank you," she finally replied. "But there's no need for you to intervene on my behalf. I get along just fine on my own."

Brandt placed a gloved palm over the handle of his cane. "I'm sure you do."

The sarcastic edge of his words was not lost on her.

As the coach rolled through the quiet streets of Londo, Veronique glared at the fog, searching her mind for a way to escape gracefully from the coach. She scanned the cityscape for familiar landmarks. Everything looked so different in the dark that she worried she wouldn't be able to recognize the new neighborhood. But then she caught sight of the spire of the abandoned church. Before Roman could stop her, she called out her thanks and jumped from the carriage.

She landed on the cobblestones and took only a moment to gain her balance. Then she dashed down the street and cut through the graveyard to save time. She hoped the bulky gravestones would conceal her from view, enough to allow her to slip into the mansion and get up the stairs before Roman could find her, if he chose to pursue her. He didn't know what unit she had rented, and she doubted he would be so impolite as to knock on anyone's door at this time of night in pursuit of her. If she could get up the three flights of stairs before he found her, she might escape him. Valuable time ticked away as she struggled with the unfamiliar lock at the back of the building. She finally wiggled the key just enough to turn the tumblers and push through the door.

Veronique galloped up the staircase that turned and grew narrower as it ascended to the third floor. At the top of the stairs, she paused to catch her breath and glance down the hall at unit 27, her unit. She still couldn't believe she had a home. A safe haven.

Ears ringing from the exertion of her run, she pushed the key in the lock, opened the door, and slipped in.

In the instant it took her eyes to adjust to the darkness, she realized how wrong her last thought had been. Out of the shadows of her so-called safe haven stepped two men. Their eyes glowed red, like the man in the churchyard. She froze, struck motionless with terror, sure the men were more agents of the Overseers, sent to capture her.

Before she could force her shocked limbs to move, the men rushed toward her, hissing and spitting like wild animals. They grabbed her arms and pulled her out of the flat and toward the stairs. She lashed out at them and kicked at their knees, refusing to be taken without a fight.

"Let me go!" she shouted. She wasn't a criminal, and she wasn't a child who could be snatched off the streets. They had no right to manhandle her like this. She writhed, doing everything in her power to keep from being dragged away.

The shorter one laughed, displaying unusually pointed teeth. Veronique dug in her heels and tried to catch hold of the rail just as Roman appeared at the top of the stairs.

The taller of the men growled. Veronique stared at him in surprise. The agents of the Overseers could be rough and intolerant.

But they had never sounded like animals. What kind of men were these two?

"Let go of that woman!" Roman demanded.

"She's ours." The taller man hissed. "We found her first!"

"Let her go!" Roman took his cane in both hands and shifted it with a smart click. In that instant, Veronique knew that Roman Brandt and the colonel of the graveyard were one and the same. Her blood ran cold.

Veronique saw a metal point slide out of the end of his cane. In the blink of an eye, he had turned the ornate walking stick into a deadly weapon. "Now!"

"It's two against one, Brandt," the tall man growled. "Didn't you learn your lesson the other day?"

"Apparently he's a slow learner," the smaller man put in. "Wants us to break something else. Eh, Brandt?"

Before Veronique could make sense of their puzzling words, the men fell upon Roman. He struck out with the cane, but his assailant deflected it with his forearm. Veronique watched, frozen in place. She'd seen a few fights in the streets, but never anything like this. These men moved with astounding speed and power, as if they had springs in their boots. They jumped on Roman, the first on his chest, the second on his back, while Roman staggered to the side, knocking one of them senseless against the wall. Soon all were rolled down the stairs to the landing, where they battled for dominance. Roman's cane flew out of his hand in the fall, and Veronique plunged down the steps to retrieve it.

Just as she rose up, she saw Roman lift one of the men and hurl him into the stairwell. She couldn't believe anyone could be that strong. But in throwing the man off the landing, Roman left his torso unprotected. An eerie warning tone rang in Veronique's ears, and she glimpsed the flash of a blade in the taller man's hand. He dove for Roman. She had no time to think, only to react. She lunged forward, whipping out the cane in front of her. Blade met flesh as Roman's assailant impaled himself on the shaft of the cane.

For a moment everyone stared. The man with a cane through his chest stared in shock that a woman had just run him through. Roman stared in outright astonishment. And Veronique stared hardest of all. She was sure she had just killed a man. But there was no blood from the horrendous wound. In fact, as she stood there clutching the cane and wondering how long she would have the strength to hold on, she watched Roman's attacker wither like a wad of paper thrown on a fire and then crumble to flakes of ash at the hem of her skirt.

"What the Name of Wanda?" Veronique gasped.

"My God!" Roman exclaimed. "You killed him!"

"But what just happened?" Veronique pointed at the ash on the ground. "He just—dissolved."

Roman ignored the question. Maybe he didn't have an explanation. He leaned over the stair rail. "The other one's gone. Good."

Veronique gaped at Roman. "He survived a three-story fall?"

"Apparently that one did." Roman glanced at her face and then looked away as he tucked in his shirt, a gesture that struck her as far too casual after what had just transpired.

Things were not normal here. Roman behaved as if the last few minutes had been a simple brawl. But she was not a fool. Normal human beings could not fight like that. Normal human beings didn't turn to dust when they were stabbed through the heart. And her ears still rang.

"Get your things," Roman commanded. "Quickly."

Veronique obeyed him without asking questions. She would save those for later. For now, it was important to get far away from this flat in case someone came back. She stuffed sheets of music into her vest and slipped the few trinkets she had collected over the years into the pocket she'd sewn into the hem of her skirt.

Roman had clumped halfway down the stairs by the time Veronique locked the door of the garret. She followed her tall companion down the stairs and out to the coach. The driver opened the door without a second glance, as if he were accustomed to his master collecting young women from tattered garrets—or perhaps that was the natural deportment of any discreet driver. Never having owned a coach, much less a hired driver, Veronique had no way of knowing.

Roman guided Veronique into the coach and then stepped into the cab. His weight jiggled the vehicle. He sat down and raked her with an annoyed glance.

"I told you to collect your things," he said.

"I did."

He inspected her again. "You aren't going back there. It's too dangerous."

Not about to admit to him that she possessed next to nothing, Veronique raised her chin. "I have what I need."

"Do you?" he retorted. "Most young ladies have more than one outfit to their name."

"I am not most young ladies."

"That I am beginning to believe."

She thought she heard amusement in his voice. How could the man laugh when he'd just been attacked, and she had killed someone? She glanced at the empty seat on the opposite side and was alarmed to discover Ruby Valentine was nowhere in sight.

"Where's Citizen Valentine?" she asked, glancing at Roman.

He shrugged. "She comes and goes. It is nothing to be concerned about."

"But that creep might be around," Veronique countered.

"Ruby can handle herself, I assure you." With a tap of his cane upon the roof, he signaled the driver to continue onward. Roman sat back. "It's you I am concerned about."

Veronique flushed and hoped the darkness hid her reaction.

"Why do you think those men were after you?" he asked.

She shrugged and struggled to come up with an explanation that would convince herself as well as Brandt that the attacks had nothing to do with her. "I have no idea."

"You never saw them before?"

"No. Never."

"They seemed to know you." He scowled. "What about those men in the alley?"

Veronique leaned forward. "I didn't know them, either."

"Two random attacks in a single evening?" Brandt purred. "I find that difficult to believe."

"I find it difficult to believe as well."

"And there's no reason for someone to be after you?" His cool eyes bore into her. "Tell me the truth, Miss Bishop."

"I am!"

"You are not."

"I am."

"I can see that you are hiding something, that you are upset."

"Of course I'm upset. I just killed someone!"

She glared at him, worrying what he might see in the darkness. She was in such a state of shock that she couldn't concentrate. Her thoughts kept returning to the moment she had impaled the man with Roman's cane. She had killed a man. And he had dissolved. *She had killed someone.* Her head spun.

"Miss Bishop."

Roman's voice tugged at her consciousness.

"Miss Bishop."

She struggled to turn her attention to him but couldn't break from the violent tableau playing in her thoughts.

A gloved hand encircled her wrist. "Miss Bishop, do not torment yourself." His fingers tightened around her arm, compelling her to come into the present.

She turned to stare at Roman. His face materialized before her as if he were stepping through a bank of fog. His light eyes shone through the mist like beacons as his gaze fastened on hers.

Just as before when he looked at her with more than a passing glance, he drew her toward him. She knew her body still sat on the seat opposite him, but her spirit flowed toward her male companion like smoke to an open window. She blinked, tearing away from the memory of the incident in the stairwell as she succumbed to Roman's gaze.

She heard music—it sounded like Debussy. The haunting melody transported her to a woodland full of flowers and birds. Somewhere in the distance she heard a woman laughing in delight. Where was she? And how could she know what a wooded glen looked like? She'd never been in a forest. Her jumbled thoughts plowed into one another, piling up on themselves and merging into nothingness, until her mind became as clear as the brook that gurgled at her feet. All was calm. Her spirit quieted. Nothing could trouble her in the woodland.

Roman's grip eased on her wrist. "Miss Bishop?"

She slipped from his grasp. "Yes?"

"Are you all right now?"

She broke from his stare. "Yes. I'm fine. I—"

"You must stop thinking about the man."

"But I killed him," she replied. Her voice drifted in a dreamy cadence. It sounded as if someone other than herself were speaking. "I must turn myself in."

"You will do nothing of the kind." Roman leaned forward. "Do you hear me, Miss Bishop?"

His voice hummed in her head as the music swelled around her, seducing her again.

"You will not go to the authorities. And you will not bother yourself about that person. You will cease to think of him. He is nothing. He is dirt."

Some of the things Roman said did not sound right, but she couldn't quite pinpoint what bothered her. She wanted to argue with him, but his voice held a strange power over her. She couldn't form a complete thought.

"Do you understand, Miss Bishop?" he added.

She nodded.

"Tell me that you understand."

"I understand."

"I understand, *Roman*."

"I understand, Roman." When she said his name, she fastened her stare upon his mouth. The act of speaking his name was much like a kiss. She said his name a second time and was overcome with the desire to kiss him—to feel his lips on hers as she murmured his name again and again and again. She pushed against the cushion of the seat, intent on closing the distance between them.

His gaze slanted off her face. The music cut off. The lushness vanished. She snapped to attention as if she had just been pushed through a door into the freezing cold.

For a moment, she couldn't remember where she was. Then she saw the cane in Roman's hands, and she recalled that two agents had grabbed her, and that she could never return to the flat she had rented. She would have to go back to living on the streets, with no Citizen Carson this time to help her, and no church to hide in.

She shot a glance at Roman. He sat in the shadows, his face impassive as ever, his gaze unfocused on the world outside as if nothing out of the ordinary had passed between them.

Veronique needed to think. She needed to come up with a place Roman could take her. The only friend she had in Londo was Jane. She couldn't ask Jane's family to take her in. Their two-room flat was crowded as it was. Where could she go? Whom could she turn to?

"You obviously can't stay at that flat," Brandt put in, as if he had read her mind again. "Is there a place I can take you? Relatives? Friends?"

Veronique's heart twisted in her chest. To admit that she had nowhere to go was never easy and was never more difficult than at this moment. She usually lied about her living situation. But for some reason, the lie died on her tongue. She could only shake her head, mute. She expected him to grill her about not having a family, because it was such an unusual occurrence these days. But he didn't quiz her. He simply crossed his gloved hands over the top of his cane.

"Very well. Then I'll take you to my townhouse for the time being."

"Yours?" She glanced at him again. "But sir!"

He let his gray eyes meet hers for a moment, and for a moment all she was conscious of was his intense regard, as if she were gazing into a pool of the cleanest, iciest water. She felt the pull of his regard. In fact, she had difficulty remembering what she had just said to him. For the second time that evening, she longed to sink into his muscular chest and press desperate kisses on his mouth. But Roman broke off the gaze again before the fantasy could play out.

Not seeming to read her thoughts this time, he tightened his grip on the handle of cane. "I will hear no protests, Veronique. You will be safe with me. And in the morning, I will make some inquiries. I know someone who might be able to explain these attacks."

She nodded. For the time being, she had no choice but to let him take her to his home. It seemed no matter where she tried to hide, she would be found out and assaulted. At least with Roman, she had someone to help her fight off her assailants. Still, she must be on her guard. Roman might have saved her life twice this evening, but he had killed that man in the graveyard. And he didn't know she was the single witness to his crime. She aimed to keep it that way.

Chapter 10

A HALF-HOUR LATER, the coach pulled up in front of Roman's townhouse. With all her senses on alert, Veronique followed him up the walk and short flight of stairs to the massive front door. She was either walking into a refuge or a prison, and soon she would know if she had been a fool to put her trust in Roman.

Deftly, he unlocked the door and waved her through. She waited in the hush of his house as he turned and locked the door behind them. In a daze, she watched Roman slip the key in his pocket and pivot to face her. She should have felt trapped. She should be planning her next move, in case he attacked her. Instead, she did nothing as a wave of relief surged over her, washing away her fears.

She felt *safe*. The unusual feeling astounded her and confounded her at the same time.

Roman reached for a knob near the front door and turned up the lamps to reveal a house more spectacular than Veronique thought possible. The rising light transformed the décor from monochromatic shadows to midnight blues and moss greens glinting with silver accents. The luxurious hush of Roman's home spoke of substantial wealth, stability and good taste, but also of an absent master. All the furniture was draped with white sheets. He had mentioned that he'd been away. But where would a gentleman like Roman go? Only dangerous wilderness lay beyond Londo City.

"Come this way," he commanded. He headed for the wide staircase that led to the upper floors.

Awed at her surrounds, Veronique trailed after him up the stairs, her hand on the polished banister as she took in all that she could see from her vantage point on the staircase.

His house was dark—dark wood, dark drapery, and dark carpets on the polished oak floors. Even the paintings on the walls were rich expanses of color. From what she could tell from the metal tags on the frames, he favored artists of the early 1800s—Gericault, Goya, and Turner—paintings that featured ships, horses, and scenes alive with action.

At the landing of the stairs hung a stunning canvas at least six feet tall of a young Prussian soldier in full regalia, one arm akimbo at his saber, the other holding a pair of gloves, and the haughtiest of expressions on his ruddy face. On either side of the huge painting were smaller works of horses, dogs, and landscapes.

Veronique hoped she would have a chance to study each one of the paintings, and discover their provenance, as she was sure they held clues to the character of the man climbing the stairs ahead of her. She had to admit that Roman interested her. Fascinated her, in fact.

Roman led her to a room at the top of the staircase, and barely seemed winded as he crossed the carpet toward the bed. Always wary, Veronique paused just inside the threshold as an older woman appeared in the doorway of the chamber.

"Ah," Roman turned. "Mrs. Fernside."

Veronique was relieved to discover she was not the only female in the house.

"Good evening, sir." The old woman smoothed back her gray hair, which had been braided for bed hours before. She was a small, wiry woman with the worried expression so common among older Londo citizens, as if she were fearful of advancing age. No one lived past seventy these days, and Mrs. Fernside seemed to be dangerously close to that number. She had pulled a gray flannel robe over her white night dress, but she still looked chilled in the cavernous room.

"May I be of assistance, sir?" she asked.

"This is Veronique Bishop, an employee of Whites. She was attacked by ruffians this evening and had no place to go."

"Attacked?" Mrs. Fernside bustled into the room. "Oh, dear!"

"Miss Bishop needs a bath, Mrs. Fernside, and a bed to sleep in. And please have someone come up and build a fire."

"But sir, where will you sleep?"

"I'll use my old quarters at the back of the house."

"But they haven't been prepared. Or aired."

"It will be all right. You can see to it tomorrow. It is Miss Bishop who is in dire need of rest, not I."

"I shall see to her at once then." Mrs. Fernside swept out of the chamber, and within moments, a sleepy young maid stumbled into the room carrying a stack of sheets and coverlets. After her came a young man lugging a scuttle brimming with coal. They appeared to be sister and brother, with their matching brown hair and dimples. Veronique felt sorry that they had been dragged from their beds to wait on her, but she wouldn't be sorry for a fire. She was chilled to the bone.

"I will get you something strong to drink." Roman said, walking back to the door. "Will you be all right alone, Miss Bishop?"

Veronique nodded. "Thank you." He obviously didn't count the young servants as companionship for her.

The maid bustled around the bed, stripping the white sheet that protected the mattress. She couldn't have been more than twelve years old, and looked asleep on her feet.

Veronique turned to help her.

"Please, citizen," the maid said, straightening. "Mrs. Fernside will have my hide if she catches you helping me."

"Sorry," Veronique backed away in surprise. She must have violated an unspoken rule between master and servant. But how could she be expected to know such things? She'd never had a servant. In fact, she'd never heard of anyone employing servants before.

Out of her league, Veronique stood in the center of the room and felt useless and out of place. When Roman strode back into the room, the young maid ducked out of the chamber.

Veronique watched Roman cross the floor and was surprised to see his limp had transformed to an almost imperceptible hitch. Perhaps what she was seeing was just a trick of the flickering light, for surely a man couldn't recover from a limp in a single day, especially after having tumbled down a flight of stairs during a brawl.

Roman held out a glass filled with dark brown ale topped with white foam.

"This will restore you," he said, handing it to her. "Drink it down."

"Thank you."

She drank the chilled brew as she watched Roman check each window to make sure they were locked. She wasn't accustomed to drinking ale—or any alcohol for that matter—but the cold beverage settled her nerves, just as Roman had said it would. After he was satisfied with the security of the bedchamber, he turned to face her.

"Will you be all right sleeping in here?" he asked. "The room hasn't been aired for a while."

Veronique glanced at the huge canopied bed with the fluffy white pillows and crisp sheets bleached to a snowy white, topped by an indigo coverlet. Would she be all right? She almost laughed out loud. She had never beheld such an inviting bed, let alone slept in one.

"It'll be fine," she replied. "More than fine."

"Good. I have business to attend to, so I must leave now. If you need anything, just pull this," he indicated a strip of embroidered cloth that hung near the bed. A tassel at the end glinted in the lamplight. "One of my staff will respond."

"Thank you, Mr. Brandt. Really—I can't thank you enough."

He didn't smile. He seemed perturbed, and she wondered if he didn't appreciate having a woman in his subdued, masculine home. His draped furnishings certainly weren't ready for guests. Perhaps he had travel plans that she had interrupted. His hooded eyes seemed more shadowed than ever as he shot a brusque glance over her. He looked as if he were evaluating her shabby clothing for vermin. Then his gaze landed on her hem of her skirt and her scuffed boots. He remained looking at them for so long, she almost shuffled her feet to hide them under her skirt.

Then his startling eyes flashed to her face. "Promise me that you will remain here until I return. And that you will not go back to that flat. It isn't safe."

"Okay, but as to the flat," she began, with the questions about the attack still in the forefront of her mind. "Who *were* those men tonight? They seemed to know you."

"Many men know me." He scowled again. "From Whites."

"But what kind of men were they? They seemed so—"

He cut her off with an impatient sweep of his hand. "I have no time for questions now, Miss Bishop." He walked past her. "I shall speak to you when I return. Good evening."

With that curt dismissal, he strode out of the bedchamber and closed the door behind him. Veronique watched him go, taken aback by his gruff behavior. He was obviously upset by her presence in his home or by her questions—or both. His chilled manner made it perfectly clear that she wasn't welcome.

Veronique made a vow that as soon as she could, she would put Mr. Brandt's frowns and finery far behind her and make her own way in the world again.

Mrs. Fernside bustled in a few moments later with a bowl of broth, cold meat and buttered bread. While the housekeeper started the bath, Veronique wolfed down the food, and was surprised at how ravenous she was.

Mrs. Fernside crossed the room to the door but turned as she opened it. Veronique noticed her out of the corner of her eye and glanced up from her nearly demolished dinner.

"Do take your bath before the water runs cold, dear."

"I will," Veronique said around a mouthful of bread. "Thank you."

Veronique's thoughts swirled as she washed her underclothes in the sink, hung them to dry, and then stepped into the tub. She had never taken a bath in a real bathtub. The prospect of bathing in the porcelain tub took her mind off the difficulties of the last two days. She eased into the water and stroked the warm lip of the tub, awed at how smooth and white it was, like the shoulder of a goddess.

As she relaxed into the steaming water, her troubled thoughts eased. She closed her eyes. She remembered Mr. Brandt's beautiful grand piano at Whites. She held up her hands and played one of her favorite pieces with her fingers tapping the air—imagining that she sat at that wonderful piano and was playing a Rachmaninoff etude for the Symphony Committee. Rachmaninoff was the most challenging composer ever, and she loved his music above all others. But then again, the Overseers had instructed that she should play the Souza march. She ran through the much simpler music, silently practicing it so it would stick in her mind.

JOANNA WILDER CAME awake, awash in sweat again. She had forgotten something so important that her heart banged with trepidation. What had she forgotten? What could she not remember? Had she failed to act in some way? Was a deadline approaching that she could not recall? What haunted her so deeply?

Or was this a new phase of her illness, one in which her heart would eventually stop beating?

She tried to move, but her body would not obey her. She panted, choking on claustrophobia and desperation. She could see her nurse dozing on a cot beside her bed, an empty wineglass still in her hand.

Joanna fought the desire to shut her eyes. If she shut her eyes, she would succumb to darkness and dreams again. Determined to cling to consciousness this time, she started to count under her breath.

One, two, three...

Blackness. And then a dream about a cake. A tiny cake with a candle on it, flickering. She heard laughter. A child giggling and clapping. Then the candle burst into flame, igniting the cake and the air around it. People started screaming. She could hear the thunder of a great blaze all round. Panic streaked through her, clamping down upon her chest and squeezing hard. She ran through a tunnel, fighting for breath, knowing if she could just get to the end of the passage, she would be safe. Someone would help her. She pushed through the viscous air of the tunnel, her feet like lead weights, her lungs bursting.

Then blackness.

VERONIQUE DIDN'T REMEMBER getting out of the bath. She didn't remember walking to the bed to slip under the voluminous covers. All she remembered was hearing a noise by the side of the bed and waking up to discover Mrs. Fernside laying out clothes on a nearby chair.

"There you are, Citizen Bishop," the old woman said softly, "Mr. Brandt has returned and requests that you meet him in the dining room at your earliest convenience."

Veronique rose on an elbow and blinked, surprised to see it was still quite dark in the room, but the fire had burned down in the grate. The timing seemed off.

Regardless of the puzzling time of day, she was certain of the actual date. Her birthday had arrived. She was eighteen years old today. She had successfully evaded the Overseers for ten long years, and her running days were over. A wave of joy and relief washed over her, but she kept her emotional reaction to herself, schooling her features to reveal nothing, as she had learned to do over the years.

"What time is it?" She sat all the way up.

"Seven, Miss Bishop."

The hour surprised her. She felt unusually rested after only a few hours of sleep. Maybe it was because of the luxurious bed. Sleeping in a cloud had been a new experience for her, and one she hoped to repeat.

"Mr. Brandt sent up some clothing for you," Mrs. Fernside said as she arranged a gown on a chair near the bed. "If you wish, I will have the clothes you were wearing yesterday laundered."

"That would be wonderful. Thank you." Veronique slipped out of bed, still wearing the flannel robe she had found folded up and tied with a ribbon in the bathroom, awaiting a female guest.

She wondered how often Brandt entertained women. Probably all the time. The thought disappointed her, even though she knew she shouldn't care what his social life involved.

She surveyed the clothing Brandt had sent up for her and was surprised that a man would have possessed such a sensitive eye. The gown was made of light blue silk that had a ruched ruffle at the low neckline, down the bodice, and at the hem of the split skirt. She was sure the startling color would set off her white skin and pink lips. But she had never worn, much less touched, such a fine garment. When she picked up the gown, she discovered a set of leather leggings and a pair of delicate boots that would lace all the way up her shins. Delighted, Veronique turned to Mrs. Fernside.

"This is so beautiful!" She held up the garment in both hands.

"Mr. Brandt likes beautiful things."

"But I couldn't possibly wear it!" She gaped at the dress, dying to know what it would look like when worn. "It is far too colorful to be allowed. Surely!"

"It is what the master asks you to wear."

"I suppose I don't have a choice then." Veronique smiled, happy that she had no recourse but to put on the clothes. "I wouldn't want to insult Mr. Brandt, not after he's been so kind to me." She gathered the dress close, snatched up the undergarments and boots, and hurried to the bathroom, eager to see what she might look like in the clothing of a fashionable lady. Being able to merely put on such a gown was the finest birthday gift she had ever received. She would indulge herself just this one day.

A half-hour later, Veronique stepped through the doorway of the dining room and held her breath for the instant it took for Roman to realize she was there. He turned.

Chapter 11

ROMAN STOOD NEAR THE fire, holding a book open on his palm, and when he looked up, his eyes changed from serious concentration to guarded appreciation. For a moment, Veronique felt like a queen basking in the glow of his regard. And for a moment, his gaze drank her in—from her upswept hair to the fitted waistline of the gown, and down to the smart and perfectly-sized boots. Then, as always, he caught himself and broke off his gaze.

"The gown suits you," he remarked, shutting the book with a soft plop.

"It's beautiful!" Veronique stepped forward, feeling socially presentable for the first time in ten years. "See how it catches the light!" Holding out the skirts on both sides, she pivoted, her spirits lighter than she could ever remember. Even a street urchin like her knew the gown was overly fine for a morning dress, but she didn't care. She was sure she looked lovely, and she couldn't hide her delight.

He threw a sidelong glance at her antics, as if he were trying to ignore her display but couldn't resist looking at her. A half-smile tugged at his mouth.

"And I can't believe how it fits!" she added.

"Over the years I have become a good judge of the female physiognomy."

"But the color, sir." She stopped twirling. "Are you not concerned the Overseers might fine you?"

"The Overseers be damned," Brandt replied. "I do what I like in the confines of my own home."

"Citizen Brandt!"

"And you may express yourself with equal freedom here, Veronique, without consequence."

She stared at him. No one she had ever met had uttered such blasphemy. All citizens of Londo lived in fear and respect of the Overseers and their strict moral code. To defy them meant a stiff fine—or worse—removal to the Norsea work camps. When a person was shipped to the work camps, they were never heard from again.

"You stare, Veronique."

"I have never heard anyone say such a thing."

"The Overseers are not the end all, be all. One day their power will pass. One day people will have to think for themselves again. Why not start now?"

"Because you could get in serious trouble!"

"Serious trouble is letting someone run your life," Roman lifted a green bottle from a glass bucket on a side table. He poured bubbly liquid into a tall flute. "Champagne?" He held out the glass.

She glanced at the flute. "I've never had champagne."

"But do you want it?"

"I believe I would!" She smiled and reached for the glass. While he poured a second drink, she took a sip of the golden effervescence. She tried to affect a casual air, and pretend she was not completely impressed by the man and his environment, but she could not keep from grinning like a ninny when the sparkling wine tickled her nose.

"Well?" Roman asked.

She raised her eyebrows, not sure if he was asking about her plans for the future, her current predicament, or the drink balanced above her fingers.

"Do you like it?" he added.

"Oh yes!" She bobbed her head. "It tickles my nose!"

He smiled and returned the bottle to the ice bucket while Veronique fingered the stem of the delicate glass and studied him. She couldn't help but admire the wide set of Roman's shoulders and the lean length of his legs. He had long shanks and muscular calves, and large feet that were planted on the floor with authority.

Though he was quick to smile and chuckle, an overriding melancholy emanated from him. Its call was so strong that she ached to step up behind him and embrace him. She longed to snake her arms under his elbows, to place her cheek between his shoulder blades and whisper that she knew what it was like to be alone. She often felt so completely alone in the world. But she held back, sure that he would pull away if she made such a bold advance.

She understood his standoffish nature. She didn't like being touched by other people either. Besides that, she was a guest in his home and an unmarried woman. It would be scandalous if she admitted to an attraction to him while staying in his house. On top of it all, she could never forget what he had done in the churchyard.

Still, his masculine figure, so erect and powerful, drew her to him as she had never been drawn to anyone.

To get her mind off her attraction to Citizen Brandt, she pointed the edge of her champagne flute toward the book he'd placed on the mantel.

"Is that an actual book you were reading?" she asked.

"Yes. It's an adventure novel by an American author. *The Last of the Mohicans.*" He followed her line of sight and then looked back at her. "Have you never seen a book?"

She shook her head. All instruction in the schoolroom was done on slates.

"I have access to hundreds of them."

She sucked in her breath. "But how? The Overseers burned all the books during the reconstruction."

"Not all. Some of us saved things. Some of our *families* did, that is. My family had many things in storage in caves in the hills, before and after the Grave Mistake."

"But the Overseers—didn't they take your possessions away?"

"I've had trouble with them occasionally, but not as of late."

She had always wondered what life was like for those who lived in the more fashionable parts of Londo City. She had imagined that behind the crumbling facades of the once-elegant townhouses, the people who lived inside struggled almost as much as she did—with limited food and scant possessions. But here was a man who had somehow retained his wealth and dared defy the edicts of the Overseers.

Amazed at learning of a layer of society she had never known existed, Veronique took another sip and studied him over the rim of her glass. "Are there others like you?" she asked.

She was surprised to see him throw a sharp glance her way.

"What do you mean, like me?"

"People who live like this." She swept the air with a wide swing of her arm. "As you do. With so many things."

"There are a few." Roman ambled back to the fire, and she noticed his limp had completely disappeared. "Some of us try to uphold the old ways."

"Old ways?"

"Of protecting a certain quality of life. Some of us believe that literature, art and education do not necessarily lead to moral decay. In fact, I believe man's creativity exalts him."

"You're a rebel!" she gasped, unable to hide her delight. The champagne was certainly going to her head.

Roman lifted his glass in salute. "That I cannot deny."

Before she could say anything more, a manservant carried in a tray piled with covered dishes.

"Please," Roman pulled out a chair. "Sit, Miss Bishop. Your dinner has arrived."

"Dinner?" Shocked, she glanced at the servant and then at the draped window. "But I thought it was morning."

"Hardly." Roman chuckled. "You slept the entire day."

"The entire day?" The question hung in the air as she sank to the chair he had pulled out for her.

He scooted in her chair and took a seat near her elbow at the head of the table. The servant placed a covered plate before her, but nothing in front of the master of the house.

"It's no wonder you slept so long. I suspect you've had a traumatic few days." He took a sip of his champagne.

The servant set a bowl on the charger and whisked away the lid to reveal a fragrant sea of creamed soup. Her mouth watered, and she couldn't help but stare down at it in awe. There were croutons swimming in the center, topped by a sprinkling of green herbs. The dish was as beautiful as a carefully wrapped gift.

"Eat," Roman urged, smiling down at her.

"Are you not having dinner?" she asked.

"I dine very late, and usually out."

She flushed, feeling like a schoolgirl who was being fed before the adults left for a social event. She was *not* a child, and she would have to make that clear to Roman Brandt. Soon. But she wasn't going to quibble about that now. She was far too hungry.

Veronique stared down at the forest of silverware on either side of her plate, wondering how in the world she would know which implement to use to eat the various courses she was sure would arrive. Her champagne-muddled brain didn't help matters.

Roman chuckled again. "Just work from the outside. And if in doubt, use your fingers. I don't stand on protocol, Miss Bishop."

She chose the soupspoon. At least she could recognize *that*.

For a few minutes, Roman let her eat in peace. She tried not to wolf down the soup or spill any on the gorgeous dress. It was difficult to hold herself back and draw the spoon slowly through the luscious cream of mushroom soup, instead of leaning close and paddling it into her mouth as quickly as she could. But she managed to control herself. She didn't even spill anything on the gown—which was a miracle.

After the soup, came a tiny little glass filled with purple ice.

"A palate cleanser," Roman nodded at the dish. "I believe it is plum sorbet."

"Oh my!" She dipped a tiny spoon into the slush. She'd never seen anything like it. It looked like fairy ice. Not that she'd seen much ice in her life. She had never seen snow, as it hadn't snowed in Londo City for hundreds of years. Roman watched her, obviously enjoying the sight of her eating the dishes he had ordered.

Roman leaned back in his chair. He regarded her, his gray eyes glinting. Light from the fire danced over the edge of his black suit and lit up the planes of his handsome rugged face.

"You have red hair," he commented.

Startled, she straightened and ran a hand over her temple, wondering that he could see her roots in the gentle light of the lamps. Wary of questions about her background, she shot him a glare. "So?"

He shrugged a muscular shoulder. "It is unusual these days."

"Then I must be unusual."

His eyes glinted again, but softer this time. "Why do you conceal it?"

"To blend in. To get by."

He shifted in his seat. "I don't mean no pry, Miss Bishop, but it is also unusual for a young woman to have no parents."

The chill of the sorbet streaked through her chest. She had never admitted to anyone but Jane and Citizen Carson that she was an orphan. But today was her birthday. She was eighteen years old. A genuine adult. She could say anything now. Even the truth.

"My mother disappeared when I was eight," she replied. "I think she was taken because she was ill."

"And your father?"

"I never knew him. Mother said he worked in the north somewhere and couldn't come home."

"Really?" Roman sat back in surprise.

She nodded.

"Did you believe her?"

"I tried to. But I always wondered. She was so evasive about him. She refused to talk about him."

"How did your mother manage?"

Veronique shrugged. "Looking back, I'm not sure. We lived a modest life, but she didn't have to work in the fields like most women. She was always at home. She bottled herbs, mostly. That's what I remember her doing."

"Someone must have sent her money," Roman mused. "Not to offend, but was she someone's mistress?"

"I don't know. She never went out alone. And no one ever visited that I recall. In fact, we never stayed in one place long enough to get to know our neighbors."

"Why?"

"My mother was worried that we would be discovered, because she didn't have a husband. We moved every few months."

"Of course. A single woman with a child is highly unusual." He studied her. "But after your mother disappeared, where did you go? You were eight, did you say?"

"Yes." Veronique put down the tiny silver spoon as the memories of her younger days rushed back in a dark cloud. She had spent countless nights shivering, hungry, and lonely, weeping for her mother. But after a couple of months, she had learned to shut off her grief and get by on the streets. When she was twelve, she had found Citizen Carson and his secret room. But more importantly, she had found music. Music gave her a safe place where the cold world could be set aside. In music, she was no longer an orphan and no longer bound to an Earth that was dark and unforgiving. Music had saved her life. But it had also saved her spirit.

The servant swept into the room with a dish covered by a silver dome. He whisked away the sorbet glass and replaced it with the plate. When he lifted the dome, he released a heavenly cloud of flavor. Veronique looked down at a breast of chicken nested in a mound of potatoes, and slathered with a rich, creamy sauce. Saliva flooded her mouth.

"It was not an easy time, I take it," Roman put in, breaking into her thoughts.

She shook her head, as she cut through the tender white meat. "I lived on the streets."

"But you were just a child. Surely someone took you in."

"I couldn't take the chance of telling anyone I was an orphan." Veronique glanced up at him. "I would have been taken away by the Overseers."

"Unconscionable." The word rasped out of him, sharp with outrage.

For the second time with this man, Veronique felt an unusual kinship, as if he understood her on a visceral level that Jane or the rector never had. She chewed the meat, but barely tasted it. Her mind was too occupied by the conversation to focus on the food before her. Besides, being watched as she ate by the handsome man at her elbow set her senses on edge.

"So tell me," Roman asked, as she cut into the chicken again. "How did a young lady from such humble origins learn to play the piano as you do?"

Veronique took a bite of chicken and looked at her host, wondering how to explain without sounding mentally unfit. She decided to come right out and tell him the truth.

"This might sound crazy," she began. "But I think I was born with the gift."

"What do you mean?"

"The moment I put my fingers to the keyboard of a piano, I knew what chords were. How to integrate the bass notes. The difference between a third and a fifth. There were songs in my hands that I had never heard anyone play."

"But how?" He leaned forward. "Did your mother own a piano?"

"No."

"Where did you practice? Surely, you couldn't play the way you do without some instruction."

She struggled to capture a mound of potato on her fork, not sure how she could tell the rest of her tale without revealing her connection to the murder in the churchyard. "When I was living on the streets, I came across an old man who played the organ in a church. He was my teacher."

"Only one teacher. Amazing." He finished his drink.

"I was never good at anything else," Veronique put in, anxious to gloss over her years at the church. "I was terrible at school. I could never sit still in class. And in the middle of the day I could never stay awake. I was punished so many times. The teachers hated me."

"I can't see it."

"They did! I got terrible marks. That's why everyone thought I was meant to work in the fields and nothing more."

"They were wrong to think that of you."

"My best friend Jane believes that working with plants and being in the sunshine—however weak it is these days—is the truest way to live—the most genuine human existence—even if it barely pays the bills."

Roman looked thoughtful. "There's something to be said for that, I'll give her that much."

"But it isn't what I want," Veronique planted her fists on the edge of the table. "That's her way of life, not mine. But she just can't see it."

"It's a universal theme, Miss Bishop." Roman smiled and stood up. "When you are ready to stretch your wings however, you must do what your heart tells you to do."

"I'm ready now!" She jumped to her feet.

"Really?" He raked her with a dubious gaze. "How old are you?"

"Twenty-one," she lied.

He looked down his nose at her while he tipped up her chin with the edge of a gloved finger. For a moment his ice-water gaze swept over her. She froze, wondering what he searched for in her expression.

"You are afraid," he murmured.

"No, I'm not." She met his stare full on and forced herself to stay in place instead of giving in to the urge to pull away.

"Your heart is pounding. I can see its flutter along your neck."

"It's not because I'm afraid of you."

"What else would cause your heart to race?"

"I have no idea," she lied again. Being this close to provocative Mr. Brandt was almost too much to bear. Mere inches separated her lips from his.

"I believe you are lying." His finger still angled her chin toward his face.

She held her ground but felt her spirit rushing toward him again. "About what?" she managed to blurt.

"Your age." His gaze lowered to her mouth. "Perhaps more."

"Why would I lie?" She ached for him to kiss her.

"So I might think you are older than your actual years. You seem mature for a young woman, but I suspect you are younger than you say."

"I suspect you are younger than you make yourself out to be as well," she retorted.

Roman sobered, as if he had suddenly snapped out of the peculiar trance they had fallen into. He released her. "You are seventeen, if you are a day."

"I'm eighteen. And you?"

"Old enough to know what's good for you." His eyes glittered.

"Really? How? You barely know me. You couldn't possibly know what I want out of life."

He shook his head and the melancholy returned. "Do not make the mistake of thinking of me as your peer."

"So you're too good for someone like me?" She planted her fists on her hips. "Go ahead and say it. I know what I am. Where I came from. Don't mince words with me, Roman."

"I did not mean it in the way you think."

"You don't know what I'm thinking," she flung back at him. "You might think you do, but you don't."

"I see." He slanted a dark glance at her. "My mistake."

"I never said I was interested in you either," she retorted. "Or that I even think of you like that."

"Again, my apologies." He bowed slightly. "The lady knows best."

She stared at him. In acquiescing, he had suddenly gained the higher ground. How had he managed such a feat? She struggled for something to say to regain the upper hand, but he cut her off.

"A toast then, Miss Bishop, instead of this bickering." He smiled as he refilled her glass. "To our differences and our similarities. Both of which I find...provocative."

"To our differences," she repeated, raising her glass.

"And if we are mindful of life's limitations, there will be no reason to regret having made each other's acquaintance."

He clinked her sparkling glass, and she looked up at him, not sure what she thought of the last few puzzling moments. But she knew one thing: she would never regret having met Roman Brandt.

For a moment, his serious gray eyes locked on hers. She felt that odd sensation again of being swept into his gaze, of being pulled into a vast, timeless world far different than anything she had ever known, a place where life was primal and exhilarating and unapologetic. His gaze streamed into hers, and her ears filled with a thunder of sound: strains of music, a battlefield, snarling beasts, ecstatic breathing, and a man calling Roman's name from far, far, away—all rolled into a wave of noise. But above the cacophony, Veronique was highly aware of his eyes and the way he drank her in. Her heart thudded, and her breath caught in her throat at the hunger and denial she saw burning in Roman's intent regard.

Then he broke off his disconcerting gaze.

"You should finish your dinner," he said, his voice gruff.

"I should." It took a great deal of effort to disengage from the sounds that had swept her into Roman's inner world, and an even greater effort to slough off the effect of his stare. Her breath came unevenly, as if she had just run up a flight of stairs.

"It will grow cold. Unpalatable."

"Yes."

"I am going out. But I will be back. Promise me you won't go anywhere until I return."

"All right." She gulped her champagne.

"Feel free to go anywhere you desire in the house. If you wish, Mrs. Fernside will show you the music salon."

"Do you have a piano?"

"Of course. And I expect that you will make good use of it."

She smiled. "Oh, I will."

"Then I bid you good night." With a curt bow, he left her in the dining room and called for his hat, coat, and cane.

Forgetting about her dinner, Veronique trailed after him into the front hall, where she watched him sweep out of the house in a flap of wool and a flash of satin. All too soon he was out of sight. She put a hand on the newel post of the grand staircase, waiting in the wake of his leaving for something she wasn't quite sure she would recognize if it appeared. All she knew for certain was that Roman Brandt had a cast a spell over her.

Her good sense told her she should return to the dining room. She was never certain where her next meal would come from. And to waste such wonderful food would be idiotic on her part. She took a step back to the dining room.

But she paused to look over her shoulder at the now silent door. Roman had been gone only a matter of seconds, and yet she couldn't wait for him to return. His presence in a room or a coach lit up the air around her, energized her, and mystified her. She wanted to spend more time with him, wanted to know more about him.

Then she caught herself. Where was her head? She had lost her good sense to Roman's magnetic personality and two glasses of champagne. She had the audition to practice for, without a moment to spare. And no matter how kind and generous he'd been to her, she couldn't forget he was a cold-blooded killer.

Chapter 12

VERONIQUE TRIED TO put Roman Brandt out of her mind as she returned to the dining room, but she was still thinking about him as she finished her chicken, and then a salad and dessert. This must be what it was like for Jane after she had spent a stolen hour with her boyfriend Lawrence and came back all starry-eyed and bubbling over with funny things he had said. Veronique had never understood the allure of a male, or how her friend could become so caught up by another person that she actually lost a bit of herself in the process.

Until now.

She was alarmed at how easily she could fall under Roman's spell. From here on out she would have to remain unaffected by him—especially if she intended to throw herself into study. If she worked as hard as she could for the next few days, she would play even better at the audition for the Overseers. A rigorous practice schedule would demand her every waking moment, leaving no time for daydreaming about men. Besides, girlish daydreams and romance were a waste of time. The Overseers chose mates for young women. Romance or personal attraction never had anything to do with it.

Men and boys are not for sport. Mates are chosen by the court.

Roman might defy the Overseers with his books and lavish table, but Veronique was too poor to be a true rebel. It would be best for her if she played by the rules and stuck to her plan of raising herself up using the one strength that set her apart—her musicianship. Dallying with an off-limits man would only complicate her already stressful life. Besides, Roman was dangerous.

That night, Veronique practiced for hours. But it was more pleasure than work. Roman's grand piano was flawlessly tuned, and the acoustics in his music salon added a rich dimension that she had never heard before. She had never stayed up so late playing, either.

As the hours flew past midnight, she discovered the energy of the night nurtured her in a way the daylight hours had failed to do in her previous eighteen years. In the stillness of the evening, with the soft notes flowing from her hands, and the lamps set low, she felt amazingly at peace—and for the first time in recent memory, she did not feel alone and abandoned. The night, with its patient undertones and attentive ear, was a companion like no other.

She played through the Souza march over and over again, trying to pinpoint the emotional heart of the piece. That's what vaulted a performance from the ordinary to the extraordinary. But try as she might, she couldn't find the soul of the march. All the while she played it, she visualized a brigade of agents marching through the streets of Londo City, tramping inexorably after a citizen who had not committed a crime, or a young girl who had just lost her mother. After playing the march until she knew each measure by heart, she switched to her pre-Reformation favorites.

Not until light filtered through the cracks of the drapery did Veronique realize dawn had arrived. Shocked that she had spent the entire night at the piano, she pushed back the bench and stood up. Her rump ached from sitting so long on a wooden surface, but the rest of her felt remarkably renewed. This must be what life was like when a person was well fed, warm, and clean—and all at the same time.

Smiling, she lowered the cover of the keyboard, turned to leave, and choked back a screech.

A man lay on a divan in the shadows at the side of the room. His left elbow covered his eyes and one long leg sprawled over the seat to angle down to the floor. The rising light glinted along the sleek line of his boot, from the polished toe all the way up to his muscular knee. He wasn't moving. And then she realized who she was looking at: Roman.

For a moment she stared at him, shocked that he had come into the room and she hadn't noticed. She wondered how long he had been lying there in the dark, listening to her play. She wondered if she had disturbed him, and he had come down to lodge a complaint but was waiting for her to finish the piece. Then she realized that he was fast asleep.

She paused, debating whether or not to wake him. Surely, he would be stiff and sore from spending the night on such a small couch. But something told her to leave him be. Besides, she intended to visit Jane this morning, and she didn't want anyone to know what she was up to. It was better for her if Mr. Brandt continued his slumber unaware.

Veronique stole up the stairs and searched her bedchamber until she located her old clothes. Mrs. Fernside had folded them neatly and put them on a chair near the wardrobe. After having worn the fine clothes Mr. Brandt had given her, Veronique realized just how dingy her gabardine skirt and velvet vest must have appeared to him. She held up the threadbare vest. The purple and black striped garment had always been her favorite piece of apparel. But now it hung in her hands like the moth-eaten rag it really was. How quickly a person's perspective could change.

Not good. She might have to go back to her moth-eaten life one day. She couldn't allow herself to grow soft.

She frowned. The sooner she left the townhouse, the better it would be for her. To grow too accustomed to Mr. Brandt's way of life would be dangerous for a young woman like her. Having experienced rich food and a luxurious bed, it would be difficult to return to her world of bread crusts and lumpy pallets. Yet, if all went well, she might not have to return to such a life. By the end of the week, she might join the upper echelon of society. And then Roman Brandt would be dining at *her* table and cleansing his palate with *her* plum sorbet. Now that was a picture. She had to smile.

Heartened by the thought, Veronique buttoned the tattered vest over her frayed white blouse and pulled on her skirt. But she didn't take off the beautiful leather boots with their fine heels and laces. No one was going to make her relinquish *them*.

Back in her shabby outfit and feeling the weight of her old life like a shell she longed to slough off, Veronique headed down the stairs of the townhouse.

Roman's brick townhouse sat across the road from Scotland Yard, the only greenbelt in Londo City that contained large trees. Most all other trees had been cut down for fuel after the Grave Mistake, and the saplings that had survived had not received enough sunlight to grow more than a couple of feet. But no one had dared to touch the trees of Scotland Yard. The families that lived along its borders had guarded the old growth plants well. Even so, the towering oaks, beeches and yews were scraggly from standing in the incessant fog. They made the park look more like a haunted forest than a playground. No one had time to play anyway.

Veronique kept to the pavement beside the greenbelt and set off toward the Thames. She'd been in this neighborhood before. In fact, one of her old hiding places—a deserted candy store—was not that far away, once she crossed the Thames and cut through the market. She set off at a trot for Lambeth Bridge, a couple of blocks to the northeast, as the city came to life around her.

It took an hour for Veronique to arrive at her old neighborhood. She knocked on Jane's door, just as it was pulled open.

"Veronique!" Jane's mother exclaimed. She was dressed in her drab field clothing, with a black scarf holding back her hair.

"Hello, Mrs. Ulrich."

"We were just leaving for work." Jane's mother pulled the door all the way open, to allow her slight husband to pass by. He carried his lunch in a metal pail and a newspaper stuffed under one arm.

"Mornin', Vee," he greeted.

"Hi, Mr. Ulrich."

"Hear the news about Whites?"

Veronique paused on the step. "What news?"

"The manager was found dead behind the place last night."

"The manager?" Veronique choked.

"A Thaddeus Milton." Mr. Ulrich looked back at her. "Didn't Jane say you were playing piano at Whites? Did you know him?"

"Yes." Veronique found it difficult to breathe. "I just talked to him two nights ago." She blinked, finding it difficult to digest the news. "I can't believe it! What happened?"

Mr. Ulrich shrugged, "The authorities don't know much just yet. They think it was a heart attack. They found him lying in the back lot, like he'd fallen asleep."

"Oh." Veronique felt a moment of pity for the man—until she remembered how nasty he had been to her. And then her mind leapt to Roman's comment, about Milton being due for a lesson. Her blood went cold.

"Not that surprising, though," Mr. Ulrich shook his head. "Happens to a lot of men his age these days."

Before Veronique could say anything more, Jane appeared in the doorway, dressed much like her mother in a sturdy cotton skirt and scarf. Veronique stared at her in dismay. Her friend was headed for the fields with her parents, and for a life that doomed her to repeat their same footsteps. Jane's glance met Veronique's.

"You got accepted," Veronique said.

"Yes. I start today."

"We're running late, Veronique," Jane's mother put in, locking the door. "I'm afraid Jane doesn't have time to talk."

"You can walk with us to the station, though." Jane grabbed Veronique's arm and pulled her close. Veronique allowed the unusually intimate physical contact, as she didn't want her elders to hear what she had to say.

Jane's parents set off at a brisk pace for the train station, and the young women followed a few steps behind.

"Happy birthday!" Jane exclaimed. She slipped her something soft wrapped in a paper napkin, probably a stolen sweet cake that had cost a fortune.

Veronique gazed down at the gift, always struck by Jane's thoughtfulness. She didn't have the heart to tell Jane that this year her family's sacrifice hadn't been necessary. For the first time in her life, she was well fed. Overfed, in fact. But to tell her the truth would negate the spirit of the gift. That she would never do.

"Thank you, Jane. Thank you." Carefully, Veronique put the treat in the inner pocket of her cloak. "I'll eat it when I can savor every morsel." That was certainly no lie.

"It's all I could manage."

"It's more than enough. All I ever can give you are homemade cards."

"But they're so amusing, Vee. I've kept them all." Jane beamed. "I treasure them." Then she reached into the pocket of her apron and pulled out an envelope.

"And this came for you, too."

"The Symphony Committee!"

Jane nodded. "Here." She slipped it into Veronique's hands before anyone could take notice of the transaction.

"Thanks." Veronique smiled sadly at her friend. She couldn't stop thinking about the future, and how everything would be changing for them, now that they were entering adulthood. "For everything, Jane. For all the years. For being there for me. I mean it."

"It was nothing," Jane replied, but Veronique could tell she was putting on a brave front while she held back tears.

They walked in silence for a few moments. Then Jane turned to her. "Have you found somewhere to live?" Her tone glinted with artificial brightness.

Veronique stared straight ahead. She didn't want to worry her friend on her first day of work. It was difficult enough working in the fields for ten long hours, but a troubled mind would make the task even harder.

"Yes, something temporary," Veronique hugged her friend's arm. "And by the way, thank you not blabbing to your folks about my audition."

"What are friends for?" Jane replied.

"I hope we can stay friends."

Jane pulled back. "What do you mean?"

"We won't be spending much time together, now that you'll be going to the fields every day. Things are bound to change."

"I had to apply, Vee." Jane sighed. "I know you disapprove, but Father's getting too old to work. We need the money."

"No one's blaming you, Jane. You have to do what you have to do. That's life."

Jane nodded. "But let's not let life pull us apart, Vee. Let's not lose touch."

"Never."

Jane tipped her head against Veronique's shoulder. "Promise?"

"I promise."

They walked in silence for a few moments, until Veronique saw the telltale puff of steam from a locomotive waiting at the station. They didn't have much more time for conversation. Veronique couldn't help but feel that she was seeing Jane Ulrich as she knew her for the last time. The thought filled her with anguish.

"Jane!" she cried, wanting to keep change from touching everything in her life, especially the one person who had been a steadying constant the past few years. Had she been more of a physically expressive person, she would have flung her arms around her friend. Instead, she clutched the envelope in one hand and stood immobilized by despair while steam billowed around them.

"Good luck, Vee," Jane said, acting as if they would see each other at the end of the day, just as they always did. She patted Veronique's shoulder and then dashed after her parents.

Veronique remained at the side of the tracks and watched the train chug away. She tried to locate Jane's face in the crowded car, but the press of passengers had already fogged up the windows. Even so, she waved until the train disappeared around the bend, taking the last shreds of her childhood with it. The clickety-clack of the train diminished to nothingness in the mist, abandoning the station to silence, and leaving Veronique standing alone on the platform.

She pushed away her anguish by focusing her attention on the envelope in her hand and the future it might hold for her. She slipped a finger beneath the flap and broke the seal. While her heart pounded in her chest, she drew out the card and read it.

Congratulations!
Your audition has been scheduled for:

Date: Friday, October 20th, at 7:00 pm
Location: Garrick Theatre
Additional Instructions: Please arrive at 6:00 pm for check-in procedures.
You must bring this card with you at check-in, along with one form of personal ID. No sheet music will be permitted. If selected, you will be transported immediately to the Central Compound. Please bring any required personal belongings with you to the audition. Only a small bag will be permitted.

Good luck,
The Symphony Committee

Carefully, Veronique replaced the card in the envelope and slipped it into the inside pocket of her vest. After today, Jane would have her new life, and with any hope, Veronique would soon have hers.

But Friday.

Friday was only a day away. There wasn't much time left to prepare. She hoped Roman would let her remain in his home until Friday so she could practice. She also had to come up with a new ID card, the kind carried by adults, and not the red-stamped juvenile variety that she possessed. She'd manufactured a crude one long ago that she used only to flash before an agent's bored regard, never at close range. For the Overseers, she would have to make a forgery. She hurried through the deserted station and headed back to the townhouse on Scotland Yard. With any luck, Roman's household could provide the tools she would need.

Chapter 13

SOMETHING AWAKENED Roman: the absence of sound. He slid a stiff arm to the side and opened his eyes as the old familiar silence pressed down on him, heavier than ever. He blinked it away and sat up.

Veronique was no longer at the piano. In fact, she was no longer in the salon. She had vanished, taking her music with her. His melancholy, never far away, edged closer like an ink stain on silk. Roman got to his feet, struggling to outdistance the inner darkness that plagued him.

Outer darkness, however, was long gone. Light peeked through the velvet curtains across the room. He must have slept on the divan for hours. And she must have seen him there, hanging around like a besotted fool, hungry for the sweetmeats her hands and heart could so easily provide. He flushed and vowed that he wouldn't let her beguiling music cast its spell over him a second time. It was important that he stay on task, no matter how slippery and unpredictable life had recently become.

Still healing from the attack he'd suffered upon his return to Londo City, he limped the few steps to the door of the salon. Silas and his goons would have to do better if they expected to waylay him in Londo a second time, especially now that he'd discovered Miss Bishop.

It was odd to be up this time of day. He didn't want to risk blinding himself by looking out the window at the morning fog, but it cheered him all the same to know that daylight had arrived, and he was part of it. He missed the morning hours, especially the early sun of summer. How he had loved to step out of his country home and suck in the fresh air of a new day. He couldn't remember exactly how many years had passed since he'd known such a luxury. But it had been hundreds of years.

By the time Roman gained the hallway, the recent injury quit complaining, and his gait smoothed to its usual even pace. He opened the door, called for Mrs. Fernside to bring in tea, and walked to his desk. There were still more packets of mail to plow through. Mrs. Fernside had saved every note he had received in the last ten years, in hopes that he would someday get out of prison. Roman had promised himself that he would sort through the piles a bit each day, until he made certain that nothing important had escaped his notice.

He sat down at his desk, untied a packet of letters, and swiftly went through them as he sipped the fragrant brew. He never failed to appreciate the beverages he could once again imbibe. He loved the variety. He loved the way the steaming fragrance fanned his face and brought back memories of his former life. But he set down his cup with a clatter when he caught sight of a familiar scrawl. A chill passed over him.

Gabriel had written to him? When? Roman snatched up the envelope and looked at the post office cancellation stamped on the back flap. He could just make out the date of October 10, 2515 in faded blue ink. The message must have arrived the day after he'd been arrested and dragged to the north the second time.

It was if Roman held the ghost of his old friend in his hands. His heart twisted in his chest. He hadn't realized until this moment how deeply he missed the scientist/musician he had counted as his best and only true friend. He tore through the wax seal, pulled out the letter and unfolded it with his gloved fingers.

My dear friend,

If you are reading this, something has happened to me. And I have a great favor to ask.

First, I want you and only you to know that the Commensalist Project was not a complete failure. But in its success lies my greatest anguish. Against my better judgment, I fell in love with a human female, and together we conceived a child. A vampire and a human, Roman. The result we were looking for.

I do not know if this miracle occurred because of the way the virus is changing our physical beings or because of the depth of feeling I have for my partner. Perhaps love succeeded where science did not.

My partner suffered through a full-term pregnancy. Her child lived through the first months of life and did not shrivel and die like the rest of them. I was never so happy and yet never so conflicted about anything in all my years on this earth—because to protect this child, I had to hide her from everyone, including myself.

I never told the others of the survival of this child. I wanted her to live a natural life as you always said we should live. I didn't want her to be prodded and studied or sacrificed for the greater good. I recorded her death with all the others. I arranged for her mother to disappear into Londo City with an assumed identity. Mother and child moved constantly to evade detection.

For eight years I secretly supported my little family. No one knew of them. Not even you. But my partner disappeared suddenly last week and my child never came home from school. I have reason to believe they were taken to Port Pennwood, a remote facility on the southern coast. I am going there to rescue them. Thus this letter.

If someone delivers this letter to you, it means I have not returned from Port Pennwood as expected and may need your help.

You said once that you owed your life to me, that you would do anything for me. I am calling in that favor now. You know who my partner was, but I did not disclose to you that I had a daughter. She goes by the name of Veronique Dunn. She has red hair like mine, but her mother always dyes it brown. She has a mole at the base of her spine. You will recognize me in her when you see her, I am sure.

I beg of you, Roman, find my daughter and her mother. You have a knack for such things. Please find them. Take care of them until my return, or forever, in the case of my demise. Guard them until my daughter is old enough be told the truth. Or guard her from the truth. I leave that up to you to decide.

I pray that you will find them soon. My daughter is just a little girl. If she is picked up as an orphan, you know what will happen to her.

You are my one true friend, Roman. I know you will not fail me.
G.

Dear God. Roman swallowed and sat back in his chair, struck dumb by the information he'd just read. The letter hung from his left hand, nearly forgotten. The Commensalist Project had not failed after all—it had produced a child. His red-headed friend, Gabriel Stone, had produced a child.

But the letter had been opened ten years too late. Gabriel's partner and child had never been rescued. And Gabriel Stone had been declared dead, given a public funeral and was slowly being forgotten by all but those who held him dear.

The child must be eighteen years old now. She must have been quite a scrapper to survive all those years on the streets. But she had. And she called herself Citizen Bishop.

Even without seeing the mark at the base of her spine, Roman was certain Gabriel's little girl had just walked into his life in the form of an alluring young musician. Unbelievable. But what was he supposed to do now?

He knew one thing. He would protect his friend's daughter with his life, just as Gabriel had requested. But if Neal Moray was looking for a girl, what were the odds he'd discovered the truth about Veronique? Probably high. But how had Moray found out about her?

Roman flipped over the envelope, searching for signs of tampering. He couldn't find any. Still, someone could have removed the wax seal and replaced it with a second one. He'd done as much himself. Who had read the letter? And when? His mind raced over the images of servants and acquaintances but didn't settle on anyone.

It wouldn't serve any purpose to learn the identity of the snitch. It would be a better use of his time to figure out how to keep Miss Bishop—or should he say Miss *Dunn*—safe from harm. It might be best to leave Londo City for a while, even if he had to take her against her will.

He had no intention of telling Veronique about her past. The less she knew, the better it would be for her, and the greater her chances for living a halfway normal life. God only knew what kind of blood flowed through her veins or what the future held for her.

"You will thank me one day," Roman murmured, just as Mrs. Fernside knocked on his door and stepped in to announce the arrival of a visitor.

A visitor could never be good, especially this early in the day. He put down the letter, wondering who would dare make a call at this hour.

"Mr. Moray to see you, sir." Mrs. Fernside remained just to the side of the door.

Roman stood up, stuffed the shocking letter in the top right drawer, and headed for the front of the house.

Roman strode to the parlor where his housekeeper had shown the guest. He had half a notion to keep walking right out the door and let Moray grow impatient and leave. But in the end, curiosity overcame his reluctance to entertain the man he now considered his greatest nemesis. He opened the parlor door.

"Don't get comfortable," Roman growled.

Neal Moray, in the act of sitting on the settee before the fire, checked his downward motion. He straightened and let out a mirthless chuckle. "Still the boor you've always been, I see, Brandt."

Roman crossed his arms over his chest. He wasn't happy about chatting with Moray, especially now that he knew it was Veronique he'd been pursuing. The question was, how had Moray found out about her? Roman planted his booted feet far apart as he fought through his grogginess. He was not accustomed to being awake at such an early hour. And he wasn't in the mood to entertain this particular person, no matter what time of day it was.

Fire burned in his gut as he surveyed Moray's perpetual smirk and darting hazel eyes. The skin on his face was as tight as a drumhead, stretched over his narrow skull and bulbous eyes. But he looked worse for wear from the last time Roman had seen him at the riot. Scars marked both sides of Moray's mouth, and his nose had been broken and not set properly. Eventually his vampire constitution would mend all physical trauma, but it would take years, especially if the virus had compromised his regenerative system.

"State your business and get out, Moray."

"Harsh, Brandt! We haven't seen each other for ten years!" Moray held his arms out at his sides, as if asking Roman to accept him. What was he expecting—a hug? Roman would never embrace this man or his friendship. "And this is the greeting I get?"

"You're lucky I haven't run you through."

"I heard rumors about that exact thing happening the other night."

"I heard a rumor, too—" Roman strode to the window and looked out where the light was still gray enough to tolerate. Veronique was not in the house. Now that he was fully awake, he could sense it. But he had no idea where she had gone, and her absence worried him. "—that you are looking for a young lady."

"I am." Moray scuttled across the floor to the fireplace. He reminded Roman of a crab, nervously skittering around on spindly legs, never at ease.

"Why?"

"Silas got wind of a secret. That the Commensalist Project might not have been a complete disaster after all."

"In what way?"

"We've been informed that there might have been an unrecorded but successful birth."

"You've got to be joking." Roman hoped he sounded convincing.

"Apparently there's a girl. Probably eighteen years old or so." The man was never at rest, physically or mentally, and had a busy mind that was always plotting as he chewed his cuticles to the quick. "If she's a successful hybrid and is still alive, she could be the answer to our prayers."

"As if you pray to anyone." Roman looked up and down the street in front of his house. Wherever Veronique was, he hoped she would not make an appearance until Moray had left the premises.

"Silas is desperate to find the girl. Her genetic material could save his life. Yours, too, one day. Mine." Moray shrugged one shoulder.

"And at what cost?"

"Does it matter?"

"She might think so."

Moray snorted. "She's just a freak. A lab rat."

Roman threw him a dark glance. "You never change, you selfish son-of-a-bitch."

"Listen, can we just table the bad blood?"

"Is that what you call it?" Roman countered. "Bad blood?"

"Hey, I wasn't the one who ran you out of town."

"Hmm," Roman's lip curled with hatred as he scanned the borders of Scotland Yard, hoping he wouldn't glimpse a familiar female figure coming back to the house. "A new metaphor for murder, that. *Running him out of town*. Makes it sound so...so civilized."

"You were causing too much discord." Moray stepped closer, as if to gain Roman's full attention. "First the riot. Then your objection to the Commensalist Project."

"I did not cause that riot. Or fight for the humans."

"But you did object to the project."

"At the end, who wouldn't have?"

"Well, Silas thought you were impeding progress."

"Oh, Silas thought so. I see." Roman let the lace panel fall. He turned. "And who jumped me upon my return this week? Whose men were those, Moray?"

"How should I know?"

Roman glared at him, pinning him in place as he searched for the truth in Moray's scarred face.

"Don't play the innocent lackey with me, Moray. With Gabriel gone, someone must have acted as Silas Stone's right-hand man. Don't tell me you know nothing of the goings on at the Central Compound."

"You know Silas. Iron fist. Suspicious. I couldn't persuade him to back off."

Moray bit a cuticle. He was lying.

"So Silas ordered the attack."

"He thinks you're a threat."

Roman shook his head in disgust. "Silas does or you do?"

Moray flushed.

"And what, exactly, happened to Gabriel?" Roman watched Moray's face for another flush or tick that would show he was lying.

"No one knows." Moray shrugged again. "His assistant said he was headed to Port Pennwood. That was the last anyone heard from him."

"Did anyone search for him?"

"Of course."

"And?"

"Didn't find a thing. After a month, we had a public funeral for him. We had to. The public would have become suspicious, seeing how he was their only doctor."

"A pity." Roman smiled. "Him dying."

Moray flushed. "Goddammit, Brandt, why are you so goddamned smug about death?"

"Because it's a natural consequence of being human," Roman shot back. "And the sooner you people accept it, the better the rest of your lives are going to be—however short they become."

"No!" Moray pinched the air with his spidery fingers. "That's not how it's going to work! I won't accept it!" Frustrated, he strode to the fireplace and pivoted. "You, with your sabers and snuff. What would you know?"

"Perhaps being older, I am wiser."

"No, you come from a mindset of accepting needless death as a way of life—smallpox, infection, childbirth. All needless deaths, Brandt. All preventable. This virus problem is just another blip we have to figure out and get over."

"That is not my philosophy, Moray, and you know it." Roman walked to the other window where he had a wider view of the street. "And I can't imagine you would come here to try to convince me otherwise."

"I'm here because I need you, Brandt. Silas is on his deathbed."

The news didn't take Roman by surprise, as Moray probably thought it would. Even as far north as Roman had been, stuck in prison, he was not completely out of touch with the goings on at the Central Compound. In fact, the decline of their leader was the reason he had dared to come back to Londo City. "I have heard he isn't doing well."

Moray shot a quick glance at him, as if surprised that Roman knew anything at all. "Well, you realize there will be pandemonium when he dies. We'll spend another ten years bickering and not going forward."

That was true. Roman scowled. He might not agree with Silas' desperate attempts to live forever, but at least the man had kept order over the years. That had been no small feat, considering the disparate personalities involved.

"So?"

"So?" Moray scuttled across the parlor. "Wasting time means not going forward. And not going forward means we're all going to die!"

"Again, that is not my problem."

"You're going to just let things progress?" Moray nibbled the already short nail on his right index finger. Roman wondered if the man was even aware of his nervous habit.

"Yes. And enjoy what's happening to my body."

"Knowing what's in store in the end?"

Roman shrugged. "Why do you think you're so special, Moray? Death waits for no man."

"No!" Moray paced back to the fireplace. "That's old school talk. I *am* special. *You* are special. The old rules don't apply, and I'm going to find the way out."

"And spend the last years of your life on earth scrambling for time?" Roman shook his head. "I'm going to enjoy mine."

"You're an idiot!" Moray blurted. "A reactionary idiot!"

"So be it."

"I thought after all the time spent up north, you might have changed, might have come to your senses."

"And I, you." Roman crossed the room to pick up Moray's coat and hat. He held them in the air. "This discussion is now closed."

Sighing, Moray strode to the door of the parlor and snatched his outer garment from Roman's outstretched hand. "Will you visit

Silas, at least? He wants to see you." He pulled on his coat. "He wants to settle things."

"Tell Silas he can go to Hell."

Chapter 14

VERONIQUE WALKED UP the side of the greenbelt, with part of her attention trained on the shrubbery at her right, and the rest of it captivated by the grand façade of Roman's house ahead. His brick townhouse was three stories tall and took up half a block. The main entrance, which was capped by an ornate dormer, boasted a marvelous arrangement of round, rectangular, and bowed windows interspersed with decorative friezes and four-foot high marble statues set in alcoves. On either side of the arched doorway were massive wings of the house, topped by chimneys and cupolas. Each column, tower, and rooftop was tipped with an iron spike topped with a ball. Roman's home was stately and imposing, but as it rose to the sky, she recognized the whimsy of the architect who had built the place so long ago. She wondered if man would ever regain such *joie-de-vivre* again.

She was so busy gawking at the impressive building that she nearly ran into a thin man crossing the street with his head down and a hand on his hat as he hurried to an awaiting carriage.

"Pardon me!" Veronique gasped, as she skittered out of his path. Strange, but her ears started to ring again. She wondered why her ears had begun to ring lately. Perhaps from lack of sleep. She had to start taking better care of herself.

The man shot a glance at her, his face purple with anger. "Watch where you're going!" he snapped.

Shocked by his rude behavior, Veronique watched him bustle to his carriage. Had she been dressed in the blue gown and leather leggings she would have bet the man would have treated her with more respect. Burning with indignation, she marched up the stairs to Roman's front door with her cheeks blazing and her ears flooded with the high-pitched tone.

At the door, she suddenly realized she hadn't heard the vehicle pull away from the curb. She looked over her shoulder and saw the man in the hat watching her from the carriage window. The minute she caught him staring, he dropped the curtain, and the coach lurched to a start.

With all her senses on alert, Veronique squeezed the latch. She had left the door unlocked on her way out, but someone had locked it again. She had no recourse but to knock, which would announce her presence. Steeling herself for a confrontation of some kind, she lifted the knocker. She was anxious, angry, and obsessing over Jane's lot in life. If anyone so much as looked at her sideways, they were going to be sorry.

Luckily for everyone concerned, Mrs. Fernside opened the door.

"Citizen Bishop!" she exclaimed, obviously alarmed to see her outside. But the old woman quickly contained her surprise. She swept open the door.

"Good morning, Mrs. Fernside." Veronique strode into the mansion, half-expecting to be grilled regarding her activities of the last few hours. But Mrs. Fernside merely stepped out of her way and waited to shut the door behind her.

Relief swept over Veronique. Maybe coming and going from the Brandt house wasn't going to be as difficult as she had assumed. She headed for the staircase but had taken only a few steps when a deep voice stopped her in her tracks.

"Where in the blazes have you been?" Roman demanded behind her.

His imperious tone frayed what little patience she had left. She turned to face him, her cheeks flushed and her chin high.

"Out on personal business."

"In the middle of the night?" Roman crossed his arms.

"I'll have you know it's eight o'clock in the morning!"

"For a person who was up all night playing the piano, I'm surprised you had the energy to go anywhere."

She crossed her own arms. "For a person who was up all night spying on me, I'm surprised you're even awake!"

She saw his mouth twitch. Was he angry or amused? She couldn't read his expression.

"After what has happened to you lately, you should be doubly careful, Miss Bishop."

The man didn't have to state the obvious. She was not an idiot. She took a frustrated breath, and bit back the sharp words that burned on the tip of her tongue.

"No going out alone, young lady."

"It's my life. I'll do what I see fit."

"Not while you are under my care."

"I didn't ask to be taken care of." She planted a fist on her hip.

"It seems I have volunteered." His glance darted away.

"As to that," she said, taking advantage of her anger to press forward. "I have to stay here until Friday evening. I trust that's all right with you."

His left eyebrow rose as he surveyed the version of herself that she could finally present to the world. His eyes glinted with curiosity. "You can stay as long as you like."

"All right, then. Thank you."

"But you must promise one thing." He held up a hand.

"What?"

"That you will throw that outfit in the rubbish bin and wear what I have provided for you."

She planted her other hand on her hip. "I couldn't have walked the streets in that blue dress. I would have been attacked or arrested."

"My point exactly, Miss Bishop." Roman pulled at his cuffs to straighten his sleeves. "Should you decide to go on personal business again, you will ask Mrs. Fernside to summon the coach for you. And you will kindly inform me that you are leaving. There is danger afoot. Surely you realize it."

She stared at him, amazed that he hadn't interrogated her on the subject of her personal business and even more amazed at his generosity.

"Now then," he added. "I'm glad you are safely home. Mrs. Fernside will provide breakfast for you in the conservatory." He indicated the direction with a brisk wave of his hand. "I shall join you in a moment."

"Fine." Veronique swallowed. He had said he was glad to see her home. *Home.* The word alarmed and pleased her at the same time. She should not be considered more than a guest in this household, but he had just made her feel as if she belonged here. She had never had a stable home, and she'd never realized until this moment that she wanted such a place—and badly. Still, she couldn't let him know. She'd learned never to expect anything from anyone, or from life itself. "Thank you, Mr. Brandt."

"It's Roman."

"Thank you," she tipped her head regally as she imagined a lady would do. "Roman."

She held his gaze, determined to meet him on equal ground from this moment forward, however great the distance between their social circles and their ages. No one was going to tell her to watch where she was going. No one was going to tell her she had to work in the fields for the rest of her life. She was an adult now. She was going to go where she wanted and how she wanted. She could feel her newfound determination blazing out of her eyes.

He held her glance, his eyes flashing as he drank her in, and she could tell that she had captured his complete attention, just as he had captured hers. Standing there staring at him, she realized she could read his expression clearly now—or was he allowing himself to be read? Her brazen behavior did not annoy him. It amused him. Warmth poured over her as it dawned on her that she wanted to amuse him and make his melancholic eyes sparkle like this—if only for a moment.

After breakfast, Veronique was too tired to stay up a minute longer. Her long night and dash across Londo City had worn her out. Arrangements had been made for her own room, now that Mrs. Fernside had more time to prepare for guests. Her new bedchamber was just down the hall from the huge master chamber where she had spent the previous night. Mrs. Fernside offered to have the servant girl show Veronique up the stairs and help her get ready for bed, but Veronique countered that she could fend for herself. She stumbled up the stairs to bed.

When Veronique opened the door to her room, a smile blossomed on her face. The room was smaller than the chamber at the top of the stairs, but this room was done all in a soft rose color, from the carpets on the floor to the lighter paper on the walls. The four-poster bed, wardrobe, and secretary were delicate pieces crafted of walnut, carved much the same way as the fantastic piano at Whites, with lion feet legs and a flower motif. Beneath the velvet canopy of the bed, carved vines and flowers coiled around the posts, all the way to the floor. A rose medallion graced the headboard like a huge sunburst. The coverlet on the bed was a garden of rose blossoms in all shades of red, set off by sheets and pillowslips of the snowiest white. Veronique would guess the pillows would be as soft as clouds and smell faintly of bleach and bluing. She couldn't wait to crawl into the bed.

As she passed by the wardrobe, she opened it and was shocked to find it full of dresses, blouses, skirts, and leggings—all fashioned in jewel tones that would complement her ivory skin. A dozen pairs of footwear were arranged on racks at the bottom, from dainty slippers to sturdy boots. The drawers at the side were full of underclothes, wraps and gloves. She sucked in a breath, awed that someone would have the resources to procure such finery at such short notice.

A door at the side of the room led to a large bathroom that boasted a dainty claw-foot tub and shower, powdery-pink walls and white woodwork. Veronique stripped, took a shower, and then slipped into the white nightgown hanging on a hook on the bathroom door. Then, as the day rose outside, she crawled into the fresh-smelling sheets of the rose-garden bed and closed her eyes.

Her last thought was to thank her lucky stars that she had met Roman Brandt, and that he was such a generous man.

When Veronique woke, night had fallen. She rose and dressed, feeling more rested than she could remember. She attributed her satisfying sleep to the wonderful bed she had slept in. Before she left the room, she straightened the sheets and coverlet, taking care to leave them exactly the way she had found them. The next time she came back to this room, she wanted to see it just as she had the first time—perfect in every way.

Veronique flowed down the stairs, her heart much lighter than it had been in a very long time, and her body more energized than she could ever remember. As she reached the bottom step of the stairs, her stomach growled. She glanced at the grandfather clock under the landing of the stairs and was surprised to find it was already 10 o'clock. She wondered if Mrs. Fernside was still up and could arrange a small plate of food for her. She hadn't eaten since breakfast earlier that day. Then again, she didn't want to awaken the housekeeper if she had already retired. The old woman kept long enough hours as it was.

Veronique saw a light in a room across the hall from the conservatory. Wondering if Roman might still be home, she headed in that direction.

The room had been shut earlier that day, so she didn't know what kind of salon it was. But now, the door stood open with the reflection of firelight dancing on its panels. In a rustle of silk, she crossed the threshold into what she guessed was Roman's sanctuary.

It was a dark room, paneled in walnut, with a massive desk along one wall, surrounded by shelves that at one time must have been filled with books. In front of a large bowed window stood a bronze sculpture of a horse, at least five feet tall, its metal eyes and flaring nostrils so lifelike that she sucked in a breath. Weapons of all description, from daggers to sabers, were displayed in frames hanging on the walls, along with oil paintings of rugged mountains with unbelievably brilliant snowcaps and blue skies. A stuffed bear, rearing on his back feet inside a glass case, dominated the wall opposite the door where she stood. At the base of the case glinted an old-fashioned coat of arms in blue and green. And to her right, where a cozy arrangement of furniture ringed the fireplace, she spotted the master of the house sitting in a big chair, holding a book in one hand and a small glass of sherry in his other. He was watching her.

Taken off guard, she reached for the latch of the huge door.

"Pardon me," she stammered. "I didn't mean to intrude."

In a motion so fluid and quick she didn't actually see it happening, he got to his feet. "Now that you are here, come in." He swept the air with the hand holding the book.

She flowed forward. "I can't believe I slept the whole day again."

"You will soon be following my regimen," he chuckled. "Up all night. Never seeing the sun."

"It's rare to see the sun anyway."

"True," he remarked. He motioned toward a small chair that was closer to the fire. "Join me for an aperitif?" He lifted a decanter. "I've rediscovered sherry and am quite enjoying it."

"I've never had sherry," she answered, arranging the rose-colored skirt of her dress around her as she sat back in the chair.

"Then you must try it. Try everything in life." He handed her a delicate crystal glass that was not much bigger than an eggcup. "You only live once. And it will go by so quickly."

She nodded as she accepted the glass of dark amber liquid.

"How are you faring?" he asked, sitting back down. "Have you recovered from the other night?"

"Yes." Veronique took a sip of the sweet nutty liquor. "I can't remember the last time I felt so relaxed. And all those plants in the conservatory. I have never seen so many actual flowers."

"Good." He tipped his glass to his wide mouth. "Mrs. Fernside has done a marvelous job keeping those plants alive over the years."

"It's like a haven in the conservatory," Veronique put in. "Like being in a magical forest."

"Some of those plants are no longer in existence in the natural world," Roman sat back in his chair and propped his wrists on the ends of the arms. "They didn't survive the climate change. And some are from my homeland. Did you notice the blue flowers, the cornflowers?"

"Yes. They were the same color as the dress you had me wear yesterday."

He nodded. "They were the national flower of my country."

"I guessed you weren't from Londo City. I could hear it in your speech."

He nodded. "I once lived in a place called Prussia. But that was a long time ago. Lifetimes ago, it seems." He closed his eyes and sank his head against the wingback chair, lost in thought.

She studied the planes of his face—his smooth skin, his prominent cheekbones and chin, and his gleaming dark hair—and wondered why he spoke in terms of being so old. Surely he wasn't much older than thirty, if that.

Confounded again by his remarks, she sipped her sherry, and waited until he came back to the present on his own time.

A few moments went by before he opened his eyes and slanted his gaze down at her, with his head still propped against the cushion of the chair.

"You're a quiet one," he commented.

She shrugged one shoulder. "I am not accustomed to company."

"I am not as well." He remained gazing at her as he took another drink. "Yet, a young lady such as yourself is usually inquisitive. Are you not curious about me?"

She looked down at the sherry glowing in her delicate glass. She was more than curious. But people had their secrets these days. Veronique had been raised to be circumspect, in all ways.

"Time reveals all things," she replied. "That's what my mother always said."

He gave a soft chuckle. "True."

"And if I ask you questions, you will certainly ask me some."

"Is that a problem for you?"

"The less we know of each other, the better. Our paths will part soon, and we'll never see each other again."

"Why are you so sure of that?" He lifted his head from the back of the chair.

"Look at the way you live," she swept the air with her free hand. "You live like a king."

"So, does that mean we cannot be friends?"

"Until a few days ago, I had no idea that people like you existed in Londo. I thought everyone was in the same boat, just scraping by. Living like dogs."

"I am an exception."

"What about those other men at Whites? And your friend, Ruby Valentine?"

"For lack of a better term—the lucky few."

"Well, I'm not among the lucky. I have had nothing my whole life." She stood up, annoyed that he could speak so casually of the chasm between their life experiences and the horde of poor people she represented. "What could I possibly have in common with someone like you?"

"Music."

She stared at him. There it was again. That kinship.

"Your gift sets you apart, Veronique. You know that it does." He stood up and set his empty glass upon the table near his chair.

"Do you know that long ago a person of your talent would be sponsored by kings? You would have lived like royalty because of the pleasure you bring to the human heart."

She could not take her stare off his mouth. She couldn't believe the words he was saying. A flush swept over her.

"You have brought me such joy these past few days," he murmured, "That it is I who am indebted to you." He reached for her hand.

Before she could back away, he grasped her fingers gently and raised her hand. His gloved fingers were cool as he brought her hand close to his mouth. Instead of kissing the back of her hand, however, he turned her wrist and pressed his lips to the dish of her palm.

She stood frozen in place, every sense attuned to the way his cool, dry lips felt upon her skin, like the brush of moth wings. Delight shimmered through her and constricted her breath. She gazed at his lustrous hair as he straightened and slowly lowered her hand. He seemed reluctant to lose contact with her.

"Veronique," he murmured, still lightly clutching her fingers. She knew she should pull away and say something clever to break the spell she was under, but she couldn't make a move. "Each day you bless me with your music is a day that I look forward to. You do not know how I–" he broke off and withdrew his hand. He sighed. "But I say too much. Forgive me."

He stepped backward, his head bowed, while she stared at him, shocked by the raw emotion in his voice. She knew she was seeing the part of his personality that he kept tightly in check, and that he did not want her to witness his moment of weakness.

"You can say anything you like, Roman," she said softly. "I don't stand on protocol."

He shot her a glance, and for a moment the serious expression lingered on his sharp features. Then in another instant, he pivoted and strode to the fire. She wondered if her words had amused him or offended him.

She trailed after him, perplexed by his behavior. "Why do you hold back so much?" she asked. "I can feel it every time we talk."

"You are young. Too young to understand."

"I'm not that young!" She came to a halt directly behind him. "You can barely look at me sometimes. You look everywhere but in my eyes."

"And why do you think that is?" he retorted without turning around.

"You tell me." She planted her hands on her hips. "Is there something repulsive about my face?"

"God, no."

The vehemence of his response made her flush all over again. For a moment, she was lost for words.

"Then what is it?" she finally asked.

He turned, his body slowly spiraling as if she were watching him inside a dream. Standing so close to him accentuated the difference in their heights. She felt dwarfed when confronted by his large shoulders and chest. She noticed his breathing came more rapidly now in the rise and fall of the lines of his vest. Seeing his reaction to her made the tempo of her own heart accelerate.

"Then look at me," he commanded. His voice was raspy.

Veronique dragged her gaze up the white buttons of his shirt, over the knot of his cravat, around the prominent line of his jaw, and into his shimmering eyes. The moment her gaze met his at such close proximity, she felt the tug of his undeniable magnetism.

"I'm looking," she murmured.

"What do you feel when I look at you like this?"

"I feel drawn in," she replied, already hearing the singsong quality seeping into her voice. Her mind wandered, and she flashed once again upon the woodland she had seen before. "I...I hear things when you look at me."

"I can make you do anything I desire, Veronique," he said. "That is *my* special talent. I can make you or any other person do anything I want, just by staring at them."

She knew she should be afraid or repulsed by what he was saying, but all she could think about was rising on tiptoe to kiss him.

"Is that so bad?" she asked, her voice barely above a whisper.

"It is when you tire of the uneven playing field."

"Then you *do* want to play," she murmured, intoxicated by his gaze. "What if I want to play, too, Roman?" She reached for him, intending to throw her arms around his neck, but he caught both of her wrists in his hands.

"You shouldn't." He held her arms above her head. "Not with the likes of me."

"How do you know?" She taunted. She knew she shouldn't tease him when he was being so serious, but she couldn't keep from testing her newfound power over him and seeing how far she could go with it.

"Because I know what kind of man I am."

"Maybe I am intrigued by the kind of man you are." Somewhere in the back of her mind a little voice reminded her of the night in the churchyard, and how Roman could stab a man through the heart and say that he deserved it.

"You don't know me. You don't know what you're saying." His hands tightened around the bones of her wrists. She wondered if he was trying to control her or was struggling to contain himself.

"Close your eyes," she said. "If you think you have so much power over my senses, close your eyes."

A smile twitched at the corner of his mouth. She thought he was going to release her and step away. Instead, he slowly lowered the lids of his hooded eyes. Veronique watched in amazement as the noise in her head faded away, and the dreamlike atmosphere cleared. Yet the ache to kiss him remained, just as she had known it would.

"See?" she whispered. "Your eyes are closed. But I am still affected."

"In what way?" he murmured.

"I still want to do this."

She leaned forward, and strained upward until her mouth met his.

He froze.

She pressed into his wide lower lip, wanting much more from him, wanting him to bend over her, to kiss her like he meant it, and sweep her into his arms.

"Don't," he said against her mouth.

She felt his grip sag at her wrists. She took the opportunity to tug at her arms, enough to draw her hands to the wide lapels of his jacket. He allowed his hands to curl around her wrists and pull her into the wall of his body. And for a moment the kiss changed into a wild, slanting crush of their mouths. But the next moment, Roman threw back his head.

"No!" he gasped. He stepped backward, shaking his head, and releasing her. "No, this is not right. This is not—"

"You see?" She stepped back as well, shocked at the animal nature of their kiss. "Your eyes don't hold the power you think they do."

"You were still under their influence," he retorted, tugging down the hem of his vest. "You couldn't help yourself."

"I could if I had wanted to."

"I beg to differ."

"Then we will just have to try the same thing another time, before you ply me with drink and honeyed words, and turn my head."

"You are playing with fire, young lady."

"Tell me that you didn't like it," she shot back.

"You know that I did." He glanced down at her. "But I warn you, Veronique, that some things once started are very, very difficult to stop."

She met his gaze. "I'm not afraid."

"I don't think you are," he replied. "And that's what worries me." He broke off and strode to the door. "Come," he said without looking back at her. "Your dinner awaits. And I must leave soon."

Still aroused by their encounter, Veronique followed him to the door of his den. She might be young and inexperienced, but she had read his expressions correctly. He was a man of deep desires and a wolfish animal nature, tempered only by his amazing self-control. But she knew now that behind all the control and in spite of her humble upbringing, he wanted her. The thought sent a bolt of desire streaking through her.

She slipped by him and out to the hall. As she walked to the dining room, she wondered which of his traits would win out in the end, and if she would ever come to know the real Roman Brandt. She had until tomorrow afternoon to find out.

Veronique was disappointed when Roman did not sit with her while she ate dinner, as he had the night before. Instead, he waited at the hearth until her first course was served, warned her to stay in the house, and then excused himself.

At the dining table, Veronique ate in silence and wondered if Roman would make it a point to stay away from her now. Frustration tainted the excellent roast beef and Yorkshire pudding she had been served. Peas escaped her fork with maddening ease as her thoughts spiraled far from the meal before her. Good manners and even better sense dictated that she shouldn't have kissed her benefactor, but she didn't regret it. If she went through life never being kissed again, that single wolfish moment with Roman would be enough to sustain her fantasies for a long time to come.

She hurried through her tasteless meal. Now that Roman was gone, she could return to his study. Surely, she could find the supplies there to make a forged ID card. But it would not be a simple task, not if she wanted to produce a card that would withstand the scrutiny of the Overseers.

She imagined the Overseers were a small group of serious old men dressed in black, with no senses of humor and even less patience. With a botched ID card, she might never get to play for them. She couldn't let such a small detail ruin her chances, not when she could copy signatures and forms with the best of them.

After her meal, Veronique opened the large doors to Roman's study and softly closed them behind her. The fire still flickered in the grate, throwing the shadow of the bear across the room, all the way to the door where she stood. She felt like an intruder, even though she had no intention of abusing Roman's hospitality in any way. All she needed was heavy paper, a good pen, a pencil and a ruler. She could copy lettering with amazing skill and had a typesetter's eye for spacing and letter shapes. Still, she didn't feel right about being in this room on her own.

She forced herself to pass through the shadow of the bear and hurried toward the desk. When she got to Roman's big leather chair, she paused. Guilt washed over again. Sitting down in his chair and using his equipment seemed like a violation of his privacy.

She scoffed at herself. Why would a man begrudge her a piece of paper and a few drops of ink after he had showered her with fine clothing and gourmet dinners? She shook her head and sat down, determined to continue with her ID card mission. She pulled out the right top drawer, hoping to find something heavy enough to pass as cardstock.

Her glance fell on the wings of a letter lying half open in the drawer. She knew it was bad manners to read someone else's mail, but her gaze was snagged by an enigmatic phrase before she could avert her eyes.

...just a little girl. If she is picked up as an orphan, you know what will happen to her.

For an instant, Veronique froze, one hand on the desk blotter and the other on the knob of the drawer. She stared down at the letter, all her faculties focused on the beginning of the sentence.

...just a little girl...

Was there a little girl lost in Londo City? Her chest constricted. She knew what it was like to run through the dark streets, frightened and alone. She wouldn't wish that fate on anyone. Anxious to know more, Veronique pulled out the sheet, her entire being consumed with concern, just as someone opened the door across the room. Startled at having been caught snooping, Veronique glanced up, blushing.

"Oh, it's you," Mrs. Fernside said, folding her hands under her breasts. "I thought Mr. Brandt had left the lamps on."

Veronique fought down the blush that burned her cheeks. "I was just looking for something to write with. I need to write a letter."

"There are stationery supplies in the secretary in your room."

"Really?" She rose. "I didn't even notice a desk in the room."

"Just left of the window seat."

If Mrs. Fernside hadn't appeared, Veronique would have folded the letter and hidden it in the neckline of her bodice. But she couldn't very well steal the note while the housekeeper watched. Sighing, she pushed the drawer shut and slipped around the edge of the desk. She would have to come back later.

"Thank you, Mrs. Fernside."

"Ordinarily, I wouldn't chase you from a room, Citizen Bishop, but Mr. Brandt is particular about his privacy. I'm surprised he left the room unlocked, in fact. It isn't like him."

Perhaps Mr. Brandt had been unusually flustered the last time he'd been in his study. Veronique thought back to their kiss and had to fight down a second flush. The kiss had certainly affected her.

"I didn't mean to intrude, Mrs. Fernside."

The housekeeper nodded as she reached for the knob near the door and turned down the lamps.

Frustrated at having to leave the letter behind, Veronique hurried to her bedchamber. She would have to make do with whatever supplies she found there to craft a new ID card.

Hours later she held the new card up to the lamplight and studied her work. The card was passable. If the lights were low on Friday, and the agent was tired after a long day, she might just pass the scrutiny of an identity check.

Glad to have the task behind her, she slipped out of her bedroom and down the stairs to practice as long as her strength would allow.

As she hunched over the keyboard, playing a difficult series of fifths with her right hand, she caught a movement in the shadows out of the corner of her eye. Hoping Roman had come back, Veronique paused and peered over her shoulder.

Chapter 15

GLINTING IN SATIN AND sequins, Ruby Valentine materialized out of the darkness. Veronique stared, wondering how the woman had got into Roman's house, and why she would visit at such a late hour. Unless...

"Don't stop," Ruby purred, gathering up her skirts to brush through the doorway. "It's beautiful—as far as funeral music goes, that is. I can see why Roman keeps you around."

Veronique didn't know whether to take the comment as a compliment or insult.

She watched from the bench as Ruby flounced to the fireplace and turned. The fire illuminated the petite woman in flashes of color and curves. She was wearing a wine-colored outfit again, but this time the skirt was split in the front to reveal skin-tight leather leggings and boots that went all the way to her slender thighs. Like before, she wore a bustier over her claret-colored blouse. It twinkled in spirals of purple sequins and rhinestones, setting off her generous bosom. A velvet choker hugged her white neck, and from the band hung a golden locket. Between her breasts dangled a second necklace comprised of a cluster of antique objects—a pocket watch, a quizzing glass, parts of a charm bracelet, and a tassel made of delicate silver chains.

"Is Mrs. Fernside still up?" Veronique asked, wondering how Ruby had entered the house. "Did she let you in?"

Ruby let out a small snort and reached into the velvet bag hanging from one wrist. She pulled out a silver cigarette case.

"My dear Miss Bishop," she shot an indulgent smile at Veronique. "I come and go as I please."

"Oh."

Ruby tilted her elaborately coifed head. "Did Roman not give you a key? All his friends have a key to this house." She waved a free hand in front of her before she reached for her lighter. She wore lace gloves dyed purple to match her skirt.

Veronique pushed back the piano bench and stood up. Ruby had come to confront her about something, and she could guess what that something was. She slipped to the side of the grand piano and placed her right hand on its curving outer edge, hoping the massive instrument would add the impression of bulk to her inexperience with catfights.

"If you're here for Roman," she began, trying to affect a friendly tone, when she felt nothing but distrust for Ruby. "He left long ago."

Veronique reached for the pocket watch she wore around her own neck and was surprised to see it was three o'clock in the morning. What kind of woman made social calls in the middle of the night? She glanced at Ruby, who was busy lighting her cigarette. "Hours ago, in fact."

"That's all right. I can wait." Ruby picked a fleck of tobacco off the tip of her tongue. Her lipstick was as red as blood, contrasting sharply with her bone-white skin. Her mouth looked like a wound.

"I'm not sure when he'll be back."

"Like I said, sweetie, it doesn't matter. Keep playing." Ruby took a deep pull on her cigarette and held her breath when she said, "Pretend I'm not even here."

"I'm practicing a passage over and over again. It isn't meant for an audience."

"I don't mind." Ruby smiled and blew smoke out of her nostrils. She flicked a gloved hand. "Go on. Sit your pretty little bottom down on that bench."

Veronique was confused. She had thought Ruby had come to put her in her place in regard to Roman. But that didn't seem to be the case. Apparently, Ruby was waiting for Roman, just as she had claimed.

Veronique didn't wish to be rude, but the last thing she wanted to do was sit with Ruby Valentine and make small talk until Roman arrived. Hours might pass before he came back—hours she should spend rehearsing. Her best recourse was to ignore Ruby and get back to work.

"Very well." Veronique sat back down on the piano bench. "I'll just keep practicing, then."

"You do that, sweetie," Ruby said. "And I'll just stand here and enjoy my smoke."

Veronique angled her feet above the pedals and found her mental place in the music. She hadn't played for more than a minute when Ruby drifted across the room and leaned over the piano, uncomfortably close to Veronique's left hand as she pounded her way down to the bass register. Ruby hovered closer.

"So you play music all night while Roman's away?"

Veronique nodded and plowed forward with the difficult passage she'd been working on before she'd been interrupted.

"That's ambitious of you."

Veronique didn't answer. Every time she was supposed to play a B-flat, she always hit B-natural. She clenched her teeth and began the few measures again. She would play it until the correct series of notes became part of her hand. But it was hard to concentrate with Roman's friend staring at her.

Ruby's small eyes watched her. She took a long drag on her cigarette and blew it out. As the noxious fumes billowed around her, Veronique hit the B key again. In a cloud of frustration and cigarette smoke, she sat back and glared at the woman in red.

"Please don't blow your smoke in my face, Ruby."

"I'm sorry, did I?" Ruby held the offending cigarette in front of her nose and gave it a look of surprise. "I didn't realize it."

"You did. I can't practice if I can't breathe."

"What are you practicing for?" Ruby picked up a dish from a nearby side table. She tapped the ash off her cigarette into the delicate piece of porcelain cast in the shape of a seashell. Veronique was certain the dish was not meant for use as an ashtray. "Roman said you weren't playing at Whites any longer."

"Whites is not the only venue in Londo City." Veronique kept pounding the keys.

"Really?" She surveyed Veronique with her cold eyes, as if calculating her height, weight, and cup size. "Do you have a job somewhere new?"

"Not yet. But I'm hoping to get one soon."

"I'm surprised Roman will permit you to play anywhere but for him."

"Roman has no say over me." Veronique shot the other woman a sharp glance. Fired by anger, she pushed through the difficult passage. She played B-natural again. Damn.

Ruby tittered and tapped her cigarette ash into the shell again. "Don't be too sure about, that Miss Bishop. He's a man of many surprises."

"He seems like a gentleman to me."

"Does he?" Ruby cupped her elbow in her hand and blew smoke toward the ceiling. "My dear, how much you have to learn."

Veronique frowned. This was not going well. Not only was Ruby cutting into her practice time and polluting the air, she was also annoying her. Polite requests had fallen on deaf ears with Ruby. Cutting words would merely encourage her to come back with cutting retorts. The only thing Veronique could think of to drive Ruby away was to play music she might not like.

With her hands poised above the keys, Veronique whipped through her mental library of music. What composer would be an anathema to Ruby? She looked like a woman who favored smoky taverns and hungry men, lewd jokes and garish cosmetics. What music would she not understand or appreciate? Bartok. Veronique chose the most driving, atonal piece she knew and ripped into it with a vengeance.

Thunder rolled out of the piano. Ruby staggered back from the hammering keys. No one could make conversation when Bartok was on the menu. Out of the periphery of her eye, Veronique could see Ruby hurrying back to the fireplace, her gloved hands over her ears. Veronique grinned and played harder.

Bartok wouldn't help her with the Rachmaninoff piece, but any practicing was good for her fingers and brain. She'd play Bartok for hours if it that's what it took to keep Ruby and her cigarette smoke at bay.

Roman heard the music all the way out in the street. He paused at the gate and looked up at the bowed window where the music salon was located. *Bartok*. He hadn't heard Bartok in years. He was surprised that a young woman like Veronique even played the composer's work. It took a powerful soul to conquer such music, and an ear for the challenges and ironies Bartok made in response to the more old-fashioned composers. Bartok was to music as Van Gogh was to art. And Veronique was playing his work like the maestro himself. Roman took the stairs two at a time, anxious to get into the house so he wouldn't miss another note.

He slipped through the front door, hoping Veronique wouldn't hear him come in. Then he smiled at his own idiocy. How *could* she hear? The house rang with the discordant bangs of Bartok, each chord shaking the windows like cannon blasts. He was surprised Mrs. Fernside wasn't standing on the stairs pleading for him to make it stop.

His grin widened. He strode across the hall to the music salon and pulled open the door. His grin vanished.

Ruby Valentine sat in the shadows with her booted legs crossed, while she stamped out her cigarette in a 15th century Venetian dish worth a fortune.

Still in the doorway, he intensified his gaze until she glanced up at him. He crooked his finger at her. Smirking at him, she stood up. With her lips painted a deep red, her face looked like a white mask in the darkness. A cruel white mask. No matter how Ruby smiled, she could not hide her predatory nature from Roman. He'd known her far too long.

Without waiting for her, he walked to his study and turned up the gas wall sconces by the settee at the end of the room. Then he stood inside the doorway until Ruby appeared. She flounced toward the light as he closed the door behind her.

"I thought you would never get here," she said, plopping down in a chair.

Roman watched her slouch to one side. Ruby had had years to acquire some manners, but if anything, she had grown more and more casual in her deportment. He was surprised that she didn't fling one leg over the arm of the chair.

He walked to the liquor cabinet behind the matching wingback chairs. "Whiskey?" he asked.

"God no," she waved him off. "I need something cold after all that racket." She glanced back at the heavy paneled door. "At least it isn't so bad in here."

While Veronique's music shifted to a much gentler tune barely audible through the thick walls, Roman poured two glasses of whiskey and handed one to Ruby. "Sorry, this is the best I can do. I don't wish to awaken Mrs. Fernside to fetch something from the cellar."

Ruby glanced at the scotch as if it were poison but snaked her gloved fingers around the glass. "How do you stomach this stuff?"

"Stuff?" Roman lifted his crystal glass to the lamplight. "It's the finest of the Outer Islands. My pride and joy."

"When you took over the distillery, you could have at least changed the stupid name." She glanced at the bottle he'd left on top of the cabinet. "Laph...Laphra," she shook her head. "I can never remember how to even say it."

"Laphroiaig." He took a sip. "And you don't rename a classic. No matter what the Reformers said."

"Always a troublemaker, Roman." She took a gulp of the whiskey.

No wonder the woman didn't like it. She drank it as if it were ale. Roman shook his head and strolled to the fireplace.

"What are you doing here, Ruby?"

"Just paying a visit."

"At three o'clock in the morning?"

"I thought to catch you before you retired." She held the glass to her lower lip and gazed at him. He supposed it was her best provocative look, but it fell flat with him.

"You've been scarce, Roman," she pouted. "And now I know why."

"I've been busy. I just got back to town a few days ago, as you well know."

"And already you have a pretty young thing playing your piano." Ruby narrowed her eyes. "That had better be all that she's playing."

He ignored her threat. "So what do you know about Gabriel and Joanna?"

"Gabriel and Joanna?"

"Their disappearance."

Ruby picked a piece of tobacco from the tip of her tongue. "Nothing. No more than anyone else knows."

"So, they just disappeared."

"Well, I did hear that Joanna was ill at the time. Very ill."

"Did agents take her? Cull her?"

"That's possible."

"But you don't know for sure."

"No. I'm not privy to what goes on with the big boys." Ruby shook her head. "Only with you."

She shot a smile at Roman, but he didn't acknowledge the expression.

"It's a pity, though," Ruby continued. "I rather liked Joanna. She had pluck, you know? Kind of like your new little pet."

"Pet?" he retorted, even though he knew very well what she meant.

"She's not much more than a child, Roman."

He glanced over his shoulder at her. "She's none of your business, that's what she is."

"She is when she's staying with you." Ruby took another gulp and scowled. "What's she doing here, anyway?"

"I'm keeping her safe for the time being. Two hooligans roughed her up the other night."

"Hooligans?" Ruby swirled the liquor in her glass.

"You know what I mean."

"And they didn't touch your precious ingénue?"

"No."

"So, what are you going to do with her?" Ruby watched him carefully. "She can't stay here."

"I know that." Roman sipped his whiskey. He didn't actually know what he was going to do with Veronique, and he'd been putting off thinking about his limited options. To keep her safe, all he could think of was to get her out of Londo City. But where would he send her? The wilderness was no place for a young woman. But it was plain to see she couldn't stay here with him. Especially after what had happened between them in this very room earlier that night.

"Does she know about you?" Ruby asked, her voice full of amusement.

"Of course not."

"Hadn't you better tell her?"

"I don't see that it's necessary. No."

"But how can you resist her?" Ruby got to her feet and put down her glass. "All that freshness. All that luscious pale flesh…"

"Enough, Ruby."

"I'm amazed that a man of your appetites hasn't seduced her by now." Ruby poured herself another whiskey. "Really, Roman. You surprise me." She turned to smile at him. "Or have you finally decided to dedicate yourself to me—at last?"

Roman shook his head and turned away. She would never give up. And he would never give in. She thought she had rights to him, for saving his life in the past. If there had been some way to repay his debt to her, he would have happily forked over a fortune. But some debts had to be paid in kind. He knew that and so did Ruby. She used his honor like a weapon against him.

"If you don't tell her, I will," Ruby said, marching toward him. The tops of her boots brushed her muscular thighs. Another man might have been aroused by her provocative outfit, but Roman had never been attracted to her—not when he was younger, and certainly not now.

"Don't," he growled.

"Why keep her in the dark?"

"There is no reason for her to know." Roman scowled and finished his drink.

Ruby evaluated him for a moment and then a sly smile crept over her face. "Oh, you like it. That's why. You *like* pretending, don't you? And with her not knowing the truth, it makes it almost real, doesn't it?"

Her words mocked him. He'd been chiding himself for the last twenty-four hours for doing that very thing.

Before Roman realized that Ruby had sidled too close, he felt her hand shoot out to cup his groin. "Now that some parts of you are working better, you think you might have a taste?" She caressed him. "Have you tried out the equipment yet? Hmm? You know that I would be happy to oblige."

"Remove your hand," he said. Long ago, he had ceased trying to be nice to Ruby. She needed a firm hand, much like a headstrong mare.

She squeezed him, laughed, and pulled back her fingers.

Roman glared down at her. "Don't ever do that again."

"Oh, Roman! Say it again!" She threw her head back and laughed. "You're so fetching when you're angry!"

"You haven't seen me angry."

She ran around the back of the settee and crouched down, like a cat wishing to play. She wiggled her ass. "Come then, be angry. Show me what it's like when Roman Brandt loses his famous control."

"It's time for you to go, Ruby."

She tilted her head. "Wait until I tell the others what a sweet little thing you have stashed away here in your house."

"Please don't."

"Then convince me not to." Ruby trailed her fingertips along the top of the upholstered settee. "I don't ask for much."

Roman clenched his jaw. "That's emotional blackmail."

"A girl has to do what a girl has to do." She sidled around the end of the settee and pursed her lips in what she probably thought was a provocative expression. She caressed her left thigh, all the while staring at him. "I am just as hot-blooded as you. And wanting you more than you could know." She cupped her own groin. "Come on, Roman. While we still can."

He glared at her hand. The last thing he wanted was to have carnal relations with Ruby, much less kiss her. She reeked of cigarette smoke and a cloyingly sweet perfume. He could smell her halfway across the room. He guessed her hair would be as brittle to the touch as it looked. And that mouth. He would never want to kiss such a mouth.

"My key." He held out his hand. "I want it back."

"Your key?"

"You've just lost your privileges."

"What?" The smile dropped from her face. "You can't mean that."

"My friends are allowed to use this house when I am away. And friends don't blackmail each other. Evidently, you are not my friend."

"Roman!"

"I want the key."

For a long moment, she glared at him, her eyes blazing. "It's because of her, isn't it? You want the key because of her!"

Roman stepped closer, still holding out his hand. "Give it."

"You're going to regret this!" She fumbled with her bag, jabbing her hand into it while she snorted and fumed. She slapped a long brass key onto his outstretched palm. "There! But you are going to be sorry!"

"Goodnight, Ruby."

"Don't come crawling to me when the effects wear off, and you need help."

"I won't. You can count on it."

"Roman!"

"You've crossed the line, Ruby." He pulled open the door and indicated the hall beyond. "Goodnight."

She flounced past him, her face nearly as purple as her dress.

He watched her slam the front door and then made certain it was locked behind her. Tired from her antics, he rubbed the back of his neck. Taking away Ruby's key was only a formality. She could get in the house if she really wanted to. And she would. She would show up again. She always came back eventually. But he hoped it would be later rather than sooner, and that she would leave him alone for a while.

But alone to do what? That's what worried him.

Roman suddenly realized the Bartok concert was no longer shaking the rafters. He glanced at the door of the music salon and was shocked to see it standing open with Veronique's slender figure outlined in the doorway.

"Is everything all right?" Veronique asked.

For a moment, Roman was lost for words. He couldn't take his eyes off her. After being assaulted by Ruby in all her crass glory, Veronique's rosy freshness was like a breath of springtime. But then he thought back to what Ruby had inferred regarding his motives, and his loins stirred. It had been a long time since he was forced to rein in that part of himself. He swallowed and willed his arousal to subside.

"Fine. It's fine." Feeling uncharacteristically ill at ease, he ran a hand over his hair. "That was a fine way to come home, too, with Bartok filling the house."

"Oh." She pressed against the door behind her, which made her breasts lift. The shapely orbs beckoned to him, shamelessly. "I didn't mean to bother you."

"No, I meant that I liked it. Loved it, in fact."

"Oh." Her worried face blossomed into a smile. "I was trying to drive Ruby away with it. She was blowing smoke all over me."

"She does that." He smiled back. Veronique's creative way of dealing with Ruby amused him. Her kind, open face was a refreshing change to most of the calculating expressions of the people he knew. And her mouth, as virginal and pink as the dress she wore, was a far cry from Ruby's red lips. His loins stirred again, surprising him with an ache of longing he hadn't felt since he was a youth.

"It is time I retired," he said. "You aren't staying up, are you, Miss Bishop?"

"For a while. I need to practice."

"Your dedication is commendable."

She nodded and glanced away. He wondered what was going on in her head. But he couldn't stand in the hallway another minute with her. His control would only last so long. He took a step toward the stairs, but her voice stopped him.

"Before you go?"

He paused and looked back at her. "Yes?"

"I had a question. I've been worried–"

He watched a flush brand both of her cheeks. "About what?"

"Well, I didn't mean to violate your privacy, but I saw something in your study that I–"

All thought of seducing her fled in the face of what she might have discovered in his sanctuary. He swung back to stand directly in front of her. "You were in my study?"

"I wasn't there to snoop. I just wanted some writing supplies. But I saw the letter about the girl. I happened to glance at it..."

Gabriel's letter. He'd shut it in the top drawer of his desk and had never returned to dispose of it properly. He'd practically left it out in the open, when he should have burned it immediately after reading it.

"What were you doing going through my things?" he countered, more upset at himself than at her, for having left Gabriel's letter in plain sight. He was getting sloppy.

"I was looking for something to write on. And I just happened to see a letter in the top drawer of your desk."

She knew everything. He commanded his expression to remain impassive as his mind raced through the possibilities of how he would explain the facts to her. "I see."

Veronique stepped closer, her eyes troubled. "Are you looking for a little girl? Is there a girl lost in Londo City?"

He stared at her, confused for an instant.

"Because if there is, I can help. I know a million places where a child might hide."

Relief swept over him. She had not read the entire letter after all. "Yes," he managed to blurt. "You would be an expert in such things, wouldn't you."

"If you need my assistance, I'm happy to help."

"I may." He gave her a quick smile.

"Is that what you do?" she asked. "Are you a detective of some kind? An agent of the police?"

"I am a variety of things," he answered. But he was unwilling to divulge any more than that. Now that he was certain she hadn't read Gabriel's letter, his desire for her flared into full force again. The sooner he ended this conversation, the better.

"But at the moment, I am weary, Veronique. I must bid you goodnight. Let us talk more tomorrow."

"All right." She nodded. "But the sooner you find the girl, the better."

"Agreed." With a curt bow, he swept past her and hurried up the stairs to the safety of his bedchamber at the back of the house. He had never run away from a woman to save her honor before. But no matter how much he wanted to linger and listen to Veronique play, he couldn't trust himself to behave if he remained downstairs, not after the kiss they had shared.

He had to remind himself that Veronique was in all likelihood the daughter of his best friend. That made her totally off limits. To put it in even more brutal perspective, she could be *his* daughter.

Yet, because of the strange circumstances of time and fate, she was only a handful of years younger than he was—or at least as he was physically. And because of the effects of the radiation on his race and the way the virus had turned back time, his younger man's body was now demanding to be recognized.

As a newly appointed officer long ago, his desires had been denied him much of the time. He'd spent months on marches and what seemed like eternities on the battlefield, without the company of willing females. Then had come the fateful skirmish where he'd been shot, and everything had changed.

Now he knew what the word eternity really meant. He also knew what he would face in the next few months. His old man's soul was looking forward to the end with a sort of grim relief, but his young man's body was crying out for the sexual sustenance it had never received.

In the meantime, his immediate task was to make sure Veronique was safe in the world. As her father had said, Roman owed him a favor. He hadn't been able to help her when she was a child. But he could help her now. He would have to change his will, take her on a tour of his holdings, and show her where all his belongings were stashed. She would become the heir he would never produce, the wife he would never marry, and the sister he could barely remember. When the time came for the virus to take him, he would die frustrated but satisfied, knowing he had fulfilled his debt to Gabriel.

Roman stood at the window looking out at the night, more discontent than he had ever been, as unanswered questions burned through him. If Veronique could never be his wife, why couldn't she be his lover? What was so wrong with that? He could tell she was attracted to him, even when uncompelled by his gaze. That was something. He had but to reach out for her, and she would succumb to him. Of that he was certain.

Strong people forged lives of their own making, and Veronique was as strong as they came. She could handle the pressure of swimming upstream against the oppressive society in which they lived. She had done it all her life. Why not with him? He visualized her holding out her arms to him, smiling at him, taking him into her. His loins and heart ached at the prospect.

Distraught, he looked down and caught a glimpse of his broken hands reflected in the glass and was reminded of his ruined soul. He could never ask her for such a sacrifice. Not if he cared for her. He'd known from the moment he heard her play that he would care for her. Deeply. She of all people deserved a normal life and a normal man.

He must be the one to make the sacrifice. His gift to her would be a future free of dark entanglements. He would have to be satisfied with a noble gesture and nothing more.

Still, Roman could find no peace in the solitude of his bedroom. He paced, tried to read a book, and then finally headed back downstairs. If he were quiet enough, he could avoid Veronique and the temptations she presented. Once safely ensconced in his study, he would drink himself to oblivion—or poison himself trying.

Chapter 16

"I WAS INSTRUCTED TO give you this." The burly nurse placed a wooden box onto Joanna's lap. She had recovered enough to be able to sit up now.

"Look through it. See if you recognize anything."

"Who wants to know?" Joanna watched the woman's face, looking for truth or lies in her eyes.

"The Overseers."

"Who are they? Are they the ones that keep me shackled to this bed?"

"It's for your own good."

Joanna yanked her chains. "What part of this situation is good for me? Tell me!"

The nurse stared at her, agog at Joanna's show of strength.

"You can move your arms?" she gasped.

"And a lot more," Joanna wanted to retort. It was a lie. She could move her head and stay conscious for an hour at a time. Her hands obeyed her now, but her legs were unresponsive to commands. Slowly but surely, she was healing. Perhaps her legs would regain their strength as well. But it was best to keep news of her recovery from her prison guard nurse. She didn't trust the woman.

Joanna sank back, frustrated.

"Yes, I can move them a little," she muttered.

The nurse studied her for a long moment, judging her. Then she lifted the lid of the box.

"So, look at this," she instructed, holding up a blue pocket watch. "Anything?"

Joanna glanced at the watch and looked away, stabbed by a sharp memory that spoke of loss.

"Does it mean anything to you?" The nurse dangled the watch in front of her face.

"Never saw it before," Joanna answered, staring at the wall.

Father. Father painting the watch blue to mimic an old toy, so it wouldn't be taken away. Mother mending a shirt by the fire. She remembered having parents. Long ago.

"Nothing?" the nurse urged.

Joanna glared at her. "I said I don't recognize it. What do you want from me?"

The nurse frowned and picked up another object: a filigreed ring. She slipped it over one knuckle and held it under Joanna's nose.

"What about this?"

The golden ring glinted on the nurse's pudgy finger. It was a beautiful ring, fashioned of carnelian carved in the shape of a griffin. Someone had given her that ring. A man.

Gabriel. Oh, Gabriel...

A wave of longing washed over her. Gabriel had given her that ring to wear as protection. But in the end, nothing had protected her. She had fallen ill and been betrayed yet again. And now she sat shackled in a bed, somewhere far from Londo City, kept alive for reasons she could not fathom. And where was Gabriel?

When she tried to bring his face into focus, his image kept slipping away. She remembered how she loved his smile. His eyes. But she could not conjure them. Why? Had something happened to him, something serious enough to break their bond?

Her memory was coming back in a flood. But it was of little use to her when she was held prisoner.

"You remember this ring, don't you?" the nurse said. "I can see it in your eyes."

"I wish I could," Joanna retorted. "So I could remember how to get out of here."

"You're never getting out of here unless the Overseers release you."

"Why are they keeping me here?" Joanna couldn't remember the non-personal part of her life. Was it because of the drugs they were feeding her? "Why are they keeping me alive?"

"I don't know, citizen. I'm just the nurse." She closed her fist around the ring. "So nothing? This ring means nothing to you?"

"Not a damn thing."

"Citizen!" the nurse pulled back, aghast at her language. "You are asking for punishment. I could report you."

"Would it matter?" Joanna sighed and rolled her eyes.

The nurse pulled a third object out of the box and held it up, gazing at it, curious herself. It was a knitted sweater, a tiny white sweater with tiny white buttons. Joanna stared at the garment, galvanized by the sight of it.

Veronique. Her daughter. Veronique. That was what haunted her dreams. That was what she had forgotten to take care of. Nica. Her little girl.

"How long have I been here?" Joanna demanded.

"So you remember this, do you?" the nurse jiggled the little sweater.

"How long have I been here?" The words ground through her teeth.

The nurse shrugged. "Ten years? Give or take a few months."

"Ten years?" Shocked, Joanna sank back against the head of the bed.

"What does this sweater mean?" The nurse trailed it close to her nose. "What do you remember?"

"Leave me alone."

"Tell me!"

"I'm tired."

"Does this belong to your sister's child, or did you have a daughter?"

Joanna glared at the nurse until the woman stumbled backward, clutching the wooden box to her chest.

"You did have a daughter, didn't you?"

"She died." Joanna closed her eyes. "When she was a baby."

"You aren't fooling me, citizen. Clothes were found. Clothes that fit a school age child."

"Not mine."

"Liar. I will ask you again. Your daughter—where is she?"

"How would I know?" Joanna forced back tears as the floodgates of her memory swung open and drowned her. "After ten years, how the *hell* would I know?"

Chapter 17

RAIN POUNDED THE WINDOWS as Roman poured himself a whiskey and paced to the center of his study. He'd been so deep in thought he hadn't noticed until now that the house had gone quiet. Veronique must have retired after all. He wandered down the hall, sipping his drink, all the while wondering what she thought about his home. Did she like it? Would she be thrilled to learn that he would leave it all to her? Would she change it to suit her feminine tastes?

His feet took him to the music salon. Though the lamps were down, he could still make out the grand piano at the end of the room. The dying firelight outlined the left leg and the curve of the frame. He ambled forward, drawn to the instrument whose sound he loved above all others. Once, he had been a decent pianist. Nowhere near the caliber of Veronique or Gabriel. But decent.

Caught up by the strange mood she had provoked in him, Roman sat down at the piano and set his drink aside. He stared down at the ivory keys. How many years had passed since he had placed his hands on a keyboard? Lifetimes. And what had been the outcome of his love of music? Agony. Why was he here, then? Madness.

But all that didn't matter. Soon his life would be behind him, and nothing he did would matter. So, to hell with it.

He swallowed and forced himself to raise his hands. He held his fingers above the keys, willing the music to come back to him. If he had lost his music as he had lost so many other things over the years, he didn't know if he could take it. Not on a night like this.

He spread his crooked fingers. He felt the painful twinge of broken bones that had never knitted properly, but spread them nonetheless. Then he closed his eyes and let an old, half-forgotten life sweep him away.

Dvorak. The haunting notes of *The New World Symphony* spoke to Roman's own life, his journey, his waves of triumph and despair, and his ever-questing spirit. At first, the chords came out hesitantly as his mind struggled to retrieve the piece memorized so long ago. But he pressed on, in search of his old self, the boy who had been beaten into a man. Soon the notes streamed toward him, unbidden and effortless. He didn't even have to think. He merely had to let himself open up and play.

Like an old friend, the music came back to him as if it had been living in his hands for century upon century just waiting to be released. Soon he was playing the music he had learned as a boy but now was interpreting with the heart and soul of a man. He couldn't believe how much richness his experience brought to the music. He closed his eyes and let his spirit travel to a place where there was no earthly age, no past, and no future. Just music.

As he launched into the last movement where the traveler returns home to the sweet valley of his youth, he felt someone slip onto the seat next to him. He smelled a familiar fragrance and felt the hum of a provocative presence, but he didn't open his eyes. He knew Veronique had joined him, but he kept playing. After a moment, he heard a sweet melody following along with him on the upper register, echoing and embellishing the main theme with sprightly tinkles and runs.

Roman had never played with anyone before. He'd never experienced such perfect communion, as if he and Veronique spoke the same language and felt the same sensations. He didn't want the moment to end. If he could have made the song go on forever, he would have. But it ended, and far too soon. As the last notes faded into the darkness, he dropped his hands in his lap and slumped into silence.

For a long moment, neither of them said anything. Roman didn't know what to say. In fact, he was incapable of speech. He knew whatever words he might utter would break the spell he'd been under since he had sat down at the piano. If there were ever a perfect moment in life, this was it. He didn't want to tarnish it.

"That was beautiful," she murmured.

"It was."

"I didn't know you played."

"I haven't. Not for a very long time."

"Roman?"

He felt her fingertips steal across the back of his right hand. He pulled away.

"What happened to your hands?" Her shoulder touched his arm just above the elbow. The nearness of her made the side of his body buzz. He should have pulled away, should have stood up, but he didn't move.

He didn't answer either. Instead, he clasped his hands together, hiding his crooked fingers from her, and damned the desire to play that had overruled his good sense and revealed his handicap to the world.

"Roman?" She tried to lift his hands back into the light.

"Leave it," he commanded.

"Is that why you wear gloves all the time? Because of your hands?"

"Why else?" His shame made him lash out at her, when all he wanted to do was play the song again, with her lovely, perfectly formed fingers dancing alongside his.

She fell silent, and he felt her stare.

"Sorry, Veronique," he mumbled. He moved to get up, but her voice stopped him.

"So am I." She reached for his hand again and pulled on his right thumb until he allowed her to raise his hand to the light. "Someone did this to you. It wasn't an accident, was it?"

He glanced at her, warmed by the suppressed outrage in her voice.

"What bastard did this to you, Roman?"

"My stepfather."

Her brows knitted as she inspected his crooked hands. Even the back of his hand sported a lump on the side where the bone had healed at the wrong angle.

"Why?" she whispered. "Why would he do this to you?"

"Because I was a sissy." Roman allowed his cold hand to remain in her warm one. "Sissy boys play piano, you know. I had to have the sissy boy beaten out of me."

Veronique stared, her outrage more intense.

"And before a doctor could see to my hands, I was shipped off to military school. Only sissy boys complain of pain. Or run to their mothers."

"Oh, Roman!" she cried. She raised his broken hand to her cheek.

He thought he would melt from the compassion in her eyes and the anguish in her voice. Her skin was warmer than he had imagined. He wanted to let her hold him forever, with his cool flesh pressed against her lush, womanly cheek. Instead, he pulled away before he did anything foolish, and before she realized just how cold he was.

"Forgive me." Shaken, he struggled to his feet. "I don't know what came over me."

"Yes, you do," she whispered.

He stared down at her, every cell in his body vibrating.

"It's the same thing that has come over me," she added.

He tried to take a step back, but his feet seemed to be glued to the carpet. "And what would that be?" he managed to blurt.

As a vampire, he had seduced thousands of women. And yet with Veronique, he had lost both his tongue and his poise.

"A strange affinity for one another." She pivoted on the piano bench to face him. "A strange attraction."

"It's just the music."

"No, it's more than that. It's like we're soul mates."

"I don't believe in soul mates."

"I do." She rose in a rustle of silk. "I knew you were different the moment I met you." She reached out and placed a palm on his chest—taunting him, testing him. His hunger swirled around him in a red cloud. He was aware of her pulse, her heartbeat, and the musk of her desire. He sucked in a breath, alarmed by the effect her words had on him. He knew he should walk away, but instead he reached for her wrists to pull her closer.

"What I think you want from me is unlawful, citizen," he said.

"I don't care." She tipped her head back to stare directly into his face. "The law has never served me. It has only hunted me. Why start obeying it now?"

He gazed down at her, aching to believe in her logic but knowing her reasoning was flawed. "There are reasons you should stay away from me that have nothing to do with the law."

"I don't want to hear them." She took a resolute breath. "I don't care."

"You should." He squeezed her wrists. "And I do."

"Why?" Her eyes sparked at him. "Who makes up the rules? A bunch of old men I've never met. Why should I have to obey them? I don't know them, and they don't know me!"

Roman stared at her. Veronique was every bit as strong as he imagined and probably a good deal more. Perhaps she could handle the truth—about her father, about him, about everything. Perhaps he could indulge himself for the briefest of moments. He wouldn't hurt her. He would never hurt her. And then he would tell her everything. If she walked away, at least he would have the memory of her to carry to his grave.

He fought off a wave of hunger. The white flesh of her wrists beckoned to him. He could see the blood surging through the lavender lines just beneath her skin. It had been eons since he'd tasted such virginal flesh. What would it hurt to have just one small taste of her? He had enough self-restraint to keep within the bounds of safety.

Closing his eyes, Roman lifted her right wrist to his mouth and pressed his lips against her delicate bones. He could feel the transformation begin, readying for the deepest kiss of all. He sucked in a breath and moved on, pushing back his hunger. She gasped when he eased the kiss onto the mound of her thumb and pressed his cheek into the small of her hand. How tender she was. How fragile. And yet how powerfully she had played Bartok with those hands. The contrast was startling.

Even more startling was the way his body reacted to the touch of her flesh. In the blink of an eye, he forgot all about his wolfish thirst for her. In fact, what normal blood he'd managed to produce in the last few months surged directly to his loins, like the Great Flood. Good God, she had aroused him again and this time to unbearable proportions.

He could handle his vampire appetite, but he wasn't so sure he could handle his carnal inclinations, not when he had been denied satisfaction for such a long time. He had to step away to keep from devouring her on the spot.

Before Roman could raise his head, he felt her fingers push through his hair and pass over the top of his ear. She stepped into him and held him against her breasts. Her warmth enveloped him in a cloud. Her breath came in tight little gasps, inciting his own pulse to flare.

There was nothing like the warmth of a woman—so alive, so potent, so intoxicating. And Veronique's heat had a quality about it that he could not define—a special fragrance all her own. He'd never encountered anything like it. Her fragrance swirled around him in a wonderland of vanilla, cinnamon, and irises, and something sweeter that he could not identify, perhaps a product of her unusual bloodline. He wanted to burrow into her heat. He wanted to bury his entire being in her. Desire rasped up his throat in a rusty sigh.

God, how he wanted her. And she wanted him. Her expressive hands told him more than she probably guessed. Yet what was his body capable of doing with a woman? He had no idea. And the last thing he wanted was to fail Veronique in that regard. He pulled back, up and away from her heavenly heat.

"Vero-" he broke off, not sure how to explain why he might be unable to fulfill her needs—or his own. But before he mentioned possible shortcomings, he gave in to desire and bent to her mouth. The rest of her name melted between their lips. He felt his lonely spirit break apart and fall backward into the warm waters of her love. No kiss had ever shattered him as thoroughly.

Roman gathered her in his arms and dragged her off the floor. He couldn't help himself. He kissed her as he had wanted to kiss her since that first night she played at White's. She had entranced him with Chopin, made him her prisoner with Bartok, and turned the key with Dvorak. He couldn't get away from this enchantress. He didn't *want* to get away.

Veronique felt the change in Roman as his body transformed from velvet to steel. In a single heartbeat, she lost control of the situation. She sensed the power shift as Roman's kiss vaulted from a soft press of her mouth to a hard feast of her lips and jaw and neck. She dropped her head back and let him have his way. His hunger was like a drug. The more he took from her the more she wanted of him. She clung to his torso, moaning like a cat in heat. She wanted to climb beneath his clothes and embrace him until she dissolved into him.

His arms held her like iron bands. His fingers were like vices, his torso like a granite wall. His hardness inflamed her. She had not realized a man's body could turn to stone from the neck down when consumed by desire. His complete mastery of her frightened her, yet at the same time aroused her—feverishly so. He was going to ravish her, and she could do nothing to stop him.

Suddenly she was in the wooded glen she'd seen before when under his spell. She heard water. Birds. The song was louder now, bittersweet, rolling and billowing around her. Visions raced through her head: a sleigh coursing through a snowy night, lanterns blazing, schools and schools of glittering fish careening through turquoise water, sunrise breaking on a glacial lake. And a man riding toward her on a coal black horse. Riding, riding, riding as the drumbeat of the music pounded to a deafening roar.

"Roman!" she gasped as he held her against him with his right hand and closed the piano with his left. She guessed what he intended to do. "Not the piano!"

"Yes, the piano." His words were more growl than human speech.

Before she could make another protest, he lifted her off her feet.

She flung her arms around his neck to hold on, and at the movement, he glanced down at her. Their gazes met, his feverish and hers on fire. She had no idea what to expect of the moments to come, but she wanted to experience everything with this man. Everything.

He paused. The steel in his body suddenly broke.

"I can't," he breathed. "I cannot do this with you, Veronique." He closed his blazing eyes. "I can't. I can't."

"Why not?"

"It isn't right. You are too young."

"I'm an adult. I'm a grown woman."

"I am not the one who should take your maidenhood from you."

"Maybe I want to give it."

"I appreciate the offer," he replied. "But no, Veronique. I can't."

He released her. Slowly, she slid down the front of him and stepped away.

"Roman?" Her voice cracked with confusion and dismay.

"This is entirely my doing. I have let things get out of hand." He bowed. "Please accept my profound apologies."

"Roman-" She couldn't believe he could step away from the magic that had just soared between them.

"I must go out." He bent to pick up his coat.

"Roman—"

"I have my reasons, Veronique. Leave it at that."

"Reasons?" She trailed after him. "What reasons?"

"Personal ones." He tugged on his coat. "Get some rest. I will see you tomorrow."

"Do you expect me to forget what happened just now?"

He shot a glance at her. His hooded eyes were icy. Difficult to read. "You must. For your own good."

Roman opened the door.

Veronique turned her back and stared glumly at the piano. At the sight of the instrument, she suddenly remembered her audition. She had spent hours with Roman. It must be close to dawn. She was going to be a wreck if she didn't get some rest. And yet all she wanted to do was crawl into Roman's arms and continue where they had just left off.

She looked over her shoulder at him.

"Will I see you tomorrow?" she asked. "I mean, before dinner? Will you be here?"

Roman wondered why she would ask such a question. Of course he would see her tomorrow. He wanted to see her tomorrow and for hundreds of tomorrows after that.

"Actually, I am spending the day with a solicitor. I have personal affairs to arrange. My life is going to change soon, and I intend to have everything in order."

"Oh."

He was puzzled by the way her expression darkened. "Is that a problem?"

"No." She frowned and glanced at the dying fire and then at him. "It just sounds like you will be going away. Will you be?"

"Yes."

She tilted her head, much as Ruby had done, but the glint of disappointment in her eyes was totally unlike the taunting stare of his crass friend. "Were you going to go away without telling me?"

"Of course not. Never."

Her expression cleared with remarkable speed. "And you'll be home for dinner?"

"I will do my very best." He regarded her as he buttoned his vest. "Why? Will you be baking a cake for me?"

She smiled, but the expression wavered on her lips. She was hiding something. "I just wanted to make sure I would see you tonight. That's all."

Her odd behavior made him pause, long enough to allow reality to shoulder through the pleasure he had known in the last hours with her, and nearly snuffing it out. Guilt stabbed him. He should tell her everything. Right now. Yet if he told her the truth, she might turn away. Forever. He couldn't bear the thought, not after the communion they had just shared.

He would do anything to have a few more nights with her like this, with her believing he was a real man and sharing her exquisite kisses with him—even if it meant withholding the truth. What could a few more nights of deception hurt? The truth was going to shatter her, no matter if he told her now or later.

Roman studied her, knowing he was holding her glance far too long as he considered what to reveal to her and how.

"Roman," she said, one hand on the piano. "Is there something wrong?"

She was either keenly perceptive, or he had begun to wear his heart on his sleeve—which wasn't like him.

"No, what makes you say that?"

"You look as if you are going to tell me something. Something unpleasant."

So she had noticed. He should tell her. But he simply couldn't.

Like the cad he was, he switched to a much easier subject, that of leaving Londo City.

"What if I asked you—" he began, unsure how his suggestion would be received. He intensified his gaze in order to use his powers of persuasion to their greatest potential. He could take her out of the city by force if he had to, but it wasn't the way he wanted to deal with Veronique. He preferred to persuade her, and to keep their relationship as natural as possible. "What if I asked you to do something for me."

"Like what?" She studied him warily.

"To accompany me out of Londo City."

She blinked, but that was the only sign of surprise she revealed. She had amazing control over her reactions, almost as much as he had over himself. "For what reason?" she finally asked.

"I have a distillery up north that needs to be taken in hand. Since my absence, it is no longer producing as it should."

"What has that to do with me?"

"I assume you are looking for work."

"I am, but—"

"Then it's settled. You will accompany me to the north."

"In what capacity?"

"Personal musician." Roman was heartened that she hadn't flat out refused to go with him. "Music soothes the savage beast, or so they say, Miss Bishop."

Her pointed chin rose ever so slightly. "You would employ me to play the piano? That's all?"

"Yes. Unless you want more." He smiled. "And I promise not to steal the tips."

"And the salary?"

"Twenty units a day. Plus room and board. And any other fringe benefits you so require."

"For how long?"

"Until I return to Londo City. I would expect the journey to take a couple of weeks. I might not return for a few months, however, once I'm up there. If you find the work to your liking, and I find your music enriches my life, which it has so far, we can come to a permanent arrangement in the future."

She studied him as she considered his proposal. What could she find objectionable about the offer? If he had not ravished her just now, there would be no complications whatsoever, he was sure. What a fool he could be.

"Thank you for the offer," she replied, her tone cooling. "May I give you an answer on Saturday?"

"Of course." He kept his voice casual, when all the while he wondered why she might turn down such a lucrative offer. Could she have a better alternative? How could it be? And what could it be? Her reticence confounded him. "I will be leaving on Sunday. Let me know."

"All right. I will."

"I must go out for a while now." He reached for the latch of the door.

"Roman?" she called. Her voice cracked on his name.

He turned on the threshold. "Yes?"

She took a couple of steps toward him. "If I don't see you again—I mean, if we don't see each other tomorrow, I just wanted you to know how much your hospitality has meant to me. Everything, actually."

"What are you talking about—if you don't see me again?"

"I don't know how long I'll be staying."

His heart twisted. "There's no rush to leave. I trust you know that."

"Thanks, but I'm hoping I'll have a job soon. A real job."

"I just offered you a real job."

"You know what I mean. A *real* job. With a future. A career."

"You don't need a career."

"Yes, I do."

"What if I said I would take care of you, no strings attached? That you don't need to worry?"

"But I have always taken care of myself." Her brown eyes darkened, as distrust and suspicion crept into her expression. He couldn't blame her for not trusting him, after having been so hot and cold with her.

"I'm saying that you don't have to take care of yourself."

"Yes, I do." She set her jaw. "You know that I do."

She threw back her shoulders and stared at him. The steel in her determination stood in stiff contrast to the shining folds of her gown. She looked like a warrior draped in the wrong uniform. Her pride set against such incongruity made her more beautiful than any woman he could remember. He caught himself staring at her, completely entranced.

But no matter how much he admired her independent nature, he couldn't let her go. He had a promise to keep. Whatever career she had in mind, she would have to be dissuaded from pursuing it. He had to keep her safe, no matter the cost to her self-respect. If he could keep her innocent of the shadowed underbelly of Londo City as well, then so much the better.

God help him, he *wanted* to be responsible for Veronique, not just for the near future but for the rest of her life. If he could come home every night to her and her music, he would be the happiest man alive. He would be her guardian. Her mentor. Her friend.

Her father.

Shame spiked through him at the thought of his recent behavior. He had kissed Gabriel's daughter. Wolfishly kissed her. He had almost seduced her on top of a piano. What kind of gentleman lusted after the daughter of his best friend?

Roman prided himself on his decency and self-control. He had overstepped the bounds with Veronique, and he had to make sure it would never happen again. He would restrain himself. He would enjoy Veronique's companionship and keep it at that. He could conceal his true nature from her and live an almost normal life—something he had always yearned for.

The price he would pay for such a life would be high. He could never declare his true feelings. He could never make love to her. Never even touch her. It would be difficult to keep her at arm's length, but he could do it.

Besides, he wouldn't have to endure such painful restrictions for long. The days of his life were pouring through his fingers like so many grains of sand.

Chapter 18

AFTER ROMAN LEFT THE music salon, Veronique retired for the evening. As she walked up the grand staircase, her entire being hummed from the events of the day–from her run-in with Ruby, playing music with Roman, their shattering kiss, and then the confusing way Roman had cooled and backed off.

Mere days had passed since she'd come to Roman's house, but it seemed as if she had already spent a lifetime here. Roman's odd schedule had wreaked havoc with hers, which had resulted in making time stand still. Soon, however, her life would shift back to the daylight. The thought saddened her. She had enjoyed the night hours spent in this house–especially the hours with Roman.

Her musings turned from the past to that of the future as she opened the door to her bedroom and noticed light filtering through a crack in the curtains. A sharp thrill caught in her chest and then streaked through her arms and fingers. The day of her audition was dawning. Everything hinged on the moment she would sit down at the piano and play for the Overseers. *Everything.* She must not fail.

She knew she should close her eyes for a few hours and get some much-needed rest but sloughing off the anxiety that coursed though her would be difficult. She took a deep breath and reminded herself that music had never failed her. She shouldn't expect it to fail her this evening. Yet her life had always been difficult, and she had learned the hard way to temper all optimism.

Determined to master her inner turmoil, Veronique shut the door behind her and turned up the lamps. She would take a warm bath and then force herself to sleep.

Veronique headed toward the wardrobe, her head tilted downward while she unfastened the buttons at the back of her gown. She played through the Sousa piece in her mind, especially the part with the B-flat in the run. But just as she reached for the crystal knob of the wardrobe door, she heard the same high-pitched noise ringing in her ears that she had been hearing off and on for the past week. She whirled around at the same time as something leapt onto her, trapping her in a cloth that reeked of stale cigarettes and cloying perfume.

Ruby. Smothered in satin, Veronique couldn't see her assailant, but she was sure it was Ruby. She struggled to break free of the woman's grip, which was astoundingly strong for someone with such a petite frame. But she couldn't bat her way out of the folds of cloth. As she fought off the attack, she heard Ruby snarl and was shocked when the woman locked her legs around Veronique's hips. Veronique staggered under Ruby's weight, and tried to cry for help, but Ruby stuffed a wad of cloth in her mouth to muffle her. Lace rasped against her tongue. *Ruby's gloves.*

Veronique gagged and pivoted, trying to fling Ruby off her back, but the woman clung to her like a wild animal. She grabbed at Ruby's arms, but her hold was too strong to break. Then, much to Veronique's horror, she felt Ruby bite the flesh of her throat.

Shocked, Veronique staggered backward to the edge of the bed as Ruby pressed her mouth to her neck. She had thought Ruby was eccentric and overbearing, but she never would have guessed the woman was out and out crazy. And yet...and yet...

An unwelcome sensation of lassitude washed over Veronique. For a moment, all she could think about was sinking onto the coverlet and giving herself up to whatever Ruby wished to do to her.

It would be easy to give up. Even pleasurable. She heard herself sigh as her knees buckled, and she collapsed onto the bed.

Suddenly Ruby threw back her head and spat. Blood splattered the rose-garden fabric at Veronique's cheek.

"What in the Name of Wanda?" Ruby shrieked. As if she had wings, she launched herself off Veronique and landed on the floor at the end of the bed.

Veronique stared at her, still too stunned to move. Roman's friend had bitten her on the neck—and had actually broken the skin. She clamped her hand to the wound.

"What kind of a freak are you?" Ruby hissed.

Veronique would have asked the same question had she been able to speak. She was certain she glimpsed a set of fangs before Ruby snapped her mouth shut in a disgusted grimace.

"What has Roman been feeding you?" The woman in red smeared the back of her hand across her mouth and glared up at Veronique. "I haven't tasted anything that disgusting in my entire life!"

Veronique's mental fog continued to lift. She had the sense to reach for the gag. But she got her right hand only halfway to her mouth when Ruby lunged forward.

"Oh, no you don't!" She kneed Veronique in her abdomen, just below her ribs, which knocked the wind out of her in a sickening wave. Before Veronique could recover from the blow, Ruby tied her wrists with the cord of the dressing gown Mrs. Fernside had left on the bed.

Veronique gaped at Ruby in alarm, afraid for her life now, and questioning her sanity as well as that of the woman crouching above her. Ruby seemed to move at lightning speed and possess unusual strength. Not only that, she had bitten her on the neck. What else would she do? Veronique thrashed, desperate to get away.

Ruby glared down at her, tapping a finger on her chin. She sniffed the air. Then she leaned over and sniffed the air above Veronique's midsection. A flush spread across the woman's face as she stood up. Her eyes narrowed into slits.

"He seduced you."

Veronique stared up at the woman, wondering how Ruby could smell Roman's scent from such a distance.

"I can smell him on you!" Ruby hissed. "He bedded you, didn't he?"

Veronique didn't think denials would help. She kept silent.

Ruby balled her hands into fists and turned her back. Veronique wondered if Ruby was trying to control herself or was preparing herself to inflict more violence. Seconds later, Ruby turned back around, her mouth a cruel line and her eyes glittering.

"So be it," she declared. "He has a lot to answer for! And he will, by Gottfried." Then she perched a hand on her hip. "But he's good, isn't he? A real champ."

Veronique tried not to display her astonishment. Roman had slept with Ruby? She couldn't believe it.

"He's the best lover I've ever had." Ruby crossed her arms under her pointed breasts. "Insatiable." She gave a dry laugh. "What, surprised? You are." Ruby shook her head. "Poor thing, did you think you were special?"

Veronique had thought she *was* special. The possibility that Roman might kiss other women the way he had kissed her—and worse—make love to them, sent despair twisting through her chest.

"I'm afraid you aren't special at all, Veronique. In fact, Roman and I go at it like wild mink nearly every night."

Ruby surveyed her, drinking in her distress. Veronique couldn't keep disappointment from showing in her eyes.

"Too bad, but your precious lover can't help you now," Ruby's eyes flashed as red as her lipstick. "I'll teach *him* a lesson in loyalty. Boys?"

Two young men seemed to step out of the floral wallpaper and into the light. They were dressed in black suits worn green with age. One of them sported a tattered ivory scarf looped around his throat. The other wore a cap over his mousey bangs, which hid his expression—all but the cruel slant of his mouth. Veronique stared at them, terrified.

The one with the scarf ran a hungry inspection over Veronique's figure. The hairs on her neck and arms rose in fright. Both young men looked as if they were starving and she was a banquet spread upon the bed cover.

Veronique writhed, yanking at the cord that bound her wrists. She pulled up her knees, ready to kick the first person to approach her.

"What do you want us to do?" asked the one with the scarf.

"I want you to get her out of here." Ruby straightened her disheveled clothing. "Out the window before Brandt hears anything."

Out the window? Veronique glanced at the nearest window, which was hung with rose-colored velvet and ivory lace panels. Her bedroom was at least twenty feet off the ground. The only way they would manage such a feat would be if they had propped a very long ladder against the side of Roman's house.

The man with the cap ambled closer, just out of range of Veronique's feet while his companion bent closer to her head.

"Wait a minute." The one with the scarf cocked his head to study her more closely. "She's got red hair."

"What of it?" Ruby glared down at Veronique's hairline.

Veronique hadn't thought her red roots were that obvious. But here was the second person to take notice of the real color of her hair.

"I know someone who is looking for a red-headed female about this one's age." He winked at Veronique.

Veronique felt as if she were a beast being discussed at an abattoir.

"Who's looking?" Ruby asked.

"Neal Moray. Haven't you read any of the memos?"

"Why should I?" Ruby snorted. "I'm not the slightest interested in Moray's idiotic schemes."

"Because you've been hanging around Brandt too long." The young man laughed. "There's Brandt's way and the new way. I'm betting on the new way. Nothing else has worked."

"I would never bet against Roman," Ruby countered. "Anyone who would is a fool!"

"A dead fool."

The man with the cap sighed. "Not to put a damper on the exciting political discussion, but what do you want us to do with Rose Red here—after we get her out the window?"

"I *was* going to kill her." Vexed, Ruby crossed her arms. "That is obviously not going to happen tonight. I'd never get the taste out of my mouth. But she does have to go."

Full of dread, Veronique listened as they casually discussed her future, which appeared likely to end unnaturally and soon. She couldn't believe Ruby had planned to kill her—and to say so out loud like that and with such sangfroid, showed how heartless the woman was.

"Then can we have her?" the man with the ivory scarf smiled down at Veronique, his eyes gleaming. "Anyone who brings in the prize gets first chance at the antidote."

"And you believe that?" Ruby snorted.

The young man shot a glance of surprise at Ruby. "Why shouldn't I?"

Ruby shrugged and smoothed back her hair. "That's right. I forget how new you are to all of this, Edward. You couldn't possibly know what Moray's like."

"And?"

"He'd send his own mother to the Norsea mines, if he saw a political advantage in it."

"I'll take my chances," Edward retorted. "What do I have to lose?"

"Suit yourself. But if she gets away, you will answer to me. Do you understand?"

"She won't." Though Edward gave Ruby a jaunty smirk, he couldn't conceal his fear of the petite woman. He must have experienced her heartlessness first-hand.

Ruby marched to the window and yanked aside the velvet curtains. "Get her out now, then, before you lose the darkness. It's nearly dawn."

"Fine."

"And if I find out that you bungled the job, you will deeply regret it."

"You don't have to tell me twice, *mommy*."

"And don't call me that!"

Veronique stared from one to the other, trying to figure out their odd relationship and their even stranger behavior. Then the young man turned for the bed, chuckling. Veronique flipped on her back and struck out with her feet, pummeling the one called Edward squarely in the chest.

He staggered back, laughing, barely affected by the most powerful kick she could muster. His eyes danced as he caught her ankles in his hand. His fingers clamped around her bones like iron shackles while his partner grabbed her right arm and dragged her off the bed. She cried out, but the sound of her voice was no louder than a mumble.

"Ta-ta, Miss Bishop," Ruby flung open the casement window. "I won't say I'll miss your horrible music."

Veronique didn't have time to give Ruby a second glance. She was too busy worrying about how the two young men were going to climb out the window without dropping her.

"Roman!" she cried, desperate for him to hear her. But all that came out was a muffled moan.

Ruby laughed at her distress. "Don't worry about returning my gloves," she said. "I've got another pair just like it."

Ruby's voice mingled with the grunts of the men as they lifted her through the open window. Freezing air blasted through the opening and into the bodice of her half-open dress. Then to Veronique's astonishment, the men jumped into the air.

She screamed. The wadded gloves gagged her, and she coughed so hard that the lacy fabric at last untangled. She spit out the gloves just as the three of them landed on the ground.

At the last instant, the men yanked her upward to cushion her fall, almost pulling her arms out of their sockets. She hit the ground, careening forward, but they kept hold of her elbows, enough to prevent her from pitching forward onto her knees.

She gaped at them, amazed that anyone could jump from such a height and not break a bone. Yet the two men hadn't so much as sprained an ankle.

"Roman!" Veronique yelled.

Edward clamped a cold hand over her mouth. "Not a sound from you, Rose Red!"

"Yeah. Keep quiet," the other one said. "Or you'll wake the dead."

For some reason, the two men found the remark humorous. Giggling, they swept her up, one at her feet and the other at her shoulders. Like a discarded roll of carpet, they carried her out of the alley behind Roman's house and through the streets of Londo City. They seemed to know the back routes as well as she did: the unlighted lanes, the lonely passageways where good folk rarely tread, and the threadbare squares where the veil of night still draped over moldering benches and weed-filled flagstones. They snaked through two miles of city byways without encountering another living soul, until they came to what looked to be an abandoned warehouse in Brick Lane—a rundown East End neighborhood dominated by tile manufacturers and storage buildings. The two men set her on her feet.

"Hurry up and knock," Edward barked to his partner as he grabbed Veronique by her hair. "The sun is almost up."

The man with the cap banged a fist on the huge wooden door. Fog rolled around their feet as they waited for an answer. The late autumn cold didn't seem to bother the two men, even though they wore no overcoats. Veronique, on the other hand, shivered as she clutched the tops of her dress.

"Where the hell is everyone?" Edward leaned forward and kicked the door with the toe of his boot.

His companion glanced over his shoulder and squinted. Far to the east, bleak light oozed above the mist.

"We've only got a few minutes," the man with the cap said.

Teeth chattering, Veronique watched them, wondering at their odd remarks. Most people worried about being on the streets *after* dark, not during the daylight hours. Perhaps these two were afraid of being seen by agents of the Overseers. They were obviously criminals and were probably wanted by the Office of Detention.

Edward pounded again. "Hey!" he yelled. "Open up!"

After a moment, Veronique turned to him. "Please," she implored. "At least let me fix my gown. I'm freezing!"

Edward glared at her. "If I want any commentary from you, I'll ask."

"But I'm cold. Could I just button my dress while we wait?"

Edward narrowed his already small brown eyes.

"I'm not as tough as you," Veronique added. "Please, citizen."

"Oh, all right. But no funny stuff." Edward released her hair. His partner pounded on the door again.

"I'm going around to the side," he said. "Maybe the guard fell asleep or something."

He trotted off while Veronique struggled with the buttons of her gown. Her fingers were so cold she could barely feel the tiny glass discs between her fingertips.

Edward looked over his shoulder at the gray light creeping toward them between the brick warehouses on either side of the street.

"Shit." He pulled up the collar of his suit coat and pounded on the door again, harder than ever. The moment he turned his attention away from Veronique, she dashed toward the sun, hoping her abductors would not follow her. She knew she might have only one chance to get away, and she had to make it count. With her skirts flying and her heart in her throat, she sprinted down the cobbled street, with every shred of her being focused on speed.

"Come back here!" Edward shouted. His voice sounded far too close. No ordinary human being could have reacted so quickly to her break for freedom. But she had ceased to think of the two men as ordinary human beings. They were anything but. Still, she had no time to figure out who or what they were—not just now.

If memory served her right, there was an alley on the left that led to a circular marketplace with a score of doorways where she might be able to elude her pursuers. She shot toward the opening.

Something inside Veronique switched on. It was as if her strange urge to run had finally found an outlet. Her pace launched into a new level. She felt as if she were almost flying. The brick walls on either side of her blurred as tears flew out of the corners of her eyes. The cobblestones beneath her boots dissolved into a gray plane whose surface she barely touched. The morning air blasted past her, streaking through her hair as she rocketed toward the marketplace, leaving Edward far behind.

Years of living on the streets finally paid off for Veronique. Edward didn't find her. Just to be cautious, however, she hid in the shadows for an hour more before she ventured out. The light wasn't bright enough to illuminate the illegal brilliance of her rose-colored gown, but people still glanced at her with suspicion. Young ladies in sumptuous apparel did not often stroll through Brick Lane, and certainly not at such an early hour. Veronique knew her next order of business was to find something else to wear before she got arrested.

As the vendors opened their tawdry shops, Veronique could smell chicory tea brewing and potato scones frying. Her stomach growled, but she ignored it. She was accustomed to being hungry. She walked the lane, keeping to the center of the road so someone couldn't jump from a dark doorway and catch her off guard.

While she walked, she considered her options—or lack thereof. She had no money and nothing of value she could exchange for a more subdued outfit. The gown she wore was probably worth a hundred units, but no one in their right mind would buy it from her. Owning or wearing such a garment could place a citizen in serious jeopardy—including herself.

Though she hated to steal, she had no recourse but to grab a drab cloak or dress and make another run for it.

She stood in a doorway and surveyed her choices. She'd have to select a vendor on a corner, which would give her four escape routes to choose from at the last minute. In addition, she would have to find something appropriate hanging on a perimeter rack.

Veronique studied the tawdry landscape. She chose her target: a black caped coat, much like the one Roman Brandt had been wearing when he'd impaled the man in the churchyard.

Years of practice tempered Veronique's plan of attack. She waited until the vendor was engaged with two customers—a man and woman in well-pressed but over-laundered clothing. Then Veronique made her move.

Casually, she walked to the racks of cast-off clothing, tagged with colored squares of paper stapled to the collars or neckline. She kept the owner of the shop in the periphery of her sight, waiting for her moment. When he turned to hold up two items to the female customer, Veronique sipped the coat off the hanger.

The trick to successful thievery was to limit sudden moves that might draw attention. Stifling her thundering heart, she draped the coat over her arm and then strolled along the perimeter of the shop's wares, pretending to look at the other items on sale.

From under her lashes, she shot a glance at the vendor. He hunched over his cart, tallying something with a large pencil, seemingly oblivious to her. Veronique kept walking. She shifted the coat to her other arm and pulled off the blue tag. Past lines of black suit coats she walked, toward the intersection of the next streets. When she got to a rack of bulky items where she was sure she would not be seen, she hoisted the heavy coat over her shoulders and pulled up her skirts and knotted them to one side. In seconds, she transformed from a young lady in a shocking pink dress to just another faceless, nameless member of the Londo City monochrome.

Forcing her feet to maintain a maddeningly slow pace, Veronique continued toward the crossroads and never looked back. Looking back always gave a thief away. Sweat beaded along her telltale hairline. She wondered if anyone had seen her and would yell out. Even if someone called her out, she wondered if her newfound skill at running might allow her to outdistance just about anyone. She prayed she wouldn't have to test the theory.

You do not see me. You do not see me.

As she walked, she fastened the big black buttons of the coat until her gown was completely submerged in heavy wool, made heavier with a strong masculine scent. The coat brushed the tips of her boots and hung over her knuckles. But at least she would blend into the crowd now.

After a few blocks, Veronique's pulse quieted to its normal inaudible thrum. A steam clock tooted the hour. Nine AM. Ruby's thugs had obviously lost the trail and the vendor had not seen her rob him. She strolled on, headed for the other side of the Thames where the neighborhood was not so bleak.

She couldn't return to Roman's house. Ruby might be waiting for her. She would have to wait out the day until the time for her audition arrived. She had lost everything—even the shreds of clothing she had had saved from her garret room. She would have no identification and no acceptance letter to take to the Garrick Theatre. She had to brace herself for the possibility that she might be turned away without ever getting to touch a single piano key.

Heartsick, Veronique pressed onward. All she could hope for was that the Overseers might have mercy on her once they heard the story of her harrowing abduction—if, that is, she was permitted to tell it.

Chapter 19

"MR. BRANDT!"

Someone pounded on Roman's bedroom door, rousing him from his sleep. He came instantly awake and jumped to the floor, swearing. He hadn't had a decent rest since coming back to Londo City. Sheer exhaustion would kill him before the virus ever did.

"What is it?" he called, reaching for his dressing gown.

"It's Miss Bishop, sir!" Mrs. Fernside's voice rang with alarm from the other side of the door.

Roman's hackles rose. He strode to the door, yanking the belt of his robe tight around his waist, while all thoughts of sleep vanished. He pulled open the door to find Mrs. Fernside's face as white as the cotton mobcap she wore over her hair.

"What about Miss Bishop?" he asked, glancing down the hallway toward her bedroom door.

"I think something has happened to her!"

Alarm washed over him in a hot wave.

"What do you mean?" Roman stared down at his small housekeeper.

"I went in with her tea just now and found her window wide open."

"Her window?"

"Yes, and no sign of her." Mrs. Fernside clutched her arms close to her sagging bosom. "I don't think she even slept in the bed."

"Surely she wouldn't run off." Roman scowled and then plunged down the hallway. He dashed through the open door of Veronique's bedroom and stopped in the middle of the room to glance around the chamber. Nothing seemed amiss, except for the open curtains and the gaping window. The lace panels billowed in the late afternoon breeze. Roman walked past the untouched tea service, shielding his eyes from the bleak light as he approached the casement window. He glanced down at the ground. There was no sign of Veronique's escape: no knotted sheets and no ladder. He squinted down the alley that ran alongside his house. Surely, she wouldn't have run away. And yet last night she had mentioned that she might not see him again. She must have been planning something all along.

His thoughts flew as he shut the casement window. Where had Veronique gone? And why? He had treated her like a princess. What woman in her right mind would run away from the luxuries he had provided?

Roman searched the room, from the bathroom to the wardrobe, looking for clues as to why Veronique might have left the house. He found nothing, until he looked under the bed. There he discovered her satchel. She hadn't taken her possessions with her, which was strange if she had decided to run away. Maybe she planned to come back. The thought heartened him. Or maybe she had been taken by force out the window. Another wave of alarm crashed over him. If Veronique had come to harm, he wouldn't rest until he found her.

He grabbed the tapestry bag by its wooden handles and plopped it on the bed. Normally he would honor a person's privacy and not paw through their belongings. But Veronique might very well be in danger. Therefore, he had no qualms about opening the bag and searching the contents.

Roman fished through the bag, pulling out the black and purple striped vest he remembered her wearing at the club, and then a white blouse and a pair of lace panties that had been laundered so many times, the elastic had disintegrated at one leg. He held up the scrap of lace, wondering how often Veronique had worn the sad little piece of lingerie—probably hundreds of times—and marveling at how she must still value the garment if she had kept it.

He shook his head. Why would Veronique run away from the finery he could shower on her? She could have had all the lace panties she desired—and more.

Then his fingers found something more promising: an envelope. Maybe an old acquaintance had written to her. Some young buck from the streets. Maybe she had left for an assignation and a future that she intended to keep secret from him. Young love would trump lace panties any day and give a perfect explanation for her disappearance. Distressed at the possibility that a lover had torn Veronique from his life, Roman dragged the letter from the satchel, bracing for the worst.

He opened the flap. Inside was a piece of cardstock. He slipped it out and tilted it toward the light of the window.

"Congratulations," the card began. His worry eased. This was no love letter.

He scanned the short message, his curiosity piqued, until he saw the words "audition," "symphony," and "Overseers."

Damn it to hell, Veronique was scheduled to audition for the citizen symphony that she had mentioned a few days ago. He should have guessed she would try out for a position.

He scanned the rest of the invitation. She was due to play for the Overseers this very night—in a matter of hours in fact, at seven o'clock. Roman turned.

"I believe I know where I might find Miss Bishop." He held up the card. "Take her tea into my chamber, Mrs. Fernside. I'll drink it while I dress."

"Very good, sir." Mrs. Fernside bent for the tray.

Roman reached for the satchel to put it back under the bed but stopped in midair when he caught sight of a collection of purple dots splattered across the flower pattern of the coverlet. He hadn't noticed the dots until this moment. Roman bent closer and sniffed. *Blood.* His heart constricted in his chest.

He heard the clatter of the tea service as Mrs. Fernside came up behind him.

"Did you find something, sir?"

"Unfortunately, blood. There are some drops here on the coverlet."

"Oh dear!"

"We don't know if it's Veronique's. But in all likelihood..."

"Do you think something has happened to her?"

"I certainly hope not." Roman turned for the door. He frowned. "Unfortunately, trouble seems to follow Miss Bishop wherever she goes."

Night descended upon Londo City like a blind being pulled down from the rooftops. Grateful for the shadows as always, Veronique slipped out of the train station where she'd spent the afternoon and headed for the Garrick Theatre. She walked the blocks in silence, all senses on alert, hurrying past workers returning from the fields and shopkeepers closing their doors for the day. Soon the streets would be deserted, as the people of Londo City locked themselves in their homes for the night.

Veronique crossed a road crowded with steam chuggers and horse-drawn carriages and walked the half block to her destination.

People called the building the Garrick Theatre out of habit, even though it no longer provided entertainment. These days, theatres were used for disseminating information, much like churches were used for disseminating food and clothing instead of religious instruction. Veronique had never attended a community meeting, so she'd never stepped foot in The Garrick. She had no idea what to expect, or where she should go for the audition, but she pressed on undaunted. As she approached from the south, she studied the façade of the place.

The Garrick Theatre squatted in the middle of a block of stone buildings all the same height and all a dirty grey color from centuries of neglect. But the theatre stood out from the rest of its architectural companions because of a rickety metal awning hanging above its doors. She could see the remnants of light sockets where hundreds of light bulbs must have once lined the edges of the awning as well as all the windows. But electricity had been banned during the Reformation, and all bulbs destroyed.

In the old days, the theatre must have been quite a showplace, ablaze in light. Now, only soft gaslight glowed through the glass doors of the lobby and reflected in the puddles on the sidewalk. Veronique stepped around the puddles to the bank of doors. A sign taped to the middle door read:

Citizen Symphony Auditions – Main Stage

Her heart skipped a beat.

This was it. This was the night her life would either soar to heights her mother had never imagined or plummet back to her friend Jane's reality. Taking a deep breath to steady her hands, Veronique pushed down the corroded brass bar to open the door.

"Veronique, wait!" a voice rang out.

She glanced over her shoulder and was shocked to see Roman striding toward her, his coat flapping around his shining boots. The last thing she needed was an argument with Roman about the merits of the Citizen Symphony. She had enough on her mind.

"How did you know I was here?" she demanded.

"I found the card in your bag."

"You looked through my things?" She branded him with a scathing glance and pushed into the lobby. He followed, close at her heels.

"I had to. I was worried about you. Mrs. Fernside found you gone this morning, with your window wide open."

Veronique turned abruptly, and Roman nearly collided with her.

"Do you know why?" she threw at him.

"Why?"

"Your precious friend Ruby tried to kill me last night."

"What?" Roman's eyebrows shot up in genuine surprise.

"The woman's crazy, Roman. She bit my neck."

Veronique saw a shadow pass through his eyes and would have asked why, but she was in a hurry to get on with her audition.

"She had two thugs jump out of the window with me and carry me to Brick Lane."

"Why?"

"I don't know. Hold me for ransom? Sell me into slavery?" Veronique frowned. "Why don't you ask Ruby? You seem to have an intimate relationship with her, from what I hear."

She plunged forward, but he caught her arm.

"Wait, Veronique."

"Let go of me!"

"I don't know what went on with Ruby," he said as he released her, "but please hear me out before you do anything rash."

"Trusting *you* has turned out to be rash. I could have been killed last night."

"You still might."

"What do you mean?"

"These auditions," he swept the air with his hand. "This new symphony. How do you know it's genuine?"

"Why wouldn't it be?"

"It doesn't seem like something the Overseers would do."

"I'll take my chances with them. It can't be any worse than trusting you."

"I am not like Ruby." His eyes chilled with frost. "Do not make the mistake of classifying me in such a way."

"Really?" She avoided his gaze, determined to stay clear of his hypnotic eyes. Instead she threw a schoolgirl slogan at him. "*A man shall be known by the friends he calls his own.*"

Furious and unsettled, Veronique marched away, leaving him standing near the door.

"Veronique!" he called.

She ignored him. The lobby was empty, but she could hear voices deep in the building. Staircases on either side of the lobby were roped off with thick gold cords. The only route left to her was straight ahead. She squared her shoulders and strode toward the bank of interior doors that was barely visible in the low light. She thought it was strange that Roman didn't follow her, but she had no time to worry about his odd behavior.

When she got closer to the second bank of doors, she caught sight of a table at the right, where a scrawny man sat dressed in a top hat and black suit. He held a sheaf of paper in his left hand, a pen in his right and wore thick goggles, probably to allow him to read in the poor light of the wall sconces.

"May I help you?" he asked, training the goggles on her face.

"I'm Veronique Dunn." She approached the table, hoping the man was an understanding sort. She couldn't tell. She couldn't read his expression because the ornate brass and glass goggles dominated his face. "I'm here to audition."

The goggles scanned her from her fashionable boots, up the bulky wool coat she'd stolen, and over her pale face and damp hair. Thank goodness she still wore the rose-colored gown beneath the coat. At least she wouldn't look like a complete ragamuffin. If the lights were low during the audition, maybe no one would be able to see the scandalous color of her dress.

Half-composed explanations regarding her shortcomings tumbled through her mind, ready to spill from her lips if the clerk gave her the least sign of trouble. But she kept tight control of her tongue, having learned long ago that silence and a bland stare were often the best attributes when dealing authority figures.

The goggle survey left her and arced down to peer at the sheaf of papers in the man's hand.

"Dunn," he repeated. "Dunn."

The clerk took a maddeningly long time to sift through the names, time enough for Veronique to catch the muffled sound of someone playing a violin behind the bank of closed doors. She recognized the musical passage, even though the person playing the adagio rushed it to the point of destroying the intent of the composer. Probably because of nerves. Veronique winced for her fellow musician as she turned her attention back to the man at the table.

"Ah, here," he said, tapping the list. "Dunn. Veronique."

"Yes," Veronique nodded. "That's me."

The man held out his hand. "Your acceptance card?"

Veronique swallowed. "I don't have it."

"You don't have it?" The goggles swept back to her face. "You were instructed to bring it with you to the audition."

"I know, citizen, but—"

"The Overseers are adamant that all applicants abide by their instructions."

"I know, citizen, but I was robbed this afternoon. The thieves took everything—my clothes, my identification card, and my acceptance letter. Everything."

The glass lenses glinted in the lamplight as the man studied her.

"Please, sir, let me audition. My name is on the list. I'm supposed to be here."

"But you haven't followed the instructions. How do I know you are really who you say you are?"

"Does it matter what my name is?" Veronique's heart pounded in her chest. "Please let me play for the Overseers. I promise, you won't be sorry."

"Won't be sorry?" The man gave a mirthless chuckle. "I'm always sorry. What's to be happy about these days?"

The question made Veronique pause. A variety of things had made her happy the last few days: *warm baths, clean towels, handmade boots, plum sorbet, beautiful pianos, and pristine beds.* Everything that Roman had lavished on her had made her happy. But even those wonderful things barely registered on the happiness scale when compared to Roman's kiss. That kiss had altered her world forever.

A painful feeling constricted her already tormented heart. If she managed to get to the audition and then was selected for the symphony, she would never see Roman again.

She couldn't think about that now. She must put him out of her mind. Besides, he wasn't worthy of her slightest thought. He was a killer, and his friends were ruthless. She was a fool to dwell on the man or his kiss.

"I don't like this." The clerk scowled at his list. "How do I know you qualify?"

"I'm eighteen. I just turned eighteen a few days ago. Isn't that the only real qualification? My age can be verified later, surely."

"If you are playing some kind of game, young lady..."

"I promise you I'm not. I was the victim of a crime. Please, citizen, don't punish me for something beyond my control."

The goggles glanced at her and then back down at the table. He raised the pen above her name. "Oh, very well. Go inside." He waved her toward the doors at his right.

Relief swept through Veronique, but she kept her expression impassive, never wanting outsiders to know what thoughts or emotions were running through her mind. Carefully she opened the door so as not to disturb the violinist still demolishing the adagio.

The door led to an antechamber that was as dimly lit as the lobby had been. As the door closed behind her, she saw a small shape coming toward her out of the shadows. Veronique braced herself, ready to run. She'd been attacked too many times this past week to take shadowy shapes lightly.

"Last name?" the shaped asked.

Veronique could see the person's silhouette was that of a female. A badge on the woman's left breast displayed the red and blue logo of a medical officer.

"Dunn." Veronique still didn't let down her guard. Why was a medical officer at the audition?

"Remove your coat, please." The woman pulled a syringe from a pouch. "I need to take a blood sample from you."

"Blood sample? Why?"

"All symphony members must be in excellent health. No use spending time and money on educating people who will not be able to withstand the rigors of the training program."

That made sense to Veronique. She shrugged out of the coat and threw it over her right arm. The woman wrapped a cord around the top of her left arm and reached for her hand.

"Make a fist."

Veronique watched the medical officer pierce her skin with a needle and slowly ease out enough blood to fill a small vial. Veronique stared at the dark liquid flowing into the glass container. She had never seen her own blood before. She had never been badly wounded, and she hadn't ever menstruated. Jane had begun to have her womanly flow a year ago, but Veronique had not entered her menses yet. Perhaps like other young women in Londo City whose genes had been altered by radiation, she never would come to full maturity.

Many people believed radiation had changed human beings forever, but until this moment Veronique had not given the state of her race much thought. All she was concerned with was being embraced by Londo society and accepted as a rightful member at last.

"You can go now," the medical officer said, pointing toward more doors. "Be sure to press on your arm until it stops bleeding. And stay quiet until they call your name."

"Thanks." Glad to be over what seemed to be the last hurdle of audition formalities, Veronique pushed through the door with her shoulder.

A wide aisle carpeted in a swirling pattern of maroon and gold led gently downward toward the stage. Veronique's lips parted in awe at the sight of the gilt and velvet wonderland before her. She'd never seen anything so ornate—not even at Whites. The stage was two stories high from floor to ceiling and flanked by gilded boxes and sculpted columns. Lush claret-colored curtains hung from the vaulted ceiling, complemented by a crystal and gilt chandelier so large, it would have filled up most people's entire living quarters.

On either side of her were rows upon rows of upholstered seats. Behind her was a second story full of seats, as well as tiers on either side that climbed all the way to the tin ceiling high above her head. Thousands of people must have watched plays here at one time. Now, after the devastation of the Grave Mistake, the climate change and the collapse of society, the whole of Londo City could be seated here and still have room to spare.

Veronique frowned and turned off her thoughts. She didn't want to think about the terrible past. Her intent was to run headlong into the future and never look back.

Slowly, she padded down the aisle, wondering where she should sit. A few seats from the judges, she paused and looked up. At center stage stood a small young lady dressed in a gray gown and bathed in light, playing her nervous adagio. Veronique could see the girl's left hand shaking. As she played, the light turned her mousey hair to a glowing nimbus while five black silhouettes watched from the first row of seats. Veronique guessed the five judges were members of the Overseers, the powerful ruling body that no one ever saw and rarely heard from. They didn't seem to be enjoying themselves. Not one of them nodded his head to the music or tapped a finger. In fact, all five had unusually stiff posture and didn't utter a word to each other.

Chastened by the demeanor of the Overseers, Veronique sank to a seat and tried to relax. In order to give her best performance, she must put everything out of her mind except music. She closed her eyes.

Chapter 20

"TIME FOR YOUR TEST," the nurse announced.

Joanna feigned sleep. For the past few days, she had stayed awake for hours at a stretch. She knew she was almost fully healed. She could wiggle her toes, and she was ravenous. Whatever they had been feeding her through the tube was not enough now.

In a week or two, she would be able to grab the nurse at a vulnerable time. Maybe even choke her until the woman relinquished the keys to her manacles.

She heard the nurse breathing as she took her pulse. Then she waited for the tourniquet to be bound around her upper arm.

"Make a fist," the nurse instructed.

Joanna feigned deafness.

"I said make a fist."

Joanna didn't move.

"Very well, don't." The nurse jabbed the needle into the crook of her arm and moved it around under the skin, looking for a vein. Pain streaked up Joanna's arm, but she kept her expression blank.

"Two can play your games," the nurse retorted. She yanked away the tourniquet, chafing Joanna's arm.

"And now, it's exercise time." The nurse grabbed one of Veronique's feet. Roughly, she pushed her leg up until the knee buckled and knocked her in the chin.

"How do you like that, citizen?"

Seething, Joanna kept her leg cocked and drew up the other leg, unsure if her muscles would obey her for long. She felt heat race down the back of her thighs and into her calves. With a grunt, she thrust both feet forward and bashed the nurse in the stomach. The woman flew across the room and crashed against the wall, howling in pain.

"Bitch!" she panted, holding her abdomen. "You're going to get it, now."

Joanna yanked at her chains, desperate to get away.

She watched the nurse march to a valise and snatch out a syringe and a bottle. Joanna pulled at the manacles on her arms, struggling to slip her hands through the cuffs. She tugged until her bones ached and her skin abraded. But she couldn't get the cuff over her thumb joint.

The nurse charged forward, holding the syringe in the air. Then she plunged the needle into Joanna's shoulder.

"Take that," the nurse said. She grimaced and stepped back to watch as Joanna plummeted into a drugged stupor.

JOANNA'S VISION BLURRED. Shapes swirled around her. She couldn't stop the colored blobs and ceiling from circling around her. Sick with dizziness, she closed her eyes and careened into darkness.

The tunnel dream came back. She was running in the long corridor again, but she was too dizzy to keep to her feet without reaching out to support herself on the walls. Even in her dream, she shuddered at the hoariness of the passage. The sides of the tunnel were hewn from crumbling dirt and dank stone and the bottom was wet with slime. She recognized the place this time.

She was stumbling through the smuggler's tunnel in Port Pennwood.

If she could only get to the end, she would be safe. There would be no more nurses, no more shackles and no more drugs.

"You can do this," Joanna chanted to herself. "You can get through this. You can do this."

She ran for what seemed like hours, reeling and woozy. There, near the end, she could see a black lump materializing out of the darkness. A body. Unmoving.

"Gabriel!" she screamed.

Chapter 21

"DUNN, VERONIQUE."

Veronique jerked to attention and opened her eyes. Someone in the front row had called her name. Veronique glanced at the stage. The violinist was nowhere in sight. She must have missed the young woman's exit. Veronique's chest swelled with anxiety. This was it: her turn to mount the stairs to the stage and play her heart out.

Her mouth went dry as she stood up and eased out to the aisle, leaving the stolen coat behind. She walked toward the stage, reminding herself that she had played flawlessly at Whites to an appreciative audience. This audition would be no different. All she had to do was ignore the five silent monoliths in the front row and remain calm.

She could feel their stares on her back as she walked up the steps. She heard one of them suck in his breath as she flowed into the light. Her rose-colored gown lit up the stage as if it possessed its own internal fire.

"Is this some sort of joke?" a deep voice boomed.

Veronique searched for the face that belonged to the voice, but the glare of the footlights blinded her. "Pardon?" she asked.

"Do you flout the law, young lady?"

Veronique flushed. "Do you mean with this dress?" She swept the pink folds with the edges of her hands.

"Is it not obvious what we mean?"

"I am sorry, citizen. It was all I had. I mean, all I was given to wear."

"By whom?" the voice demanded.

Veronique would never disclose the name of her benefactor. He'd done too much for her to deserve to be punished by the Overseers.

"By the people who found me," Veronique put in. She had spent years making up lies about herself and her activities. She could do so again. "I was robbed today. I lost all my possessions. A good family found me weeping on the street but had nothing to spare for me but this ancient dress. I would never wear such a color if I had a choice."

"You mean to say the thieves took your clothing?"

"And more," Veronique clasped her hands together. "They would have abused me, citizen, had not my benefactors come to my rescue." That wasn't a lie, to be sure. She'd just altered the timeline a bit.

"I was desperate to make it to this audition. Even wearing this dress."

"Let her play," a second voice, reedier than the first, put in. "We can deal with the dress code violation later, if we need to."

"I agree with Moray," a third voice added. "We digress."

Moray? Though the stage lights were hot, Veronique felt a chill pass through her. Was her pursuer sitting in the audience? Was he an Overseer? She gulped back her alarm, reminding herself that more than one person named Moray could be living in Londo City. She squinted, struggling to see through the glare of the lights. But she could not make out any facial features of the judges. Besides, she had no idea what her pursuer looked like.

She suddenly wondered if instead of rushing headlong into the future, she had walked straight into a trap.

Worried and nervous, Veronique sat down at the piano just right of center stage. It was a grand piano—a gleaming black Steinway that looked as if it had never been touched by human hands. Trying to ignore the fact that her pursuer might be watching her from the front row, she adjusted the bench and placed her boots on the pedals. Then she took a deep breath to compose herself. She lifted her hands.

Take me away, she prayed to the beautiful instrument before her. *Take me away from all this, and I will play you the way you were meant to be played.*

She closed her eyes and struck the opening notes of the Sousa march. Her fingers knew the way. Her heart soon followed. No march had ever been played with such intensity or precision. Even the run flowed out of her fingers flawlessly, with no B-natural to be heard. She finished with a flourish and to utter silence.

After a pause, she glanced at the monoliths, her heart still beating a hard staccato behind her breastbone. She could see the judges conferring about something. Was that a good sign or bad? She glanced around the stage, looking for obstacles in case she had to bolt for freedom. She couldn't see anyone standing in the wings. But she couldn't see a door, either.

One of the judges cleared his throat. "Play again, Citizen Dunn. Something of your own choosing this time."

Had they asked the violinist to play more than one song? She wondered if their request was routine, or if she had made it to a second level in the audition process. At least they hadn't told her to leave.

Heartened, Veronique ran through a mental list of her favorite pieces, knowing she should choose one that would showcase her range of ability in the shortest amount of time. She raised her chin.

"I would like to play a Chopin etude. Opus 10, Number 3 in E Major. Many know it as *So Deep Is the Night*."

"Very well," the booming voice replied. "Begin."

The etude began softly, like wind lifting leaf tips, like afternoon sunlight dappling to dusk. She played the nearly inaudible notes with her eyes closed, building to the bittersweet, shattering crescendo at the center of the piece. As she pushed toward the heart of the etude and hit the climax, her breath caught in her chest in an almost unbearable swell.

She had felt this sensation before, but not while playing Chopin. She had felt it in Roman's arms. His kiss had brought her to this same piercing, poignant place. For a moment, she hung on the top note, stunned by the realization that a man had been able to take her to the same heights that music did. Then she swept down the slope of the notes, into the pool of emotion that only Chopin could evoke. The complexity of notes spoke of passion, despair, and a tortured heart abandoned at the close of a glorious love.

She loved him. After so short a time, she loved him. But she must *not* love him. He had shown himself to be unworthy of her regard. She must forget him and never look back.

Her heart cracked in two at the thought, and tears dropped from her eyes. *Roman.* How could she pursue a life with a symphony over Roman? Without him in her life, she would be as alone and devastated as the soul of this music. What was she doing here? She was barely aware when song ended.

The monoliths were silent. She dashed the tears from her cheeks, chiding herself for displaying too much emotion. From what she had been told, the Overseers were logical, strict, and unsentimental. She had probably violated another one of their precious rules, just as she had done by wearing the rose-colored dress.

While Veronique waited at the piano, she saw a small figure bustle down the aisle and hand a note to the nearest judge. Veronique guessed the figure was the medical officer who had taken her blood, but because of the bright lights of the stage and the darkness beyond, she could still not make out features on the people in the audience.

The note passed through all ten hands, until the last judge dropped his hands in his lap and looked up.

"We have found our pianist," he announced. "Welcome to the Citizen Symphony, Miss Dunn."

Veronique stared, her tears turning to sand in her eyes. Her mouth went dry. She couldn't believe what she'd just heard. For once, she didn't know what to do and sat fused to the piano bench.

"Miss Dunn?" the man with the reedy voice called out. *Moray's voice.*

Her senses rushed back to her, sharpened by fear and indecision. She had been selected for the symphony. This was what she had worked for her entire life. Why, then, did it suddenly feel so wrong? She clutched the edge of the bench with both hands. Her ears started to ring.

"Pardon?" she stammered. She rose.

"Your audition was extraordinary. You are just what we are looking for."

Chapter 22

VERONIQUE WATCHED NEAL Moray stand up and approach the stage. When his features materialized out of the darkness, Veronique had to force herself to remain standing in one spot and not bolt offstage. She'd seen that face before. This was the man who had insulted her on the street outside Roman's house. Surely, this was also the man whom Roman had discussed with the person in the graveyard—before he had run him through with his cane.

She was sure now that she *had* stepped into a trap.

Moray raised his hand to guide her down the flight of steps at the left. Though Veronique didn't want to touch the man, she had no recourse but to accept his help. His fingers grasped hers, and they were as chilly as the regard of his hazel eyes.

She took his measure as he guided her down the steps. Moray was a slight man with the usual brown hair and spare frame of most Londo City males. His hands were as delicate as a woman's, however, and the fingers that clutched hers were narrow, tapered, and soft at the tips. She wondered if he bit his nails. She glanced up at his face, curious that a grown man would retain such a childish habit. But there was nothing childish in his expression.

His face was a ghoulish mask, marked by pink scars that swept upward from the corners of his mouth. He reminded her of a snake she had once seen in Scotland Yard. His lips were thin and straight, and tipped up by the scars into a perpetual smirk. The cruelness of the smirk alarmed her.

When she reached the bottom of the steps, he released her hand. She wanted to wipe away his touch by swiping her palm on her dress, but she refrained. He would take notice. She didn't want to offend any of the Overseers. People were banned to the Norsea work camps for the slightest offense, and she had already stretched the boundaries by wearing the rose-colored gown.

"A prize as precious as you must be treated well," Moray commented. "And guarded closely."

She didn't reply. His choice of words sent a chill down her spine.

"Citizen Walsh?" he called over his shoulder.

The medical officer straightened to full attention. "Yes?"

"See that Citizen Dunn is transported safely to the Central Compound."

"At once."

The medical officer reached for Veronique's elbow.

Moray turned back to Veronique. "You will be sanitized, groomed, and subjected to a complete physical examination. We want no surprises, citizen."

"I have no medical issues," Veronique shot back.

"That may be so," he tilted his head, and she thought she saw a slight smile lift the slit of his mouth before he reined in his amusement. "But we must take every precaution."

Veronique raised her chin. She didn't like this man, and she didn't know why. But she knew one thing for certain. He was her enemy. Since he had been in pursuit of her the past couple of weeks, he must have an agenda completely different from that of the symphony selection. Once she got out of earshot of Moray, she would tell an Overseer about the bounty he had set on her head and beg them for protection. If they thought she was good enough for their symphony, they would have to prove it by ensuring her safety.

Moray hadn't joked about Veronique's physical examination when he termed it a complete one. First, a strong-armed woman subjected her to a bath, during which the woman treated her more like a dirty piece of laundry than a human being. Then another woman came in, studied various strands of her hair, and returned with a concoction that stripped the walnut dye from her locks. Every nail was cut and polished. Every hair on her body was either trimmed, tastefully shaved or removed. When the two ladies were finished, the "laundress" announced that Veronique would be taken to the medical lab next and to please lie down on the gurney. Neither of the women smiled at her, looked her in the eye or said good-bye. Veronique sank back, feeling faceless and nameless, and more than ever like a piece of laundry. But at least she was a *squeaky-clean* piece of laundry now.

Moments later, a male attendant arrived to collect her gurney. As Veronique was rushed from the bathing station to the medical facility, she caught a glimpse of herself in a window and was shocked to see her natural red hair for the first time in her life. She jerked to a sitting position to stare at her reflection.

She barely recognized herself. Her tresses flowed like gleaming flames down her back, transforming her usual far too pallid skin to ivory moonglow. She looked magical, otherworldly.

"Please lie down, citizen," the attendant barked.

Still shocked by what she had seen, Veronique sank back to the padded gurney. No wonder her mother had insisted that she do whatever it took to fit in with the rest of the Londo residents. She looked like a freak. But why? What was it about her heritage that had cursed her with such outlandish hair, pale skin, and unusual height?

At the lab, Veronique was weighed using a water device and then again using a metal scale. Every part of her body was measured with a cloth tape and recorded in a book. Her blood was drawn again, and then she was put through a score of machines that chugged and clanked and tooted, all designed, she supposed, to peer into her internal organs, make a record of her bone structure, and monitor her bodily functions. Veronique lost track of time as she was drawn into the devices on conveyor belts or pushed through them while she lay on a metal table that rolled though the medical equipment. After an hour of being poked and prodded, she felt her lack of sleep descending upon her, and as the machines thrummed endlessly onward, she succumbed to fatigue and nodded off.

WHEN VERONIQUE WOKE up, she was surprised to find herself in a totally different place. She was no longer lying on the metal table in the medical facility but reclining in a padded chair in a shrouded bedchamber that smelled of sickness and decay.

As she came to her senses, she realized someone was inserting a needle into her right arm. Though she felt unusually groggy, and the room was too dark to make out many details, she recognized the slight figure hovering over her. *Moray.*

She jerked up, commanding her dizzy head to clear and her trembling limbs to obey her will. But she couldn't move. Her wrists and ankles were bound to the chair with braided cords.

Chapter 23

"SORRY," PURRED MORAY, smiling down at her. The pupils of his glowing eyes dilated like a cat's. "I didn't mean to wake you."

"Where am I?" Veronique demanded.

"Where you were designed to be the day you were born."

"What are you talking about?" She yanked her traces, but only managed to chafe her wrists. "Let me go!"

Moray ignored her. He straightened and turned to a small machine perched on the nightstand between the padded chair and a nearby bed. To Veronique's horror, she realized the needle in her arm was connected to a tube that looped up to the machine, and that the machine was connected to two more tubes that led to a reclining figure in the bed. All she could see of the person in the bed was the emaciated skull, bony nose, and short wisps of hair of an ancient man whose face was covered with age spots and lesions.

Judging by the smell in the room, the man was either dead or close to dying.

Veronique stared at the tubing that linked her to the ancient being in the bed. What was Moray going to do? Alarm choked her as she watched him reach for a handle on the side of the machine. He cranked it around until the machine jiggled to a start. As pressure built up in the tubing, Veronique felt a tug at her right arm. A few moments later, she saw her own blood snake through the rubber tube and head for the machine. Soon, her blood was dripping into a small glass container fastened to the front of the machine.

"No!" she cried.

"Be quiet," Moray glanced down at her as he continued to crank the machine. "Or I'll sedate you. Do you want that?"

She glared at him.

"Relax, Miss Dunn. This isn't going to hurt you." He cranked harder. She saw a dark line of blood appear in the second tube and edge toward the machine. The elderly man's blood looked like sludge compared to hers. It was black and viscous and very slow to drip.

"If this works, you will have done your only relative a huge favor."

"Relative?"

"Your uncle."

She had an uncle? Veronique glanced at the old man in the bed. All this time, she'd had an uncle? Perhaps that was why Moray had been pursuing her. He'd been looking for this man's next of kin.

"I don't have an uncle," she retorted.

"Oh yes, you do."

"If I had, he would have found me long ago."

"He's been trying to, believe me."

Veronique thought back to the nomadic days of her childhood. Her mother had never lived in one place for more than a few months. She had never worked very long in one job, never made any friends and had insisted that Veronique keep her red hair dyed to a dull brown. Now it all seemed clear why she had gone to such lengths to remain anonymous. Her mother had been trying to keep her from being discovered. But why?

She sank back to the soft cushions of the chair, trying to think clearly. Judging by the way her mind lagged, she was certain she had been drugged. She should have been ecstatic to learn she had family and that she was not alone in the world, but her sixth sense told her to beware of the man on the bed and Moray as well.

"He's awfully old to be my uncle," she ventured, fishing for more information.

"He is."

"What makes you think we are related?"

"I don't think. I know."

"But how?"

"Markers in your blood." He threw a cool smile at her. "Science doesn't lie, Miss Dunn. Or should I say, Wilder."

"Wilder?"

"Yes. You are a Wilder. Daughter of Joanna Wilder and Gabriel Stone."

"You're wrong, my mother's name was Dunn."

"An alias."

"How do you know?"

"Like I said. Markers. Plus, I knew your parents. They were meddlers. Both of them."

"You knew them? Where are they? Are they alive?"

"Who knows? They haven't really kept in touch, have they?"

She fell silent, her mind whirling. She had finally learned the name of her father. Maybe he was still alive. Maybe even her mother was somewhere. In the Norsea work camps. She could find her! Maybe the supposed long-lost uncle lying beside her would help her.

In order to discover more about her parents, she would have to submit to Moray's medical procedure for now.

Still skeptical, she studied the man on the bed. "What's wrong with him?" she asked.

"He's got a rare blood condition." Moray fiddled with the man's tubing as he cranked away. "We have been looking for you for years, Miss Wilder, hoping you could provide life-saving antibodies to him. I only hope we aren't too late."

"But why me?"

"You can't give a person just any kind of blood. Certain components must match. Since you were a family member, the odds were greater that we would find those components in you."

The events of the evening were beginning to make more sense. "So that's why you had me examined by all those machines."

"Correct. Your healthy blood might give him a few more years or even cure him. That's the theory, anyway."

The argument that she was someone's next of kin was growing stronger by the minute. And Moray wasn't actually doing anything to cause her discomfort, other than keeping her bound to a chair. Her terror ratcheted down to wavering disbelief.

"So what is his name?" She nodded at the old man.

"Silas. Silas Stone."

When she didn't say anything more, he glanced at her. "The name means nothing to you?"

"Should it?"

"He's the leader of the Overseers."

She stared. Each new revelation made her pause. If the leader of the Overseers was in fact her uncle, then that made her a member of the Overseers as well. Her future was about to transform in ways she could not even imagine. But more important than any lofty social status was the concept that she was not alone in the world. If Silas lived, he would be able to tell her about her mother and father. Help her look for them. The shadowy figures of her childhood might finally come into the light. Such a possibility made her head dizzier than it already was.

"So this process could save Citizen Stone's life?"

"I certainly hope so."

"And it won't be dangerous to me?"

"It shouldn't be." Moray bent closer to inspect her uncle's face. He gave a soft chuckle. "A little blood loss never hurt anyone."

Veronique relaxed into the velvet chair as her thoughts raced over the events of the last few days. "And the audition? The symphony? What about that?"

"Just a ruse to find you, Citizen Wilder."

"What?" she whispered.

Veronique stared at him as her hopes and dreams collapsed. Everything she had worked for in the past few weeks had all been for nothing. Everything she had dreamed about had been a lie. She was so demoralized that she couldn't speak.

Moray didn't notice her shock. He filled her silence with more chatter. "Your mother ran off with you, and we had no idea where to look for you. We knew your approximate age. We suspected you might have red hair and profound musical ability. But that's all we had to go on."

"Why would she run off with me—and keep me from my own family?"

"She was reputed to be mentally unstable."

Veronique frowned as she thought back to her mother's odd way of dealing with the world. She had always seemed over-tired and worried, and certainly over-protective. But Veronique had been too young to recognize what might have been signs of mental illness. For the first time in her life, she wondered if she had been wrong about her parent. Maybe her mother hadn't been the strong, bucking-the-system single-parent she had always thought her to be. The idea made her break out in a sweat, as the memories of her childhood began to fray at the edges.

She couldn't think about that now. She swallowed back her panic and concentrated on Moray's hand, as it went around and around with the crank.

"Why would you suspect that I possessed musical ability?"

"Because your father was not only a brilliant scientist, he was also an accomplished pianist, from a long line of pianists."

"And a redhead?"

"As ginger as they come."

"Tall?" Veronique added.

"Taller than most. Like you."

"But he is no longer alive?"

"No. Sorry."

"When did he die?"

"Ten years ago."

Veronique closed her eyes. Her parents had dropped out of her world in the same year, abandoning her to a life on the streets. But her days of hunger and loneliness were over. She had been found. She was a member of the elite Overseers class. Things could only get better. Much better.

Then why didn't she feel secure?

She tried to relax, but she couldn't ease the tension in her neck and shoulders. Life had taught her to be cautious, to expect the unexpected—even if the path seemed clear. She still had a lot of questions. She still didn't trust Moray. But she would wait for the outcome of this medical procedure before she made a move. However, if she did decide to make a move, she couldn't go anywhere until she was free of the cords around her wrists and ankles.

She affected an exhausted expression. "Could you please untie me?" She pulled at her wrists. "The cords are awfully tight. I'm sure my blood would flow more quickly to Citizen Stone if I weren't so tense."

"You won't try anything?"

"Why would I?" She sighed. "The old man is my uncle. My only family."

"If you promise to just lie there—"

"Why would I go anywhere?" she retorted softly. "I have no home. No money. Nothing."

She spoke the truth. Silence hung in the air between them. Then she heard Moray sigh.

"Oh, all right," he said. "It *might* make your blood flow faster if you are more at ease." He ceased cranking the machine. The contraption wheezed and shuddered to a stop. She felt Moray unfasten the cord at her left ankle. Soon her legs were free. He made quick work of untying her wrists, and then turned back to the machine, seemingly anxious to resume his task.

"Thanks," she said, without opening her eyes.

Veronique settled more comfortably in the chair. If her uncle survived, he would be able to explain everything and protect her from Moray—if the small man was as dangerous as she sensed he was. She should relax now and quit being so paranoid. A new chapter of her life had begun. The story of the poor little orphan girl was over. She took a deep steadying breath, just as something slammed in the distance and footsteps rang in the hall outside.

The door of the bedchamber burst open. Veronique jerked to a sitting position, stunned to see a man's large frame filling up the doorway.

"What's going on here?" Roman demanded.

Moray whirled to face the door. "Brandt!"

"Veronique, get up." Roman strode forward. "This instant!"

Veronique hesitated. She didn't fully trust Roman, but she trusted him a whole lot more than Moray. Still, that wasn't saying much. She froze in place, uncertain whether to stay or flee. What if Silas Stone *was* her uncle? What if she could save his life and in doing so discover the missing parts of her past? She had to take the chance.

"Don't listen to him, Miss Wilder." Moray stepped in front of the chair and held out both arms to shield her. "You have no business here, Brandt."

"I do when you kidnap Gabriel's daughter." Roman lifted his cane off the ground and gave it a quick twist. Veronique saw the wicked blade slide out. "Stand aside, Moray, or I will run you through."

"Roman, no!" Veronique struggled out of the chair. She swayed, her head swirling from blood loss. "You don't understand!"

"Oh, I understand." His glance raked across her, hot and cutting. Then he slanted his glare back to Moray. "It is you who does not."

"This old man might be my uncle!" She took a step toward Roman, but Moray shifted his weight to block her forward progress. "He needs my help."

"He doesn't deserve your help. Moray is using you, Vee. Like a lab rat. He will use you up."

"Brandt!" Moray snapped. "I'm warning you, back away!"

"Make me," Roman growled.

"Are you threatening me? In Silas' house?" Moray planted his hands on his hips. "You dare break the rules like that?"

"No one is following the rules anymore. It's utter chaos out there. And it's what I predicted all along. No one will survive if someone doesn't restore order."

"And that would be you?"

"It has always been me."

"Good luck with that."

Veronique stared at Roman, wondering what type of man he was and what they were talking about. She had thought he was a detective. But perhaps he was some kind of policeman. Maybe that's why he had killed the man in the graveyard. Maybe that's why he carried the deadly cane. Perhaps he wasn't a cold-blooded killer after all.

"Even animals live within certain limits," Roman went on, oblivious to her regard. "So must we."

"That's where we differ, Brandt. You think we are ordinary creatures. Part of the earth. You couldn't be more wrong. We can make our own rules. You and me. Starting here and now."

"Never," Roman shot back. "Now back away from Miss Wilder."

"Make me," Moray smirked, mimicking Brandt's words.

In a lightning fast move, Roman swiped his cane across Moray's chest. A button of the small man's coat flew off and rolled along the floor. Before Moray could do more than gasp, Roman flicked the tip of his cane into position over Moray's heart. He pressed the tip closer, enough to cause an indentation in the man's wool suit jacket and vest. Roman's deadly command of his weapon sent a shiver through Veronique.

"Now as I requested earlier," Roman said through clenched teeth. "Step away from the young lady. To the end of the bed."

Stiffly, Moray minced to the side, his stare riveted to the tip of the blade, until he had moved to the foot of the bed. Roman followed, never lowering his guard. Veronique watched Moray smirk and raise his chin, feigning nonchalance in the face of the threatening weapon. "You are one against hundreds, Brandt. You know that, don't you?"

"It has to start somewhere."

"You're forever the idealistic idiot."

"Your opinion."

"It's a fact. You come alone to the house of your mortal enemy with nothing but that silly cane of yours? That's idiocy."

"It's enough to kill you, Moray." Roman tilted his head. "And I suspect you are the only one here. I doubt you would want anyone to know the outcome of your foray into medicine, especially if it succeeds."

Moray shot a dark look at the man on the bed and made no reply. Veronique stared at the two men, confounded and frustrated by their bickering. She wanted them to stop talking and continue the medical procedure so she could get answers from her uncle.

"Please, Roman, leave him alone!" she exclaimed.

"Did you tell Veronique what you plan to do with her blood?" Roman raised the tip of his cane to the soft flesh under Moray's jaw.

"Yes, he did," Veronique put in. "The old man is sick. I'm helping him."

"He is not sick." Roman retorted without looking at her. "Not in the way you think. Moray didn't give you all the facts."

Moray arched his neck, trying to get away from the point of the blade. "Tell her about Silas, Brandt, and you will have to tell her everything. I doubt you want that."

"You're right about that." Roman glanced over his shoulder, "Veronique, come. Get behind me. We're leaving."

She paused. She hadn't been able to follow their conversation just now and was confused about what she should do. Roman had protected her in the past. She had needed his protection. But it seemed clear that he had known her real identity all along—that she belonged to a powerful family—but he had never let her know. Why had he kept such information a secret? Distrust anchored her feet to the floor.

"Veronique?" Roman glanced at her again, obviously surprised that she hadn't obeyed his command.

"You knew who I was?" She glared at him. "That I had a family? And you didn't tell me?"

"It was better that you not know."

"And you thought to decide that for me?" Anger burned through her dizziness. "Who do you think you are?"

"It was for your own good."

"What do you know of good? You lied to me. You kill people! You sleep with that...that Ruby!"

"A discussion for later."

"There won't be a later. I'm not going with you, Roman. Not anywhere."

"What?" Roman lowered his cane and turned to face her, shocked at her announcement.

"Ha!" Moray grinned. "See? Even a girl has more sense than you, Brandt."

"She doesn't have enough information to make a decision."

"And whose fault is that?" Moray sneered. "It's obvious that you have told her nothing about yourself."

"Silence!" Roman roared. He plowed toward her. "Veronique, I am warning you—come with me now or you will be forfeiting your life."

Veronique could see that Roman's tight control over his emotions had cracked. His eyes were like fire. She stared at him, half-afraid of what he might do. But she did not step back. It was time he learned that he couldn't boss everyone around, especially her.

She raised her chin. "I don't believe you."

"You don't have to believe me. Just trust me."

"That's the last thing I'll ever do."

"Veronique." His gaze burned into her. She could feel him trying to bend her to his will with the force of his eyes. She turned her head aside, deflecting his powerful stare.

"I might have a family, Roman," she said. "I need to stay to find out. I *want* to stay."

"No!" He lunged for the tubing in her arm. She pivoted, careful not to dislodge the needle in her arm, and backed against the head of the bed, just as a dark force sat up behind her.

"Brandt!" a voice boomed. The chamber filled with the thunder of the old man's voice. The shadows of the room loomed into monstrous swirling shapes, blotting out her sight, as the smell of death enveloped her, sickening her. Veronique retched from the foul odor and staggered forward, trying to get away, but she was tethered to the machine.

As she pulled at the needle taped to her arm, she saw her uncle rise from the bed and land on his feet in a motion so fast, it didn't seem physically possible for a man in his condition. But her senses were too overwhelmed, and she couldn't be sure of what she was seeing. She blinked, trying to dispel the dark blobs swimming in her vision. For some reason, she couldn't make out the features of Silas' face. The outlines of his body shifted constantly, as if she saw him through wind-whipped drapery.

"You dare interfere!" Silas boomed. His voice sounded hollow and remote, like a voice from another, darker world. He raised a gnarled hand, his fingers pointing upward. Billowing darkness rolled from his palm, like night creatures being released from bondage and taking wing.

Veronique watched in horror as the dark shapes tumbled toward Roman. They pushed him backward until he was pinned to the wall. He writhed, swearing, trying to break free, but was held in place, his arms and legs akimbo. Roman had always seemed strong to her. Invincible. To see him shackled and helpless shook her to her core. What was going on? Why was her uncle being so harsh? And what kind of man *was* he? She whirled to face the entity standing the few feet behind her.

For an instant, her heart stopped beating out of sheer terror.

Chapter 24

VERONIQUE GAPED AT the creature that was her uncle. She doubted he was a human being. He stood upright, but his feet didn't seem to touch the ground, and his eyes were balls of yellow fire. All around him, obscuring the rest of his figure, was an undulating cloud of black and purple.

"Run, Vee!" Roman shouted. His voice broke off as a dark cloud surrounded his throat.

What had she got them both into?

With shaking hands, Veronique tugged at the needle taped to her arm. Fear made her clumsy and time seemed to stop as she tore herself from the transfusion machine. Behind her she could hear the thunderous breathing of her uncle as he concentrated his will on keeping Roman imprisoned. She glanced at Roman, terrified that his shadow attackers would choke the life out of him, and then saw Neal Moray snatch Roman's cane out of his hands.

"Now let's see who's the tough guy!" Moray taunted, switching the cane back to a harmless walking stick. "Let's kill him, Silas!"

"No!" Veronique whirled around to stare at her uncle, who stood near the bed in a cloud of swirling mist. She couldn't make out his features, let alone his expression. But she had no time to study him—not when Roman's life was in danger. "You can't!"

"He's a meddler." Moray backed toward the bed, holding the cane in one hand and his knife in the other. "Always has been and always will be. Let me put an end to him, Silas. He's a troublemaker. We are better off without him."

"No!" Veronique gasped. She scanned Silas' face in the mist, searching for mercy, but saw only the glowing yellow sockets. She'd seen rats with more kindness in their expressions. "I beg you, uncle, don't kill him!"

"Silence!" Silas roared. "This is a matter for the council to decide."

"And let them all know about Gabriel's daughter?" Moray countered. "No offense, Silas, but are you crazy? We'll have no chance to regulate the process. They'll pounce on her like the greedy vultures they are. They'll suck her dry."

"It is our way. It is the law."

"But the old way doesn't work anymore," Moray countered. "And you promised that things would change!"

"All in good time."

"We're out of time. Haven't you got that through your head, yet, Silas?"

"Watch what you say, Moray."

"Maybe it's time for new ways. New blood."

The atmosphere shifted in the room, and Veronique felt her uncle's concentration falter. An unearthly growl rumbled across the floor.

"Maybe the virus has affected your brain," Moray added. "I don't think you're making the best decisions right now."

"You overreach yourself, young one," Silas' voice was ominously quiet. Waves of inky blackness undulated around him. "This matter will rest with the council. Now step aside."

"You think?" Moray rotated the cane. Veronique heard the familiar click as the blade poked through the tip. "Maybe it's time *you* stepped aside." In the next instant, she saw Moray lunge for the old man at the side of the bed. Before she could react, Moray plunged the cane into her uncle's heart.

Silas' bellow reverberated through the chamber and rattled the windowpanes. The bat-like creatures holding Roman in check screeched and fluttered under the ceiling as if they had lost their senses. Then they dropped to the floor, merged with Silas' shadow, and vanished. Veronique saw Silas sink to his knees and start to dissolve from the top of his liver-spotted skull. Powdery flakes like ash from a fire filtered onto his dark nightshirt as his head disappeared. Horrified, she watched her uncle disintegrate into his clothing.

Veronique staggered backward, unable to tear her gaze off the gruesome sight. She had seen a man die like this once before, but she couldn't remember where or when. She watched Silas' shoulders disappear, then his torso. In mere moments, her uncle was nothing but a pile of dust on the floor, covered by a dark nightshirt.

The instant there was nothing left of Silas, Moray burst into action. "I'm calling the shots now!" he announced. He tossed the cane aside and grabbed Veronique by the hair. "Starting with you. You, sweet cheeks, are going to be my little secret."

"Roman!" Veronique struggled to turn to see what had happened to him, now that Silas' hold had been released. Roman slid down the wall, his chest heaving and his lips parted with exhaustion. Someone pounded on the door as Roman sank to the floor.

"Enter!" Moray barked.

Two young men burst into the room with pistols in their hands and their eyes wild with alarm. "What's going on?" one of them shouted.

"These two just killed Silas." Moray swept the air behind him. One of the men dashed to the bedside. "I managed to subdue Brandt there."

"He's lying!" Veronique shouted.

Moray jerked her hair. "Quiet, you." He pulled down her head at an unnatural angle until she cried out.

"Let Veronique go!" Roman wheezed. He struggled to one knee as the younger men with guns trapped him in place.

"Shut up!" Moray yanked Veronique toward the door. "Take this girl downstairs. Along with him." He nodded his head at Roman.

One of the young men shot a questioning glance at Moray. "Not downstairs, surely." He jerked a thumb at Roman. "That's Colonel Brandt."

"Yes, I mean downstairs. And see that he stays there. He's a menace to us all."

"The Colonel?"

Moray nodded. "It's the virus. He's gone mad. Don't believe a thing he says."

Veronique, weak from blood loss, was dragged by one arm through the cellar of the compound. Just as drained as Veronique, Roman staggered through the darkness in front of her, and was struck every other step with his own cane to keep him moving. Their captors pushed and prodded him through the cellar and then ducked into an adjoining section that was connected to the underground sewer system of Londo City.

Veronique heard water and glanced around. Her eyes had finally adjusted to the darkness, enough to see where she was being taken. Along the channel of deep black water ran a series of cells built into the tunnel system. They were to be imprisoned in a dungeon comprised of stone walls, iron bars, wooden benches and chamber pots. A dank funk hung in the air.

Veronique held the small of her elbow to her nose as she was pushed along the stone causeway. The two men shoved Roman into one cell and Veronique into the next. They shackled Roman to the back wall. Out of respect for Veronique's gender or perhaps because they didn't consider her a threat, they left her wrists free of the iron cuffs.

Veronique kept her mouth shut as the two men locked her in and left the dungeon. When all she could hear was the hushed rush of water, she walked to the wall of bars that separated her from Roman and wrapped her fingers around the cold rods. Roman's wrists were shackled to the wall. His clothes, usually immaculate, were rumpled and torn. His cravat hung untied, and his shirt had been ripped open to the low curve of his vest.

She could see the muscled plate of his abdomen. A wave of desire for him washed over her, but she pushed it back, as she had pushed back desire for food as a child.

She reminded herself that Ruby had touched Roman's abdomen. Who knows how many other women had stroked him. Being a virgin, she hadn't known the first thing about seduction. Roman had seemed to enjoy her fumbling eagerness, but perhaps he had been secretly amused with her naiveté. He *had* laughed once or twice when with her. At the time, she had reveled in the sound. But he must have been laughing at her. What an idiot she had been. What a child.

Still, Roman had cared enough to come after her and risk his life.

Veronique lifted her gaze to his face. Roman's dark brown hair fell over his forehead in unruly strands, and even from a distance, she could see fatigue shadowing his eyes.

"Roman," she called. "Are you all right?"

"Yes." He raised his head. "And you?"

"Yes." She swallowed. She had so many questions, but she didn't know how to begin asking them. Most of all she wanted to know how he felt about her. But she didn't want to risk the embarrassment of being told the truth: that she was just the comical element of his love parade, marching somewhere far in the rear. Her stomach burned.

Roman pulled at his restraints, and the sound brought her out of her dark thoughts. She glanced over at him. "I tried to warn you, Vee, about the audition. You should have listened to me."

"You should have told me everything. About my uncle. My parents. About everything."

"I thought to shield you from all that."

"I didn't ask to be shielded. And had I known—"

"Would you have done anything differently?" His hard gaze bore into her. She had forgotten how icy his eyes could appear. "Your career is tantamount to everything, it seems."

"If I had known that I had a family?" She squeezed the bars as her heart squeezed together. "That I was not alone? And that I was part of the Overseers—"

"You are *not* part of the Overseers," he countered. "You don't want to be part of them."

"That's easy for you to say, Roman. You have everything." She swallowed back a lump. "I've had nothing all my life."

"Regardless of its outer glitter, my life has its shortcomings. Make no mistake about that."

"Really? Have you ever starved?" she retorted. She wanted to shout far more personal questions at him, but she stuck to the safer subject of her past instead. "Have you ever been shivering with cold on a night that seems to last forever? Do you know how cold it can get at three o'clock in the morning, when you have nowhere to go?"

"I know what the night is like." Roman's stare slid off her and he pressed his lips together. "But you do not want to trade one difficult life for another. Believe me, Vee." He pulled at his restraints again, putting all his strength into the effort, but the chains held fast.

Frustrated and angry, Veronique rattled the bars of the door, looking for a way out. She paced the perimeter of the small cell, searching for a loose bar or a cracked stone—anything that hinted at a weakness in their prison and a means of escape.

For a long while they were quiet, lost in their own thoughts. A drip, drip, drip rang though the silence, driving her mad. It was as if the sound in the darkness was timing her, pressuring her to demand the truth from Roman—a truth she didn't want to have confirmed.

A dull ache in Veronique's forearm reminded her of the strange medical procedure she had just undergone. She gazed down at the puncture wound in the white flesh of her arm. A bruise had begun to form around the purple dot.

"So, did you know my uncle?" she asked at last, breaking the silence with another question that had nothing to do with her real torment. She returned to the wall of bars that separated them.

"As well as anyone could know Silas."

"Was he some kind of magician or something?"

Roman shot a glance at her. She wondered if the question confused him.

"The way he had you up against the wall," she added. "Without touching you. And the way mist seemed to swirl around him. I never really got a good look at him. It was odd."

"He's always been a mysterious man," Roman said. "And powerful. That's why he was the head of the Overseers."

"He couldn't have been that powerful. Neal Moray killed him pretty easily."

"Silas was in a weak state. Keeping me at bay sapped what little energy he had left." Roman sighed. "And my cane is especially suited for such a kill."

"But to dissolve like that. Into powder?" Veronique scowled. "What kind of person dissolves?"

"I didn't see that happen."

"I did." She fell silent. Then after a moment, she sighed. "Did you know my father?"

"I did." Roman watched her, wary of her new line of questioning. "He was my best friend."

"Why did my mother lie about him? Why did he never visit me?"

"To protect you. From the very thing that happened tonight."

"What was he like?"

"Gabriel was the kindest, most brilliant man I have ever known."

The warmth in Roman's voice washed over her. Tears clogged her throat.

"He asked me to look after you, in case something happened to him."

"So, you knew who I was all along?"

"When I heard you play, I suspected the truth. Then I noticed the unusual color of your hair. Like his. And your smile is unbelievably similar to his. It lights up your face. Just like his did. So, yes. I suspected you were related."

She looked down. It was wonderful to hear what her father was like, but she was still heartsick at the loss of a parent she would never know.

"So, he really is dead?"

"That's what they say. He went to Port Pennwood ten years ago and never returned."

"Port Pennwood? Where is that?"

"The southwestern coast. Far from here."

"And my mother. Will you help me look for her? In case she was sent to the Norsea work camps?"

"You know I will."

"We just have to get out of here."

ROMAN WATCHED VERONIQUE frown. Something had changed in her—besides the color of her hair—but he didn't know what was different. He swept a glance over her red tresses, the color of rust, but silky and shining. She was her father's daughter all right.

Gabriel's hair had been exactly the same burnt red. Veronique's flaming hair against her pale skin was a vision worthy of a painter.

God, she was even more beautiful than before. He could imagine that hair spread over the top of a black Steinway.

But something about her had changed. He could sense a wall between them. Perhaps, having discovered she had a family and a place in the world, she had ceased to need him. The thought sent a dagger of doubt through him. Surely Veronique had not simply been using him.

Then again, she had survived alone on the streets since she was eight years old. That took determination, guts and a staggering amount of self-reliance.

For him, their kisses had been all about love and communion. For her, perhaps their kisses had been all about hunger and sustenance. She had been forged by hunger. He couldn't blame her for wanting the things she did. Roman averted his eyes at the thought of their night at the piano, and how the joy might have been one-sided. Disappointment swallowed him, but he refused to reveal the emotions roiling inside him.

She wasn't the only one playing a game. He'd almost lapped up her virginity like a ravenous cur. He'd wanted to take a precious gift from her under false pretenses. She thought he was a man. Maybe even a good man. And he was neither.

Once again, the thought of his deception filled him with shame. Yet to fulfill the dying wishes of his best friend, he had to continue to deceive her. He had to get her to the Outer Islands where no one knew her, where the Overseers rarely traveled, and where she could have a halfway normal life. Until then he must keep up the ruse that he was an ordinary human being. He owed Gabriel his life. The least he could do was protect Gabriel's daughter as best as he could.

A flush branded Roman's cheeks. He was just like all the bloodthirsty hoodlums he hunted down and destroyed. He thirsted for the innocence of his best friend's daughter.

"Roman?" Veronique's soft voice broke into his thoughts. "What's to become of us, do you think?"

He glanced at her but couldn't muster the smile he knew he should fake to reassure her. "I'm not sure."

"Do you think Neal Moray will kill us?"

"You? Not likely. He wants your blood."

"What about you? He seems to hate you."

"In that, we share a mutual regard."

"You don't seem all that bothered that he has imprisoned you."

Roman shrugged. It was difficult to explain to a young woman on the cusp of adulthood that he didn't care one way or the other if he lived or died. He had seen all that he wanted to see. He had done all that he wanted to do—all but truly love someone. But he should have known better than to expect true love to appear this late in his life. "I am not afraid of Moray or what he can do to me."

"I am." She leaned one cheek into the brace of her knuckles. "He gives me the creeps. He smiles. But he looks like a snake to me."

"You should fear him, Veronique. In fact, you must leave Londo City the first chance you get." He thought back to the moment he'd entered Silas' bedchamber and had seen Veronique hooked up to that deadly transfusion machine and sitting back in that velvet chair with her eyes closed. He hadn't known then if she was alive or dead, and the sight had undone him.

"Roman?" her soft voice beckoned him back to the present.

"Yes?"

"I'm sorry I didn't listen to you. About the audition."

He nodded.

"I was very upset. Trusting people doesn't come naturally to me."

"Perhaps that's a good thing."

"Had I known the truth, I would never have persisted."

"I wanted to protect you from the truth."

"Why? I'm not a child, Roman."

If only that were true. If only she *were* older.

"But you're a good man," Veronique continued. "I know you usually have my best interests at heart."

God, he felt more of a cad than ever. A lump of self-loathing lodged in his craw. He couldn't say a word for fear that his voice would crack.

"Roman?"

"Don't worry, Vee. We'll get out of here. I'll think of something."

"You're shackled."

"Still, try to get some rest. You've had a long day. You've had considerable blood loss. Morning will come sooner than you think."

She sighed and her hands dropped from the bars. "Yes, well, I don't think I'll ever be able to sleep in this hellhole."

"Try."

"What about you?" She nodded at his chains. "How will you get through the night hanging from the wall?"

"Don't worry about me. I've had worse sleeping conditions than this."

She raised a brow and gave him a doubtful stare. But the concern in her eyes sent a shaft of longing through him, all the way to his toes. He couldn't remember the last time someone had looked at him that way.

Just before dawn, Roman heard a key turn in the lock of his cell. He blinked awake, surprised to see Ruby Valentine standing at the door, swinging a brace of keys in front of her breasts.

"My, my, my," she purred. "Look what Roman's gotten himself into this time."

"Ruby!" Roman glanced over his shoulder at Veronique. She lay on the cot, fast asleep, too tired to register their conversation.

"Yes. Your personal angel has arrived. Did you think I would let you languish all night in this place?"

"Thank God you knew where to find us!"

"What are you doing here, anyway?"

"Moray killed Silas and is blaming it on me."

"I heard." Her painted lips curled. "But I assumed you actually did the dirty deed."

"As will everyone else."

"Ooh. You are deep trouble, Roman. Deep, deep trouble."

"Time is of the essence." Roman raised his hands. "See if there's a key on that ring and unlock these cuffs."

"Not so fast." Ruby leaned her back against the bars. The hem of her wine-colored dress whispered across her boots. She smiled one of her nasty little smirks. "As I recall, you were quite mean to me the last time I saw you."

Roman flushed with anger. The woman wished to punish him for having thrown her out of his house. Her pettiness annoyed him.

"You try my patience," he growled.

"Then this will be good practice. You'll need a lot of patience to last in this place."

"Ruby!"

"I want my key back," she demanded, standing straight again. "And I want her—" she jerked her head in the direction of Veronique, "—out of your house. And out of your life."

"Wait a moment." Roman narrowed his eyes. "How did you know I was here?"

"A lucky guess."

"And how did Neal Moray find out about Veronique?"

"Who knows?" Ruby pushed away from the bars and paced to one side. Roman watched her closely. She was nervous. She was hiding something.

"You read the letter." Enraged, Roman yanked his chains. "You went through my things when I was away and read Gabriel's letter. Didn't you!"

"Yes!" Ruby whirled to face him, her cheeks scarlet. "For your own good! To help you!"

"Help me do what?"

"Get out of prison!"

Roman stared at her. "What?"

"I figured if I told Neal Moray that I had crucial information about the Commensalist Project but would only give it to him if he had you released from prison, that he would get you out. And it worked!"

Roman clenched his jaw. He didn't know whether to thank Ruby for saving his life or damn her for endangering Veronique. "You signed Veronique's death warrant with that little trick. I hope you know that."

"I don't care what happens to her. I did it for you, Roman! You!"

"The girl in the letter was me?" a small voice asked.

Roman turned to look at Veronique. She stood up from the cot, her hair a russet cloud, her eyes misty with sleep. She flowed to the bars that separated them.

"The letter was about me?"

"Yes," Roman answered. "Your father asked me to find you. Ten years ago. But I was in prison at the time."

"My father tried to find me?"

"Who cares?" Ruby thrust herself between them and glared at Veronique. "You were a lost little lab rat and now you are found. Ask Neal Moray all the questions you want. I'm sure he'd love to answer them."

Obviously irritated that Veronique had awakened, Ruby sorted through the keys, her movements sharp with annoyance. She never could hide her emotions from the world.

Roman watched her, anxious to get away before the morning light limited his strength. Perhaps Ruby had come to the same conclusion. She tried a key without success, swore and tried another. The cuff fell away from his wrist and clanged against the stone wall. Roman held out his left hand, and Ruby unlocked it. He was free.

"Come on, Roman." Ruby grabbed his hand and tugged him toward the opening of the cell.

He strode after her, anxious to be away, but was surprised when Ruby hurried past Veronique's cell without unlocking it.

"Hold on!" Roman reached for Ruby's elbow. "What about Veronique?"

"I'm not setting her free."

"You must!"

"I don't want to." Ruby raised her chin. "She has caused nothing but trouble since she showed up in our lives."

"We can't leave her here. Moray will kill her."

"What a pity." Ruby tilted her head and feigned a hurt expression. "Poor little Veronique."

"Ruby!" Frustrated, Roman reached for the keys, but Ruby whipped them behind her skirts. She smiled.

"What will you give me in return for letting her go?"

"Nothing!"

Ruby fell back, holding the keys above the black water that flowed beside them. "Why should I help her? She's come between me and you."

"That's not true."

"Tell me that I'm prettier," Ruby continued, "Tell me!"

"You're prettier," Roman growled.

"Promise me that you'll devote yourself to me." Ruby dangled the keys precariously on one fingertip. "To me, Roman. Only to me."

"Ruby!" Roman glared at her.

"Promise that you will marry me. That you will take me as your mate. It's what I should have been all these years, you know."

Roman glanced at Veronique's worried face and then back at the hoyden who had transformed him so long ago. He had no choice but to acquiesce to whatever Ruby asked. If he refused, he was certain that Veronique would be left to die.

"I promise," he said at last.

"And a little something so I know you mean it?"

"So help me God."

"Good!" Ruby gave a gay little hop and snatched the keys out of danger. She winked at Veronique. "He's still so devout—it's truly precious."

"Give me the key, Ruby." Impatient with her games, Roman thrust out his hand.

Ruby slapped the ring of keys on his palm. "Let Little Orphan Annie free, then, and let's get out of here."

Chapter 25

STILL WEAK FROM BLOOD loss, Veronique trailed behind as they hurried through the sewer system, looking for an exit point. Noticing her flagging, Roman grabbed her hand and pulled her along. When they had clambered up to street level, he swept her into his arms and carried her like a child. Veronique didn't protest. She was too worn out to keep up with the other two. They seemed to have far more energy than she did.

Ruby had a coach waiting on a nearby street. When they got to the vehicle, Roman lifted her into the cab and ordered the driver to take them northward.

"North?" Ruby asked as she plopped down beside Roman.

"Out of Londo City," he replied. Roman sank back against the seat and leaned his head against the side of the coach, looking as worn out as Veronique felt. "Feel free to get out anywhere, Ruby. The Overseers aren't after you."

"They will be once they find out who set you free."

"Are we going to your distillery?" Veronique asked. Roman shot a glance at her for the first time since they'd entered the coach.

"In the vicinity."

"Will it be safe?" Veronique leaned forward. "Don't they know to look for you there?"

"They might, but I don't think they'll bother. They don't like how...how remote...it is."

"Remote is another word for bright," Ruby put in.

The comment confused Veronique. "What's wrong with bright?"

"The Overseers prefer the fogginess of Londo City. It's better for their health."

Veronique frowned. "I can't see how."

Veronique let the subject of their pursuers drop, and for a while no one spoke as the coach rumbled through the coming dawn. Ruby sat beside Roman, her hand on his thigh, claiming him. Her fingers were like the iron shackles in Silas' dungeon, yet far more binding, as there was no honorable way to break free.

Ruby Valentine. The last time Veronique had seen the woman, Ruby had tried to kill her. And when that hadn't worked, she had tried to sell Veronique to a bounty hunter—at least that was what Veronique assumed would have transpired at the warehouse in Brick Lane if she hadn't escaped. She wasn't sure who was her worst enemy now, Ruby or Neal Moray.

Veronique sat on the opposite seat, her mouth set in a tight line while her thoughts whirled with all that had happened in the last few hours. Instead of subjecting herself to the gloating expression of Ruby Valentine as she claimed her prize, Veronique focused her attention on the view outside the window. Slowly the city blinked to life as people rose for the day, turned on their gas lamps and prepared for another shift in the factories and fields. The routine reminded her that she was more of an outsider than ever now, with no job and no place to live.

In the space of a week, her life had completely unraveled. She had fallen in love with a man and now must fall out love with him. She had no hope for the future, no plan, and nowhere to go. All she knew was that she couldn't go north with Roman Brandt, however much she desired to remain in his company. He had proved to be untrustworthy and high-handed. Even more, she refused to be a member of anyone's harem—and a mere dalliance—not that he had asked her to be. She wanted to be much more than that to a man she loved. She took a deep breath and fought back tears.

She was angry with Roman for deceiving her. But more than that, she was heartbroken.

Then there was Ruby. Roman had promised himself to Ruby to save her life. If he hadn't vowed to marry Ruby, Veronique would still be locked in that horrible cell. But there was a price to pay for her release, and she was the one who was going to pay it. Veronique clenched her jaw. When Roman made a promise, he would keep it. That was one thing she knew for certain about him. He would never touch her again, never look at her with warmth swimming in his mysterious hooded eyes.

Roman. She wondered what she would find if she removed the blinders of young love and examined him rationally. She would have to one day. But not yet. Not when the memory of his kiss was still sharp and sweet.

Since she could not go to the Outer Islands with Roman, she had to decide where *to* go. Veronique sighed and looked at the sky, which was as overcast and murky as ever. She would have to go back to life on the streets. At least she was an adult now. She was officially old enough to get a job, so that would make her life easier. As long as she could elude the clutches of Neal Moray, she would be all right.

As they rolled through the blocks of abandoned buildings ringing the Central Compound, Veronique bided her time, waiting to arrive in familiar territory, but barely registering the buildings they passed. Soon she would have to say good-bye to Roman. She would never see him again. Despair hung on her like chains.

Ruby did not countenance the silence for long. She shifted beside Roman and stroked his leg, all the way to his knee.

"You've been through a lot, Miss Bishop," Ruby began. "Or should I say *Wilder*. There are no secrets between us now, are there?"

"None at all," Veronique replied, her voice flat.

"Are you sure? You haven't asked many questions. If I were you, I'd be dying of curiosity about what's going on."

Veronique shot a glance at Ruby. "I am not you, Ruby. Thank Gottfried."

She saw Roman fight back a smile but forced herself to look away. She couldn't take the chance of falling under his spell. She had to cut off their friendship and make a clean break.

Ruby's grip tightened on Roman's thigh. "You're not even curious?"

Veronique was bursting with questions, but the last person she wanted to talk to was Ruby Valentine. She crossed her arms. "Not especially."

"So Roman must have told you about himself then."

Veronique shrugged a shoulder, feigning indifference.

"No?" Ruby chuckled. "He has a secret that we haven't got out in the open yet."

Veronique's heart twisted with dread. She wanted to remember Roman as a hero—the man who had endangered his own life to save her. She wanted to remember his kiss as the most thrilling moment of her life.

If she knew everything about Roman, she was certain his memory would be tarnished. She didn't want to know Roman's secret, no matter what it was. Secrets were usually bad. "Everyone has secrets," she replied, turning to look back out the window.

"Not a secret like his."

"Ruby," Roman planted his hand on hers. "Not now."

"If she knows, she'll leave us alone." Ruby raised her chin. "You can tell she won't give up that easily."

"It's not advisable," Roman squeezed her hand again, harder this time. "And it's against the law."

"As if I care." Ruby snorted. "The Overseers have been trying to run me out of town ever since I got here. And you, too, Roman."

"What law?" Veronique asked.

"Ah!" Ruby turned to face her. "At last! A question from the lab rat."

"What law, Roman?" Veronique ignored Ruby and fastened her regard on his face.

"A law that governs the Overseers."

"There are separate laws for the Overseers?"

Roman nodded. "Some more strict than the laws that govern the citizens of Londo."

"That's surprising." Veronique leaned back in the padded seat. "I think the laws of Londo City are plenty strict. But there are stricter ones?"

"Thou Shalt not Kill for Pleasure," Ruby gloated. "Ever hear of that one?"

Veronique ignored her expression. "That doesn't sound overly harsh."

"It is when killing is a person's only physical release."

Ruby sat back and smirked at her. Veronique stared at Ruby, trying to make sense of what she had just said. Surely, she had not heard the woman correctly. The Overseers had no physical release? What did that mean? That they could not make love? They could not procreate? That couldn't be possible.

"We are wasting valuable time," Roman put in as he pried Ruby's claw off his thigh. "We need to talk about the immediate future."

"Our future or hers?" Ruby nodded at Veronique. "Because I swear to you, Roman, the two are never going to be the same."

"Just a minute," Veronique leaned forward. "Are you saying that the Overseers can't make love?"

Ruby stared at her for a minute, as if she were trying to comprehend what Veronique had just said. "You mean have sex?" She threw back her head and laughed. "Making love. Good Gottfried, I haven't heard it called that for such a long time!" She wiped her eyes with a gloved finger. "And no, they don't. They can't.

They don't have sex. They don't eat. And they live for a very, very long time."

"Why? How?"

"Because they're not human, that's why."

Silence fell over the coach.

"What are they?" Veronique finally asked. Her voice cracked. Somehow, she knew what Ruby was going to say.

"Vampires. The Overseers are vampires."

That meant Ruby and Roman were vampires as well.

A chill streaked through her. Veronique had always thought vampires were part of Londo City folklore. Only tall tales. But if vampires did exist, everything made sense: the way her uncle had transformed, the odd way Ruby and Roman had moved, as if they had wings, the way Roman's limp had healed so quickly, the way her kidnappers had jumped out of a two-story house and not suffered any injuries, the way Citizen Carson had been killed, and the way Londo City shut itself up at night.

Londo City was governed by an ancient coven of vampires. For the past week, she had been eating, drinking and sleeping with vampires.

Even worse, if Silas Stone was her uncle, and Gabriel Stone was his brother, that made Gabriel a vampire, too.

Her father was a vampire?

"Stop!" Veronique demanded. She pounded on the top of the coach with her fist. "Stop!"

The driver reined in the horses with a loud "Whoa!" and a jangle of harnesses. Before the coach rolled to a stop, Veronique threw open the door and jumped to the ground.

"Veronique!" Roman called. His shoulders filled up the doorway. "I can explain!"

She glanced at him, knowing it would be her last glimpse of him—if she were lucky enough to survive the experience.

"You lied to me!" she shot back. "You have always lied to me! From the very start!"

"Not about everything."

"You're a vampire!" Veronique fought back tears. "A vampire!"

"So are you."

She glared at him, and then shot a cold glance at Ruby, whose triumphant face appeared at the window. She fluttered her gloved fingers in a victory ta-ta.

"Veronique!" Roman shouted. "Don't run off!"

Veronique held up a hand. "Don't follow me, Roman!"

She couldn't look at his face. Instead, she turned and bolted for the nearest alley. She counted on her remarkable running ability to allow her to outdistance all pursuers. In minutes, she had put a mile between her and the coach.

Roman was wrong. She wasn't a vampire. She may have a vampire branch on her family tree, but her father's nonhuman traits hadn't been passed down to her. She had never thirsted for blood. She could walk in sunlight—or at least the filtered sunlight of Londo City. The only unusual attributes she possessed were her height and running ability.

She ran, desperate to outdistance her thoughts. She had kissed a vampire. That's why Roman's skin had been so chilly. That's why he had never eaten dinner with her. He didn't need food to survive. He needed blood. Human blood. Roman Brandt killed people.

But then she knew that already.

How could she have feelings for such a beast? And yet she did. Veronique clenched her teeth and flew through the night, hoping to outrun the effect Roman had on her.

In ten minutes, she was far from Roman and Ruby and their dark secrets. She panted to a stop, her heart breaking, and looked down a familiar street. *Jane.* If there was ever a time she needed a friend, that time was now.

Veronique threw a spray of gravel at Jane's bedroom window, and stood impatiently in the fog, hoping the mist concealed her from all that hunted in the night. Now she knew why her mother never wanted her outside after dark. She must have known about the Overseers—about everything. The hair on the back of her neck rose to full attention, as if her instincts were aware of watching eyes.

As she stood in the dark, she ran her tongue over the ridge of her teeth. She wasn't a vampire. Her teeth were as normally formed as anyone else's in Londo. Then again, she had never noticed that Roman's teeth were unusual either. She dashed the vision of his sensual mouth from her thoughts.

"Come on, Jane," Veronique prayed. For the first time since escaping the dungeon, she felt the damp chill of the air close around her. She waited. Surely Jane must be up, getting ready for work.

Then she caught sight of the radiation boards moving to the side. Veronique waved. She heard the latch click open, and in another moment, Jane swung open the casement windows—just as she had done a hundred times before.

"Vee!" Jane gasped. "What are you doing here?"

"Can I come in?" Veronique clutched the points of the rickety iron fence and leaned forward, anxious to leave the misty expanse behind her.

"Of course."

Veronique climbed over the fence, careful not to snag her gown, and jumped up to the sill. In the old days, Jane's room had been the front parlor of the townhouse. But that had been before the dwellings on the street had been split into multiple units, with entire families living in three rooms on either side of the central stairways. She tipped aside the radiation boards that covered the window, opened the sash and crawled through. She wondered if Jane would be able to do the same, or if her vampire bloodline allowed her to spring so easily to the sill. Her blood ran cold at the thought of what else she might be capable of—or worse, driven to do.

As soon as Veronique slipped through the window, she closed the sash and shut the curtains. She turned to find Jane gaping at her rose-colored dress.

"Where did you get that gown?" Jane pointed at the luxurious satin, still amazingly clean after all it had been through.

"It's a long story."

Jane tilted her head to the side as she tied her scarf over her hair. "I take it you didn't get the position in the symphony. I'm so sorry, Vee."

"Don't be. There actually wasn't a symphony being formed."

"What?"

"It was all a ruse. To find me."

"Find you?" Jane buttoned her vest over her dingy homemade skirt. "Why?"

"Apparently I had a father at one time who was important. An Overseer."

"Your father was an Overseer?" Jane's jaw fell open.

"The Overseers thought I might be—" Veronique broke off, suddenly unsure how much she should tell Jane. A vision of Roman's serious face passed through her mind, as if to warn her to keep her birthright a secret—especially from an innocent human.

"Might be what, Vee?" Jane put in.

"Able to tell them what my father had been doing when he died. He was a scientist, you see. Working on an important project, just like my mother always said. But I couldn't help them." She shrugged. "I never met the man."

"So they just put you back on the street, with no reward for your trouble?"

"None at all." Veronique sighed. "I should have known, Jane. I shouldn't have got my hopes up."

Jane slipped her arm around Veronique's shoulders and gave her a quick squeeze. "What's life without a little hope, Vee? Nothing. Your audition has been all that I've thought about for weeks. It gave me hope, too, you know."

"Sorry to disappoint." Veronique ducked out of the embrace and paced to the narrow cot opposite the window. "I've been such an idiot."

"It was good while it lasted, though," Jane replied. "I wouldn't have had it any other way."

Veronique nodded, but her heart was still heavy. She looked down at the faded quilt that covered the cot and the pillow with its patched linen case—so different from the soft clean cloud of a bed that Roman had provided.

Once Veronique had thought Jane was the luckiest girl in the world, to have her own bedroom and her very own bed. Such luxury. But Roman had changed her poverty-stricken perspective. Now she knew what real luxury was.

Roman. More than anything she wished she could tell Jane about Roman. But Jane would ask far too many questions. And Veronique wasn't prepared to answer them.

"Do you mind if I stayed here today, Jane? I haven't slept for days."

"No, not at all." Jane pulled down the quilt and motioned toward the sheets. "Stay as long as you like."

"We can talk when you get back from work. You can tell me how the fieldwork is going—all your adventures."

"You mean the turnip weeding and the carrot thinning? So exciting!" Jane giggled as she reached for her threadbare coat with its mismatched buttons. As she put on the garment, she sobered. "It's so good to see you, Vee. I was so worried about you. I'm glad you came to visit."

"Me, too." Veronique sank onto the bed, barely able to keep her eyes open. "Thank you, Jane."

In the morning, Veronique would start a new life. She would create a new identity and look for a job, preferably in the records office. She would not stop looking for her mother until she found out what had happened to her. And if she were still alive, she would find her.

Chapter 26

A SOFT CLICK AWAKENED Veronique. She opened her bleary eyes, realizing that she had not rested well and had slept in short half-awake spans, fraught with worry and bad dreams. But she was not so groggy that she failed to see the tall shape at the window. A man stood to the side of the curtains, cast in silhouette as the late afternoon light outlined the edges of his long coat. Veronique jerked to a sitting position, her heart pounding.

"Did you think I would let you go that easily?" He moved away from the window in a fluid motion that she now knew was part of his otherworldly makeup.

"Roman!" Veronique gasped. She didn't know whether to be ecstatic at his appearance in Jane's bedroom or terrified that he had tracked her down to the one place she thought she was safe. There was no one to help her. Jane and her parents would still be toiling in the fields at this time of day. She pulled up her knees, ready to bolt from the narrow bed.

"How did you find me?" she demanded.

"It was easy to pursue you. Since the...piano...I can sense where you are."

Veronique flushed and dragged the quilt to her chin. "Don't come any closer."

"Why?" He opened his arms wide, without moving from his stance by the window. "Do you think I would hurt you?"

"I don't know!"

"If I had wanted to hurt you, I could have done so long ago."

"You probably didn't because you wanted to keep me safe—for your own use!" She glared at him. "Do you have that same illness—the one that my uncle had?"

His expression darkened. "Yes. It's a long-term effect caused by radiation. That much we have found out. And we all have it."

"See?" she countered. "So you want my blood, too."

"No." He held up a gloved hand. "That virus is what is making me human again, Veronique, able to react to you like a man. I don't want to be cured."

She flushed again, this time at the memory of what he had done with her and how glorious he had made her feel. Longing for such closeness fanned out deep in her belly. She had to remind herself to focus on being angry with him. But focusing was difficult, especially with his seductive fragrance wafting across the room, lacing each breath she took with pine and sage. She flung back the quilt.

"You let me kiss you when you knew all along that you weren't human!"

"I tried to stop you."

"Not very hard!" She jumped to her feet, wide-awake now. "You might have told me who you really were. *What* you really were!"

"Would that have changed the way you feel?" His eyes locked upon hers.

She tried to tear her gaze away but was trapped by his magnetic melancholy. "Maybe!" she exclaimed.

"Beneath what I have become," he said quietly. "I was first of all a man. And it is a man that I hope to become again, for however brief a time I am granted such a miracle."

"And what about me?" She marched from the bed, heading toward the door to the hall and swatting away the wrinkles of the beautiful gown she had ruined by sleeping in it. "Were you ever going to tell me that I was half-vampire?"

"No."

"Why?"

"To keep you innocent."

She turned to stare at him. "Why?"

Roman sighed. "Because the life of a vampire is dark and cruel, Veronique. And sometimes sordid. I didn't want that for you."

"How is it cruel and sordid? Your life seems pretty nice to me."

"There are times when however hard you struggle to maintain your self-control, your animal nature boils up in you, and it is quite—" He paused to find the right word. "—Disturbing. Such behavior is what our earthly laws are designed to keep in check: the lust to overpower, the lust to possess and the lust to kill."

He heaved a deep breath and looked away, consumed by his thoughts. Veronique took a step toward him to reach for his hand, aching to give him comfort. But she caught herself in mid-stride. He would be cold to the touch. He wasn't a real human being. She must keep her distance.

"It is like no other sensation on earth," Roman continued, his voice softer than it had been. "To take a human life, to taste a soul as it is released from a human body. It is the sweetest, most ephemeral sensation I have ever known." He glanced at her. "Have you ever come across that piece of music by Mendelssohn? Heilig, I believe it's called."

"Yes," Veronique said, barely above a whisper. Helig was a chorale that began like angels breathing and rose to a stirring crescendo.

"It is like that."

"It's better than making love?"

Roman turned to look at her. His expression softened. "Sex is of the body, Vee." He stroked the vest that covered his abdomen as if remembering the way he had felt with her pressed tightly against him. "Releasing a soul is of the mind." He brought his hand up in a flourish that ended in the air above his head. He smiled. "As to which is best? It depends upon what kind of person you are and where you find your greatest pleasure."

"But you thought to keep the choice from me?"

Roman's smile vanished. "When you are young, Veronique, sometimes you think you can do anything, try anything, and you will be able to handle it. But there is one thing that will damn you forever. And I mean forever."

What more could he reveal? So many fantastic notions had been revealed to her in the last few days that she was numb with shock. She stared at him, her mouth dry and her tongue stuck to the roof of her mouth.

"Once you kill for pleasure, you will never be the same because you know that you have fallen."

"Fallen? To where?"

"I don't know how to explain it. Backward. Down. Into darkness." He frowned, "You realize you have forever lost the chance to reach your full and best potential. And man is funny that way. If he knows he has no hope of achieving something, he spurns it. Do you not agree?"

She nodded, caught in his spell. Pine and sage swirled around her. His voice rumbled, reverberating all the way to her bones.

"You begin to savor the darkness, to become part of it. Darkness creeps into your heart and soul. Granted, you become stronger and unbelievably powerful, but day by day you also become more alone, as you can never, ever trust another vampire."

"Why?"

"The darker a person becomes, the more ruthless they are. The more self-absorbed. The more you kill, the more unlovable you know you are, and the more alone you become."

"You don't seem that horrible."

"That's because I cling to my human values. And I have never purposely killed for pleasure. But these days I am ridiculed for such old-fashioned ways."

"People seem to respect you."

"Only the older vampires. The newly turned ones like Neal Moray? They think I've got it all wrong. The younger ones only appear to respect me because they fear me. To them, immortality is a gift. A game."

He walked to the fireplace and looked down at the dying fire.

"God in heaven knows how strong I have been all these years. I once thought that He would realize what a mistake had been made. And that He would release me. But He never has." He glanced over his shoulder at her. "What kind of father does that make Him, Veronique? In a fashion, I have felt as abandoned as you."

She hugged her arms, her heart aching for him, but knew it would be dangerous to show how much she cared about him.

"I should never have been turned." He sighed. "I didn't ask for it. I never would have wanted it. And Ruby failed to ask my preference as she was supposed to."

"Ruby turned you into a vampire? When? Where?"

"In Prussia. In 1898." He rotated slowly, turning his back to the fire while he studied her, his eyes glittering. "She did it to save my life. However, she failed to ask me how I felt about eternal damnation."

"How did you meet her? She seems so different than you, from a totally different social level."

"She was a penniless girl who followed the army. She did anything for money. I suppose she had to, to survive. I didn't know her. I had no idea she knew who I was or had feelings for me. I never met her until the day I decided to ride for glory."

"Ride for glory?"

He shook his head and scowled. "I wanted to make a name for myself, you see. Rather like you did. So I decided to take a huge risk."

"But it didn't turn out the way you hoped."

"We rode into an ambush. My entire battalion was slaughtered." He clenched his jaw and fell silent for a moment. The memory obviously still branded his thoughts. "Ruby found me that night, lying in the forest, dying. She gave me the kiss of life. She didn't ask me if I wanted to live. She didn't ask me if I wanted to be in her debt for all eternity. She just did it, hoping I would be grateful. Hoping I would love her for it."

"And she's still trying to win your affection."

Roman's mouth twisted in a wry smile. "You've got to give her credit. The woman's tenacious."

"Well it worked." Veronique didn't smile. "She has finally won you."

"The marriage proposal, you mean."

Veronique nodded.

"She does have a certain strategic advantage. But she will give up the notion. She never stays interested in anything for very long."

"Where you're concerned, I don't think that's true."

Roman frowned and padded toward her.

"I meant to keep you from all this, Veronique. To know too much can be a burden, sometimes an unbearable one. I thought to keep you free of darkness. To never let you see the underbelly of Londo City. Or to know the ugly truth."

"Especially about you."

"Yes, especially about me."

Everything Veronique knew about her world and about Roman Brandt had turned upside down. She felt as if all vitality had been sucked from her. She sat down on the edge of the cot and dropped her head in her hands. "I don't know what to think," she murmured. "Everything you have just said—it sounds incredible. Unbelievable."

"I wish to God it weren't true. But it is."

She heard the rustle of Roman's clothing as he stepped closer to her, his vampire footsteps undetectable by her human ears. She felt his hand on her shoulder.

"I had hoped to keep your potential golden," he said, his voice thick with emotion. "I thought that if you didn't know what might live inside you, you might never explore it. And you might remain free of the life I have been cursed with."

His touch sent shivers of delight through her. She should have been repulsed by his caress, but she wasn't. Part of her screamed at her to bolt from the room, but another part of her ached to pull him down onto the cot and cover his serious face with kisses.

"Come. It is time to go." His voice rasped through her tangled thoughts. "Before Moray awakens and tracks you down."

"I can't go. I told Jane I would wait for her to come back."

"Staying here much longer will be dangerous." He stepped back from the cot and slipped off his long coat. "You must give up your old life, Veronique. Starting today." He held out the coat, waiting to drape it over her shoulders.

She knew she needed to trust Roman, regardless of his previous deceptions. For once in her life, she should fully trust another being, whether he was human or not.

She stared at him, torn by indecision that threatened to break her in half.

"Starting now," he added.

Roman was right. She remembered how her perception of Jane's bed had changed. The cot was just a metaphor for the rest of her life. Knowing what she knew now, nothing would ever be the same. She stood up and allowed the vampire to settle his heavy woolen garment around her slender frame. A cloud of his heavenly cologne eased around her like an embrace.

With a hand that was far steadier than her knees, she grasped the front edges of the coat and pressed them against her throat.

"I should leave a note for Jane." She glanced around, looking for something to write on. A pencil stub sat next to the gas lamp on the night table. She pulled open the drawer and found a scrap of paper.

Dear Jane—

I'm so sorry, but I had to leave before you returned from work. Thank you for everything, especially your friendship all these years. I will never forget you.

Veronique

Veronique stood up, folded the paper and wrote Jane's name on the front. Then she sighed and put down the pencil.

"Ready?" Roman held out a hand.

"Yes." Veronique lifted her hand to meet Roman's long gloved fingers.

A coach waited on a side street. The vehicle was black and unmarked, bereft of Roman's usual coat of arms on the door. Two men muffled against the cold sat on the driver's seat, hunched against the frosty night air. The driver held a whip in his hand as his eyes glittered with fear. Apparently, he wasn't a vampire and was afraid to be driving at night. His companion, who would share the driving during the long trip, chafed his hands.

"To the north road, as quickly as you can," Roman instructed as he lifted Veronique into the coach. "There's a bonus for you if you make the city limits in an hour."

"You got it, guv'nor."

Roman closed the door and locked it. Veronique settled into the upholstered seat and pulled the blanket over her legs, thankful to be out of the chilly night air but not so thankful to see Ruby Valentine sitting in the corner, smoking one of her long cigarettes. Veronique's ears rang, and she suddenly realized why. Her ears must ring when she came in contact with a vampire—all vampires but Roman.

"Sorry," Ruby drawled. "I couldn't talk him out of dragging you north. Believe me, I tried."

"Thanks," Veronique replied. "I'm sure you did."

"Do you mind if I smoke?" She blew a funnel cloud of fumes in Veronique's direction.

"Yes," Roman snapped. He nodded at the ash receptacle under the window. "We have a long way to go, Ruby. So put it out."

Ruby pouted but obeyed him. Veronique watched her stamp out the glowing end of her cigarette and mash the brown length into the ashtray. She was grateful for Roman's intercession.

As the coach rolled through the dark Londo streets, Roman reached for a folded pile of clothing on the seat beside Veronique and pulled out a long coat made of fine gray-green wool and lined in teal satin. At the shoulders were three capes in staggered rows, each bordered in green velvet trim. Veronique stared at it. She'd never seen a more beautiful coat in her life.

"Put this on," he instructed, holding it out to her. "It might fit you better than that old coat you're wearing."

Veronique relinquished his heavy wool coat, sad to be out from under his scent, but eager to try on the luxurious green garment.

"I swear, Roman," Ruby frowned. "You spoil her more than you have ever thought to spoil me."

"You have more clothes than you could wear in a century," Roman shouldered on his long coat and sat down. "Why would I buy more for you?"

"Because it's the thought that counts!" she retorted.

He glanced down at her. "Who's counting?"

"I am!" Ruby narrowed her eyes. "Don't think you can toss me aside so easily, Roman Brandt. If you so much as smile at the lab rat on this trip, I'll let the others know where to find her."

"I'm not a lab rat!" Veronique threw back at her as she fastened the buttons over her chest. The coat fit her as if it had been made to order. Perhaps it had been. She glanced at Roman, to find him appraising her, his eyes glinting with appreciation. The look warmed her more than the coat.

"You're not a lab rat?" Ruby turned to Veronique, happy to vent her anger on her. "And just what do you *think* you are?" Her cold brown eyes raked across Veronique's new green coat and then fixed on her face. "Tell me, Miss Wilder."

Veronique glared at her. She hadn't had time to think much about her unusual heritage, other than worrying that she might transform into a blood-sucking monster at any moment. She had no idea what kind of being she was or might develop into, and the prospect worried her. But she'd never let Ruby know that.

"I'm someone with a lovely new coat," she answered. She knew the color was the perfect complement to her red hair. Roman must have picked it out himself. "A coat that I like very much."

"Ooh!" Ruby hissed, rising to launch herself at Veronique.

Roman grabbed her wrist to stop her.

"Leave Veronique be," he commanded. "We have a long journey ahead of us. And it won't be easy. The least you can be is civil, Ruby."

"I don't have to be anything!"

Chapter 27

"KEEP IN MIND," ROMAN warned. "If there's trouble, you might need Veronique's help."

"When hell freezes over!" Ruby flounced back to her seat.

Veronique wondered what Roman thought they would encounter in the north and what possible assistance she could give a vampire.

"You'll change your tune once we pass through the Northern Lights. There's a reason the Overseers don't go north. And you're about to discover why." Roman crossed his arms and settled into the corner of the coach. "So if I were you, Ruby. I'd be nice. And rest while you can. The lights will test you as nothing else."

"What are the Northern Lights?" Veronique inquired as she rearranged the blanket over her knees.

"It's a magnetic band that we pass through to get to the north. It's an aftermath of the bomb. It's like a curtain of light, made up of glowing particles. It's beautiful, but the effect on a vampire is almost as deadly as full sunlight."

"Thank Gottfried we don't have much of *that* any more!" Ruby put in.

"What do the Northern Lights do to a vampire?" Veronique wondered if they would have any affect on a half-vampire. She supposed no one would know until she went through the experience.

"Some go crazy. Some have seizures."

"What about you?"

"I suffer extreme pain. I have at one time bitten through my lip and tongue."

Ruby stared at him and reached for her cigarette case before she remembered Roman's ban on smoking. Her hands shook. "I'm not sure I like the sound of this." She pushed the silver case back into her reticule. "How long will it take to get through?"

"An hour, depending upon the wind."

"Wind?" Ruby's painted lips pursed.

"There's a strange wind that's associated with the Northern Lights. I've been told it can reach gusts of over a hundred miles an hour." Roman turned to glance at the small woman in plum-colored velvet. "You can get out now if you like, Ruby. No one is forcing you to go through the ordeal. I'm not even certain a female vampire is physically able to withstand it."

Ruby shot a dark look at Veronique. "I'm not staying behind."

"You might not find it worth the trouble. You'll hate it in the north, Ruby. There are no shops. No nice young men or children. Barely any people as a matter of fact."

"How do you survive then?"

"If you can't fast for long periods? Then wild animals."

Ruby sat back, horrified.

"Don't say you weren't warned, my dear."

For once, Ruby fell silent. She yanked back the curtain and stared out the window, brooding. All the while, she picked at a line of sequins on her thigh, as if she were struggling to reach a decision. Veronique hoped she would decide to turn back and never bother her again.

But Ruby did not announce any such change of plan. After an hour had passed, and they rolled out of Londo City and into the countryside, Ruby dozed off and lolled her head onto Roman's shoulder. Veronique surveyed the sight, trying not to be jealous of the woman and knowing she should be grateful for her presence.

Without Ruby in the coach, Veronique would be tempted to reach out for Roman. Until she knew more about herself and her true physical makeup, she knew it was best to keep her distance from the vampire.

Another hour passed. Though darkness hid much of the surrounding countryside, Veronique knew that fields stretched out for miles in every direction, dotted by the ruins of deserted villages. This was the place where Jane and her family worked all day, coaxing meager crops to grow in the filtered sunlight, carrying water by hand from nearby streams, and chasing off birds and rodents that were as starved for food as every other creature.

Veronique glanced at Roman, who lounged with his eyes closed. Even so, she could sense that he was awake.

"How did it happen?" Veronique asked softly.

His gray eyes opened to silver slits. "How did what happen?"

"The Overseers. How did they end up ruling Londo City?"

"It was a natural progression." Roman glanced at Ruby's head on his shoulder, and shifted his weight as if she annoyed him, but she didn't take notice. He allowed her to remain lodged against his body.

"After the bomb, when so much died off in the nuclear winter, the vampires were as desperate for food as mankind was."

Veronique tried to picture a race she had considered only mythical as being part of history. She would have to rearrange her vision of the past to include Roman and his ilk. It wouldn't be an easy task to think of the world in an entirely different light and the part the vampires might have played in it.

"Food was scarce. Almost all human beings had perished by the end of the first year. The vampires knew their own existence was in as much jeopardy as that of the humans. They decided that they had to intervene. If humans didn't survive, the vampires would be left feeding on beasts. And that is the very last choice on the menu, let me tell you."

Veronique made a face. She couldn't help it. Discussing human beings as a food choice made her sick to her stomach.

"To a vampire, drinking nonhuman blood is like eating moldy bread. One can do it, but it isn't preferred."

"So you had to help us."

"Yes. The older and wiser members of our race decided to band together. It was a novel idea, because as I have told you—vampires are a solitary lot. But then there were the two brothers, Silas and Gabriel Stone. They formed the early coalition."

Veronique nodded.

"The times dictated unusual measures. The older vampires formed a group. They settled upon London as their center of operations. Many of us lived there already. It was on an island, separate from the rest of the world and defensible against the outside, should that ever be a problem. London was covered in mist, which made it possible for the vampires to move freely, day or night. Our group called themselves the Overseers. They hunted far and wide for mammals and birds to make sure a small pocket of humans living in Londo City got enough food to survive the next few years. If the vampires hadn't supplied meat, the humans would have died. Animals were so scarce, humans couldn't hunt at a great enough range to keep themselves fed. Little by little, the nuclear winter eased into a nuclear spring. The first crops were coaxed out of the ground. Building restoration began. Some roads were cleared. The group of humans survived, enough to start having children. But the Overseers had to be very careful about the ratio of humans to available food."

"I take it the vampires killed some of the humans."

"Yes. But in a very selective way. And ceremonially. We had to, Veronique." Roman sighed. "The old ones were culled. Any human born with a defect was culled. Criminals. Orphans, too. We couldn't afford to feed a human that could not or would not work in return. We had to make those decisions monthly. And it was not easy."

Veronique nodded, but her mouth was dry. She was glad she had not been born in the old days. It must have been even drearier and difficult than the life she had led on the streets. Then she thought of current Londo City society, and how retired people seemed to disappear off the streets or collapse of what most people considered heart attacks. She thought of the manager of Whites, his body found in the alley, his death a mystery. She had a fairly good idea now of just what had killed him. And who.

"Yes," Roman said, as if he read her thoughts. "We still cull the citizenry. It is cold-blooded, I know. But it must be done."

"And if I had been found on the streets as a child—an orphan—what would have become of me?"

"You would have been taken to the Central Compound and fed the most delicious food you could imagine. As much as you would have wanted."

"For how long?"

"Two weeks."

His serious gaze never left her face as she considered how gruesome her fate might have been.

"I could have been Ruby's dinner," she murmured, her stomach twisting again.

"Yes." Roman sighed. "But you would have thought you were in heaven, and that an angel had come to kiss you goodnight. It wouldn't have been terrible at all. Quite the opposite."

"But at the end of the evening, I would have been dead."

"Yes."

Veronique shook her head and looked down at the floor, her thoughts and heart churning. She heard Roman shift, and the next thing she knew, he was leaning forward with his gloved hands framing her knees.

"That is why your father and I came up with the Commensalist Project."

"The interbreeding experiment? I thought Moray said it was to search for a cure for the virus." She glanced up at his handsome face. "What's that have to do with orphans being killed?"

"Moray didn't understand the real reason for the project."

"Which was?"

"To put an end to the killing. To create an immortal food source." Roman squeezed her knees. "That's what commensalism is. It means to share a table. Two organisms living together, with benefit to one and no harm done to the other."

Veronique stared at him, amazed at the idea, and that someone could think it possible to create an entirely new race of people. And yet...and yet...here she was: half human and half vampire. And alive. A chill swept through her.

"If every vampire had a companion—an immortal companion—who would never die but who could supply blood, then there would no longer be a need to prey on human beings. In fact, there would be no need for humans as we know them. We could allow them to die off naturally. Once human beings were extinct, we would no longer have to worry about the next wave rising up to drop another bomb in some far-off century. Only the vampires and their companions would be left, never procreating, never dying. Everyone would have enough to eat. The world would at last be under some semblance of control. The earth would begin to heal."

Veronique couldn't speak. The concept appalled her but intrigued her at the same time.

"Your father had the scientific training to undertake the project," Roman continued as released her knees and sat up. "I championed it. For a few decades, we fought hard for it, even though we were getting no results. At least that's what I was led to believe. Then your father disappeared. The young vampires rebelled. And I was beaten to death by hoodlums hired to put an end to me."

"To death?"

"They thought I was dead. I might as well have been." Roman shook his head. "It took me years to heal. And most vampires can heal almost instantaneously."

"How did you get thrown in prison?"

"I was found barely alive on the street. Someone recognized me. They dragged me in front of your uncle Silas, who graciously saved my life by throwing me in prison instead of killing me. He was always such a politician. He knew if I was executed for my part in the Commensalist Project, then he would have to kill his brother, Gabriel, as well. If and when Gabriel showed up."

Veronique hugged the coat around her. "So you think I might have immortal blood in my veins—that I might live forever."

"Only time will tell."

She considered the possibility for a moment. Then a new thought struck her. She leveled her gaze on his face. "The plan would have worked, except for one small detail."

His left eyebrow rose in surprise. "Oh?"

"What if the experimental person..."

"The hybrid?"

She grimaced. The term made her feel more like a lab rat than anything Ruby had said. "What if the result of the experiment is not a sterile being?"

"Hybrids are sterile. It's a scientific fact."

"But how can you be sure?"

"Hybrids always have been. For instance, mules."

"What is a mule?"

"They're a cross between a horse and a donkey. They were once used on farms in Pre-Reformation times."

"And a donkey?"

"A small beast of burden." A shadow passed through his clear gray eyes. "What are you getting at, Veronique?"

"What if you and my father had created a race of beings who would never die but who could reproduce? You would have a population explosion all over again. And worse than before."

"Again, highly unlikely," he replied.

"What if there's a small chance that you and my father could have been wrong?"

For a moment he stared at the curtained window beside him, lost in thought. Then he turned. "You must not dwell on such a thing."

It was then Veronique sensed the stare of a second pair of eyes. She glanced at Ruby. Sometime during the conversation, the other woman had awakened. Her head was still propped against Roman's shoulder while she stared at Veronique, her gaze as cold and razor-sharp as a blade.

Chapter 28

SCALDED BY RUBY'S STARE, Veronique averted her glance and turned her thoughts inward as the coach jingled through the countryside. The ancient road was rough, not from overuse but from centuries of the earth heating and cooling beneath it, causing cracks and bumps that no one had time or money to repair. Veronique let the rumble of the coach lull her into a trance in which Ruby and Roman did not exist.

The night flew by. Veronique's stomach growled, but she ignored it. She was accustomed to staving off hunger. She hadn't eaten since before the audition, nearly two days ago. It seemed like lifetimes ago.

She thought of her mother and sifted through her memories for visions of the nomadic life the two of them had led. Her entire childhood had to be examined and recast, now that she knew she was the offspring of a vampire and a human. Had her parents loved each other? And how had her beautiful mother survived, if not helped in some way by a benefactor? It was hard enough for a family to get by with both parents bringing in a salary. It must have been impossible for her mother to have supported herself and a baby. Her vampire father must have provided for them, but Veronique could not recall ever seeing him.

She wanted to think of her father as a good man. She wanted to think that her parents had loved each other.

She was just about to ask Roman if he had been acquainted with her mother, when the coachman yelled out "Whoa!" and pulled up the horses.

Roman yanked back the curtain. An eerie green glow lit up his profile. Veronique snapped out of her trance and came to attention. To her consternation, her ears started to ring, alerting her that vampires approached.

"What's going on?" Ruby inquired in a sleepy voice as she struggled to an upright position. "Is it the Northern Lights?"

"Yes, but we shouldn't have stopped. You never stop." Roman reached for the door, just as it was pulled open.

"Out!" a voice commanded.

Veronique peered through her window. In the dim light of the autumn dawn, she saw a slender man standing in the road with a mask concealing his face. Behind him stood three henchmen, also wearing masks, as well as wide-brimmed hats. Ahead of the coach undulated a ghostly curtain of light that shifted between yellow green and magenta. Dawn glowed on the eastern horizon.

"Out!" the slender man repeated, indicating the direction with the end of a pistol. "And no tricks, Brandt."

Veronique's heart sank. She recognized the reedy voice. Neal Moray must have guessed where they were going and had positioned himself on the southern side of the Northern Lights. Now, masquerading as an old-fashioned highwayman, he would take her prisoner, and the human coachman would never guess she had been kidnapped by a vampire agent.

"What took you so damn long?" Moray snapped.

"Sightseeing," Roman retorted.

"Funny." Moray tilted his head. "Now, if you're done showing Miss Wilder around the countryside, hand her over."

"Sorry, not quite finished." Roman leaned out the door. "Drive on, citizen!" he commanded.

The coachman raised the reins to carry out Roman's order, but Moray fired a shot over his head. "Stand by!" Moray shouted. Then he turned back to Roman. "You've given me no choice."

The henchmen edged closer.

"Get him," Moray nodded at Roman.

It took all three men to wrestle Roman out of the coach. Veronique hung in the doorway, desperate to help him as he kicked his attackers off again and again, but she was not sure what she could do. She knew what was coming. The men would beat Roman to the brink of death again, perhaps beyond it. The virus that was transforming him back to a human being would make him easier to destroy. He might get himself killed in defending her.

"Don't hurt him!" Veronique cried.

"Fine." Moray shot a smile at her. "Just come with me, Citizen Wilder, and I'll let soldier boy go without harming a hair on his head."

Roman struggled to look back at her, even though one of the men clutched him by the hair. "No, Veronique! He'll kill you!"

"I'm not going to kill anyone." Moray rolled his eyes. "You're always so melodramatic, Brandt."

Veronique didn't believe a word Moray said, but she could see no other recourse than to do what he asked. "Let Roman go, and I will come down."

"Good choice." Moray saluted her with the gold handle of Roman's cane, which he held in his left hand. "We can make this easy and spare everyone a lot of trauma." He looked up at her. "But ladies first. I insist."

Veronique picked up her rose-colored skirts and stepped down from the coach.

"No, Vee!" Roman thundered. He lunged toward her, dragging all three men with him. They punched him in the face and gut, but he fought back, elbowing one in the jaw so hard that the man lost consciousness. He kicked a second one in the stomach and sent him sprawling on the ground. The third man jumped on him, but Roman struck back, pummeling him in the ribs and kidneys and flinging him against a tree.

Moray watched as Roman fought off the thugs, even without benefit of his special cane and in the faint light of dawn, when a vampire should be at his weakest. For a moment, the slight man let his attention center entirely on the fight.

Veronique took advantage of Moray's lapse and leapt forward to snatch the cane from his grip. Just as quickly, she darted away. He whirled to face her, enraged.

"Give me that cane!" he hissed.

Veronique hurried backward, toward the Northern Lights, hoping and praying that she wouldn't trip and give Moray the opportunity to reclaim the cane. As she approached the curtain of light, she felt a warm wind rustle her silk gown. The Northern Lights didn't seem that threatening. They felt as if they would be more like a warm bath than a test of a vampire's pain threshold.

"Call off your dogs, Moray," she warned. "Or I'll throw this cane into the Northern Lights."

"You wouldn't!"

"I would!"

Moray's eyes narrowed to slits above his mask. His glare struck terror in her, but she stood tall and refused to let him see the fear in her heart. He lowered his head and focused his stare on the spot between her brows. He was trying to hypnotize her, as Roman had done in the past. She forced her mind to go blank and looked away, refusing to answer the demand of his vampire eyes. It wasn't easy to refuse the call. She sweated under her coat, and her limbs trembled. She knew she couldn't withstand his stare much longer. She could feel her attention being pulled toward him.

Then a miracle occurred. As Roman fought the last and most brutish thug, the autumn morning blossomed around them, sending rays of sun through gaps in the clouds, streaming through the bare limbs of the stunted beech trees and spilling over the dead grass.

For a moment, Veronique gaped at the landscape. She had never seen day emerge from night like this in a glorious golden glow. She had never been outside the city limits. She had never worked in the outlying fields. Her whole life had been spent in a world of fog and mist where full sunlight never quite broke through. She squinted, unaccustomed to such brightness, and then realized she couldn't take a deep breath. The hair on her forearms pricked. A voice in her head urged her to run, to get out of the sunlight, and to cover herself immediately.

She was a vampire after all.

At the sunbreak, Moray swore and whirled around to look at Roman. Two of the henchmen stumbled into the shrubbery, their clothes steaming. The third struggled desperately to escape from Roman, who hunched over him, strangling him, while his head and back smoldered in the sunlight.

"Damn you, Brandt!" Moray exclaimed. He raised the pistol and fired at Roman's chest. Roman flew backward and crumpled to the ground. The third thug fled, leaving Moray to finish the job. Moray staggered toward Roman, firing again. Roman struggled to get up but collapsed on his back. The fight, the sun, and the gunshot had all taken a toll on him. Grimacing, he rose to his elbows to drag himself out of range.

Moray stepped closer. "You just had to butt in!" he exclaimed. "You could have kept out of it and this would never have happened."

"And pigs would fly," Roman spat.

"But now I'll have to kill you. We can't let Silas Stone's murderer go unpunished." Moray squeezed another shot. He hit Roman in the midsection. Roman gasped and had to stop to gather enough strength before he could move again. His feet were now in full sunshine. Veronique saw flames flickering around the soles of his boots. A few more moments of sunlight, and Roman would be burned alive.

Moray squeezed off two more shots.

Veronique had to do something. Moray would keep shooting, pinning Roman to the ground until he was engulfed by sunlight. Though her exposed skin felt hot and prickly and her legs were heavy with a strange lethargy, she staggered forward, twisting the cane between her hands. The blade clicked out, as sharp and lethal as ever. Sunlight glinted off the tip, blinding her.

Moray fired again, hitting Roman in the neck. Blood splattered over Roman's snow-white cravat.

"No!" Veronique cried. Horrified, she ran toward him. The world glowed with a sudden burst of color as the clouds parted to expose a brilliant patch of blue. Her chest felt like a block of lead. She could barely see now, but she blinked back her tears and kept running.

Moray whirled to face her, with his right arm still pointing the gun at Roman, his chest exposed. Smoke rose from his shoulders and hair.

Veronique swept up the cane as she remembered Roman had done with the vampire in the churchyard. She doubted she was a match for Moray's male strength, but she was taller than he was. It was an advantage. She had only to bring the cane down and plunge it into Moray's chest and she could kill him. She knew how to do this. Somehow, the act felt familiar, but she had no idea why. She planted her feet as Moray turned to fully face her. He swung his weapon in an arc to aim at her point blank.

"Moray!" Roman bellowed. A blur of flames ran up his legs.

Moray fired, but the revolver clicked on an empty chamber. His face paled as he pumped the trigger again and again.

"You bastard!" Veronique glared at Moray, straight into his snake-like eyes. Then, using every shred of strength she possessed, she plunged the cane into his chest. The shaft pierced through him, as if he were made of butter instead of flesh and bone.

For a moment he stared at her, his eyes wide with outrage. Had he not thought her capable of killing him? He had woefully misjudged her. Then his stare shifted to terror as he realized he was a dead man. He sank to his knees and fell backward, but the cane kept him upright, facing the light as if he were praying to a sun god.

"No!" he wailed. His face burst into flames, the metal buttons of his coat melted, and his hair caught on fire.

Veronique couldn't watch while the morning sun incinerated him. Roman could be next. *She* could be next. She had to get Roman out of the sunlight and into the coach.

"Ruby!" she screamed. "Get out here!"

Veronique didn't wait for an answer. She dashed to Roman's side. He lay in a patch of crumpled thistles, unconscious. His right arm was black and withered. Veronique's heart surged into her throat at the sight of him.

"Roman!" she murmured. She fell to her knees beside him, shielding him from full sunlight while her own back burned. She patted his cheek, desperate to find some sign of life in him. His eyes remained closed. His skin felt oddly hard, as if his life force had vanished, leaving alabaster in its place.

Ruby didn't materialize, but the driver ran up beside her.

"What's going on!" he exclaimed. "Who are these people?"

"Never mind right now," Veronique replied. "Help me get Citizen Brandt into the coach."

"He's dead."

"No, he's not."

"I know a dead man when I see one."

"I don't care if he's dead or not. I want him in the coach." Veronique struggled to her feet and reached down for Roman's burned boots. She fought down a surge of nausea as the stench of smoldering leather and burned vampire flesh nearly overwhelmed her. "Please," she added, glancing down at the doubtful driver, "just help me."

Frowning, the driver reached for Roman's charred shoulders. He grunted and lifted Roman's bulk off the ground. They half-carried, half-dragged the vampire toward the coach. Veronique forced herself not to examine Roman's wounds too closely and not to think the worst. He couldn't be dead. She wouldn't let him die. He could heal, given time and darkness. He had to.

Ruby opened the door of the coach. "I'm really sorry," she said, her drawl completely gone and her voice contrite. "I can't go out in sunlight, Veronique. I'm very sensitive."

"So are we all," Veronique shot back. She crawled into the coach while the driver dragged Roman into the vehicle and hoisted him onto the seat. Veronique adjusted his legs and stood up.

Ruby looked down at her longtime companion. She held her gloved hands to her face as she took in the damage he had sustained. "Oh, Roman!" she cried. She draped herself across his charred, bloody torso and sobbed hysterically. "Roman!" For once, the woman didn't seem to care about her appearance. She hugged him fiercely and pressed her painted cheek into the small of his bloody neck.

Veronique turned as the driver hopped to the ground. "Drive on," she commanded.

"You don't have to ask me twice, citizen." He sprinted toward the horses. She felt the coach jiggle as he jumped to his seat. With a whistle and a slap of the reins, they were off, hurtling into the curtain of light.

"No!" Ruby sat up. Her pale face was smeared with Roman's blood. "I can't!"

"Be quiet!" Veronique held on to the leather strap at the door, blocking the exit, and kept her balance as the coach roared into the Northern Lights.

"I can't do it!" Ruby cried, her eyes sharp with fear. She stood up, and nearly fell when the coach hit a bump. "Let me out!"

"You're not going anywhere," Veronique snapped. "Now sit down. We need to save Roman's life."

For a long moment, Ruby gaped at her, as if she couldn't understand what Veronique had just said. Then she licked her lips and frowned. "What?" she asked.

"We need to save your boyfriend's life. You want to save him, don't you?"

Ruby's white face contorted. For a moment she stood in the middle of the coach while she went through an emotional upheaval that was terrible to witness. Veronique stared at her, knowing she should look away as the woman in front of her literally fell apart, but she was too fascinated not to keep watching.

Ruby's cocky pride twisted through her features, turning her eyes to dark triangles and her mouth to a twitching red gash. Lines puckered her flawless skin, at her forehead, at the sides of her nose, and under her lower lip. Her pretty face transformed into a grotesque mask of pain and despair. And then tears burst from her eyes as Ruby Valentine's brittle shell disintegrated to reveal the scared and lonely young woman that still lived inside her.

"He's not my boyfriend." She dashed her tears away with the back of her gloved hand. "He never was." Then she sank to her knees and threw her arms around Roman's lifeless body. "Oh, Roman!" Sobs wracked her slender ribcage. "What have they done to you?"

Watching Ruby touch Roman sent a hot wave of jealousy through Veronique. She released the strap and stepped toward the rear seat, anxious to get to work and to get Ruby away from the man she wanted to hold and cry over herself. She reached for Ruby's shoulder to pry her away, but Ruby's voice stopped her.

"He never loved me." Her voice was thick with tears. "He never looked at me twice. But I loved him the moment I saw him. Oh, Roman!" She broke into uncontrollable weeping again, squeezing fistfuls of his singed coat in her tiny hands.

Veronique stared down at Ruby's delicate back while relief mixed with chagrin washed over her. She had fallen for the oldest trick in the world. She had believed Ruby when the woman had claimed she and Roman made love every night, when in reality Roman had probably never even kissed her.

She could almost feel sorry for Ruby, except for the fact that the woman had tried to kill her.

"Ruby, get a hold of yourself," Veronique clutched both of her thin shoulders. "Get up. We've got work to do."

"Work? What work!" Ruby kissed Roman's closed mouth and hugged him. "My love," she whispered. "My dearest, my only love!"

Impatient and heartsick, Veronique pulled her back. "Ruby, get up. Get away from him."

"Why?" Ruby turned, her eyes burning with anger. "We're going to die in the lights!"

"No, we're not."

"Yes, we are. And I'm going to spend my last moments with Roman."

The more time Ruby wasted blubbering, the more time was lost for a chance to revive Roman. Veronique felt an urgency she had never known, as if the most important clock of her life were ticking away, about to gong her final hour.

"Ruby, get up. This instant!" Veronique stabbed at the air with her finger. "We're going to save him."

Ruby looked up at her, shocked by the vehemence in Veronique's voice.

"But he's dead."

"No!" Veronique felt grief scald her throat.

"Vee, he's dead." Ruby looked up at her, compassion and pity swimming in her tear-filled eyes. "Trust me. I know. I'm an expert."

Chapter 29

"NO! I DON'T BELIEVE it." Veronique's voice caught on the phrase. She choked back a sob. It was her turn to break down, but she knew she had to fight back her grief and focus on what she had to do for Roman. "Stand up, Ruby." She shrugged out of her coat, ignoring the way the garment chafed her burned skin. "And bite my neck. Now!"

"What?" Ruby's jaw dropped.

"Bite my neck. I'd do it myself, but I'm not a contortionist."

"Bite you?" Ruby retorted, aghast. "You've got to be kidding. Your blood tastes like shit!"

Above the clip-clop of the horses, Veronique could hear wind whistling around the coach. Soon they wouldn't be able to hear each other. She leaned closer to Ruby. "Now! Before we run out of time."

"You want to die with Roman—is that it? No! I'm not helping you with that. You can't leave me to face the Northern Lights alone!"

"I don't want you to kill me. I want to save Roman's life," Veronique grew impatient with Ruby's insistence that Roman couldn't be helped. "I want you to suck out my blood and give it to Roman."

"You mean...in his mouth."

"Yes. Like resuscitation. Only instead of air, we're going to use blood. My blood."

Ruby propped her hands on her hips while the green and magenta light pulsed through the cracks in the curtains. "You have to be kidding."

"My blood has special properties. Maybe it can bring Roman back from wherever he is." She glanced at him as her heart constricted. Maybe she could be Roman's commensalist. It was worth a try. She'd do anything in her power to save him.

Veronique paused as a thought occurred to her. What if Roman didn't want to be saved? Good Gottfried, she was no better than Ruby in her desperation to bestow the gift of life on the man she loved, purely for the sake of keeping him in her world.

If Roman were conscious, she would ask him what to do. But he wasn't even breathing. So it was up to her to make the decision to try to revive him or let him be. She shut off the second-guessing that whirled in her head.

"Please, Ruby. If you love Roman, you will do this."

Ruby glanced down at Roman and then heaved a heavy sigh. "Okay." She pointed at the opposite seat. "Sit down over there. You're too tall if you stand up."

Veronique plopped onto the seat while Ruby bent over her, her top lip curling back in disgust.

"I don't know if I can actually do this."

"You have to." Veronique scooted to the edge of the seat. She tilted her head to expose her neck and closed her eyes, not wishing to witness Ruby's transformation into the ferocious creature that had attacked her in the bedroom.

"This had better work and work fast," Ruby warned. "I'm getting a terrible headache all of a sudden. Are you?"

"No. Just do it." Veronique held her breath as Ruby hissed and swooped down for the initial bite. She felt two hot pricks and then the softer and much cooler flesh of Ruby's lips as she sucked the blood from Veronique's neck as quickly as it would come. The wind screamed around the coach, buffeting them. Veronique could hear the driver struggling to maintain control of the screaming horses—whipping them and shouting over the wind.

Seconds later, Ruby pulled away from Veronique's throat, pivoted, and bent over Roman. It appeared to Veronique that Ruby was kissing him deeply as she slanted her jaw over his. Then she stood up, swore and wiped her mouth on the sleeve of her coat. "Good Gottfried, that's horrible!"

"Again!" Veronique demanded.

This time she felt Ruby's vampire spell envelop her. Swirls of crimson and tangerine swam in her vision. She heard as well as felt a deep throbbing drumbeat. She couldn't be sure if the sound was a rhythm echoing from the depths of Ruby's past or if it was the desperate surge of her own heart.

For a moment she forgot all about Roman as the swirling lights and driving percussions blotted out her thoughts.

Ruby transferred two more draughts to Roman. In a daze, Veronique watched her feed him. She squinted, trying to discern a change in him, but Roman hadn't so much as blinked since he'd been carried him into the coach. With every passing moment that he remained unresponsive, Veronique's heart broke a bit more. But she refused to give up hope.

"Again!" she mumbled. She felt light-headed and weak and wasn't sure she could get to her feet should it become necessary.

Ruby scrunched up her nose. "I don't know how much more of this I can take," she exclaimed. "I'm going to be sick!" She clung to the leather strap at the door as her face switched from white to green and back again. The Northern Lights flashed through the drapery and cast the side of her face in a ghostly glow, making her appear even more sickly. The wind sounded like a train barreling by at full speed. Every piece of wood and metal of the coach rattled as if it would fracture at any moment.

"Just one more time, Ruby. One more!"

Veronique was relieved when Ruby bent down for the fourth time. She took a long draught from Veronique's neck, probably hoping it was the final draw. Then she turned to kiss it into Roman's mouth.

Veronique's senses swam. She felt nauseated and giddy at the same time, but she couldn't tell if it was due to blood loss or the magnetic storm outside. "Again!" she whispered. But this time her tongue felt too thick to properly pronounce the word.

Ruby stared down at her as she hugged her thin arms around her ribcage. "One more might be asking for trouble, Veronique."

"I don't care. Just do it."

"You might die," Ruby panted. "I can't take the chance. I'm not going through these lights alone! I can't!"

"One more!" Veronique murmured, barely able to keep the other woman in focus. "Please."

Ruby shook her head. "All right, but this is the very last one. I mean it." This time Ruby knelt at Veronique's side, as she was too overcome with pain to keep on her feet.

Veronique closed her eyes. She felt Ruby's cool breath on her throat. She smelled the metallic odor of her own blood on Ruby's mouth, and then she succumbed to a strange dream in which she played a piano in the clearing where Neal Moray had died.

She kept playing while the sun rose higher and higher, burning her face and hands. She heard her mother calling her name.

"Veronique! Veronique! Nica!"

Was that her mother, or was it Ruby calling her name? Someone grabbed her hand and collapsed beside her, crying hysterically and babbling nonsense into the top of her sleeve.

But Veronique couldn't stop playing. It felt too good to stop. Delirious with pleasure, she surrendered to Chopin and slipped all the way into the music until there was nothing left of her. No flesh and blood. No thoughts. No worries. Just a tinkling melody spiraling into the beautiful, terrible light.

Roman blinked awake. For an instant, he had no idea where he was. It felt as if he'd been on a long journey alone in the coldest, darkest place he'd ever ventured—colder than the Alps in the dead of a winter afternoon, colder than the light of Orion at dawn. Then he felt the swaying of the coach on its springs and realized he lay on the seat of the vehicle, and that he'd been shot by Neal Moray. Numerous times. But much worse, he'd been subjected to the sun. He tried to move his head to look down at his body, but he could not command his muscles to obey him. He was in the vampire mode of repair, where all he could do was wait patiently for regeneration to occur and hope that it would not take years to mend whatever damage he'd sustained.

He could sense Veronique close at hand. But he couldn't move his head to see her. He also couldn't hear her breathing, which was odd, because his highly-attuned vampire senses could always hear the sounds a human being made—even the sound of their blood swirling through their veins. Fear for her fanned over him, but he could do nothing but lie there.

He could also sense Ruby's presence. But she, like Veronique, emitted no signs of life. All he could be sure of was there were two other beings in the coach, bumping along in the dark with him. But he had no idea what condition either of the women was in. He could do nothing. He could only lie on the padded seat, willing his body to mend as quickly as inhumanly possible.

Darkness surrounded the vehicle. They must have passed through the Northern Lights and were continuing to the northwest now. He had to hang on. In a few more days, they would arrive at a tiny harbor on the western shore of the Anglo Territories. There, they would find the boat he had arranged to take them to his sanctuary in the Outer Islands.

Roman closed his eyes and willed himself to remain calm. He had to concentrate on healing. He had gone through enough restoration periods to know that he had to expend his energy as judiciously as possible. He took a deep breath and sent a series of commands to the far reaches of his body.

He had to survive. He had to heal enough to help Veronique—if she were still able to be helped. God only knew what had happened to her and Ruby since the ambush on the road. Veronique could be dead. She could have gone mad. He shut off the possibilities of what might have transpired during the ride through the Northern Lights. He couldn't think about that now. He had to concentrate on fighting for his life.

If he had been able to move, he would have smiled at the irony of the situation. He was going to fight for his life. And for Veronique's. And for that matter, Ruby's.

Good God in Heaven, he wanted to live.

Chapter 30

NOVEMBER 2525

Veronique felt a cool hand on her forehead. A big hand. A gentle hand.

"Her fever is down," a deep voice commented.

She couldn't quite identify the owner of the voice. It surely didn't belong to Citizen Carson. But who else would touch her like this? Who else would seem so familiar to her? She tried to open her eyes but didn't have the strength. She tried to ask who was there, but her lips remained stuck together, mute.

She heard the brush of cloth upon stone and sensed that someone else was staring down at her.

"Do you think she will make it?" a female voice inquired. The woman was slightly familiar to Veronique, too. Jane? No, not Jane. Someone else.

"She's come this far," the man replied. "Why wouldn't she pull through?"

"Because like you said, there is no telling what the lights and the blood loss have done to her. Or what the long-term effect might be on a hybrid like her."

Hybrid? What were they talking about? She should know, but she just couldn't retrieve the information from her memory. The facts were so far back in the mist that she might never be able to see them clearly. Too exhausted to think, Veronique rolled her eyes behind their lids and drifted off to sleep again.

Chapter 31

OUTER ISLANDS—DECEMBER 2525

As the winter solstice approached, Roman stood in the dark, looking at the tall woman leaning against the parapet. She stared at the moonlit sea, her shoulders wrapped in a heavy woolen shawl, her pale face still drawn by the ravages of her injuries. Though Veronique had almost died on the journey north, her comeliness had never waned. In fact, the suffering she had endured had sculpted her youthful prettiness into an almost unbearable beauty. Her eyes had grown luminous, her brows and cheekbones more defined, and her skin, so flawless and creamy, had taken on a glow as if she were lit from inside.

Silvery light streamed over Veronique, playing in her fiery hair and dancing off the planes of her ethereal face. He barely recognized her as the young woman who had entranced him with her music. She was a woman now—a calm and confident woman.

A woman who had withdrawn from him.

Roman's heart twisted with despair. He had fought so hard to recover his faculties and the use of his limbs. He had wanted to live as never before so he might have the chance to deepen his relationship with Veronique. But all that they had shared—the music, the kisses, and the close brush with forbidden love—all those memories had been swept away like so much dust.

Veronique had healed. Outwardly, she was as good as new. Better than new. But inwardly, something had changed. She had come out of her suffering with a coolness of character that alarmed him. She'd been so compromised that he hadn't pressed her for anything, hadn't asked her what was wrong.

Perhaps she had decided she wanted nothing more to do with him, now that she knew he was a vampire. He couldn't blame her.

With each day that passed, when she avoided his eyes and kept to herself, he felt her slipping farther and farther away from him. And each day he would start to reach for her hand, longing for the connection they had shared, and then let his arm drop.

When he had met her, he had barreled toward her virginity, too caught up by his own sexual desire to hold back. Now, however, he was determined to maintain his usual restraint, especially since Veronique had changed her mind about him. It was better for both of them. Veronique was the daughter of his best friend. He must keep his distance. Forever.

Roman watched Veronique brush her hair back from her face and walk toward the south tower. He should have taken her somewhere else. Somewhere warmer. His small castle on the coast was a moody place, with ramparts overlooking a pounding sea and grounds overgrown with brambles and gorse. It wasn't a fit place to recover a sunny outlook. But at least at night, the sky was usually clear and sprinkled with stars. The moon sailed across the twinkling field, almost like a sun. Each night the sky opened up in a glorious display that sent his spirit soaring. He might not be able to walk in sunlight. But starlight, especially the starlight here in the north, was almost as marvelous.

That's why he came to this tower each night—to smoke a cigar and contemplate his universe. Perhaps that was what Veronique did each night as well, as she walked the ramparts in her shawl. She was nurturing her spirit with a freedom it had never known before.

Roman heard a step behind him and was surprised to see Ruby striding across the floor toward him. He hadn't seen much of her since they'd arrived at his small stronghold. She'd surprised him by turning into quite the huntress and spent most of her nights chasing down animals. It was Ruby who had supplied the meat for the broths that had sustained Veronique through her illness.

Having brought no clothes with her to the north, Ruby had exchanged her sequins and satin for some of Roman's old clothes, which she had tailored to fit her much smaller frame. Oddly enough, the masculine attire suited her. In fact, as she walked toward him dressed in a pair of brown trousers and vest, with her hair pulled back in a French braid, she looked far more provocative than she had ever appeared in her gaudy attire.

"Does she know how you spy on her?" Ruby asked, nodding at Veronique on the other side of the window.

"I certainly hope not."

"Staring at her won't solve anything."

"I know." Roman turned away from the scene on the rampart and walked to his desk. "Cigar?"

"Don't mind if I do." Ruby swept forward and plopped down in a chair. She flung her leg over the arm while she watched Roman clip the ends of the cigar and then light it. He leaned across the desk to give it to her, and realized he felt relaxed. It was much easier to be in Ruby's company these days. She'd been so busy keeping Veronique alive that she had apparently put aside her pursuit of him. He hoped she'd never again take him up for sport.

"Thanks." She took a solid pull and released the smoke in tight little circles.

Roman lounged against the side of the desk and lifted his cigar.

"So what are you going to do?" Ruby asked.

"About Vee?"

"What else?"

"Nothing."

"What do you mean, nothing?" She took a draught of the cigar and squinted at him.

"I never should have involved her in our lives. Now is my chance to rectify that mistake." Roman focused his attention on the burning cigar between his fingers. "I never should have seduced her, and by some miracle I have been given the chance to make up for that transgression."

"You have to be joking." Ruby swung her leg off the arm of the chair.

"I'm not. My initial intent with Veronique was to keep her safe and keep her innocent. I've been given the chance to return to that agenda. And I will."

"You aren't going to tell her about you and her?"

"No. I have decided to find her a position in Dundonnon. I hear there's a thriving colony over there now. She can make a life for herself there."

"Without you."

"Yes." Roman flipped his hand at the window behind him. "She wouldn't miss me for a moment."

"But you would miss her."

Roman nodded.

Ruby frowned. "I can't see why you are doing this, not after what you two have been through."

"Because it is for the best. She should have a new life, Ruby. I will carve one out for her, as I should have done months ago. She deserves the best possible life I can give to her."

"She deserves *you*, Roman."

Roman flushed and shot a quick glance at Ruby. He couldn't believe his ears.

Ruby smiled and shook her head. "Shocked?" She looked at him from the side. Gone was her sly, come-hither expression. Instead he saw cocky friendliness flashing in her eyes.

"I never thought I'd hear you say such a thing."

"Neither did I." Ruby tipped the ash off her cigar. "But the truth is, Roman, that Vee wasn't the only one to change on that ride through the Northern Lights."

"I've noticed."

Ruby swallowed and raised her gaze to the figure in the moonlight. "She showed me what courage looks like. And hope. And sacrifice. And...and what real love is all about." She sighed. "I hated her, Roman. I'll be the first to admit it. But on the trip, I changed my mind." She paused and looked up at the ceiling. "She made me go through the lights. She made me test myself—really test myself. And you know what?"

Roman raised an eyebrow.

"I made it through. And now I know that I am a lot stronger than I thought I was."

"Sometimes it takes a crisis to find such a thing out."

Ruby nodded and looked thoughtful. Roman marveled at the change in her. "These past few weeks, being up here in the wild, I've discovered something else about myself."

"Oh?"

"All the time that I wanted to be with you? I think it's because I was terrified of being alone. You were so strong, so solid, and so accomplished—I was desperate to be part of your world, even if I didn't belong there."

Roman puffed his cigar, uncomfortable with her confession but listening nevertheless.

"I realize now that I was attracted to you as a father figure."

"Good God," Roman rolled his eyes.

"Not that you are *that* old. And you *are* somewhat attractive."

"Somewhat?" He glared at her through a puff of smoke, hoping she would see that he was teasing her.

"But I see now that I need to be with someone more..." She frowned, searching for the right word. "More fun."

"Fun?" Roman snorted. "You're saying I'm not fun?"

"You are far too serious for a girl like me." Ruby waved the air in front of her. "With your whiskey and music and your stuffy old books and such. I could never put up with those for long—especially if you wanted to talk about them for hours on end."

"Are you saying what I think you're saying?" Roman felt a flutter of relief take wing in his chest. "Are you breaking our engagement?"

"Yes." She sighed and looked up at him. "It never would have worked out."

"No," he smiled at her gently. For the first time since he'd met Ruby, he believed they could be friends. "It never would have, Ruby."

"So you're free to have the life you want."

"If only it was that easy." Roman shook his head and gazed down at the tips of his boots.

"You have to make it happen, Roman." Ruby stood up. "That woman out there loves you."

"Maybe once."

"Deep down she still does. She has to."

"That's taking a leap of faith."

"She risked her life for you, dammit!" Ruby jabbed her spent cigar at him. "She didn't give up on you so easily!"

Roman flushed.

"She would never want to be with anyone else. I know it!"

"She never told *me* as much."

"When would she have had the chance?" Ruby closed her eyes and shook her head. "Believe me, I know love when I see it, Roman. And she loves you."

"She's Gabriel's daughter. It's wrong. She is far too young."

"No, she isn't. She has lived an unusual life, Roman. She is far older than her years. Even I know that."

Ruby's conviction warmed him, but he couldn't share her sentiment. He hadn't been privy to Veronique's actions in the coach.

All he knew was that she had saved his life. He was grateful, but she might have done the same for reasons other than love. He wasn't about to base his behavior on The World According to Ruby Valentine—no matter if she had turned over a new leaf or not.

"So don't go sending her off to some colony, Roman."

He sighed. "But it may take forever for her to warm up to me, if she ever does."

"Time is what you have plenty of, my dear." She winked at him. "Unless the virus interferes."

He nodded and crossed his arms over his chest. "Unless," he mused, suddenly thinking of something that hadn't occurred to him until this very moment. He couldn't believe what a complete fool he could be.

"Unless what?"

"I could get through to her. Get through that wall she's built around herself."

Ruby put out her cigar in a dish on his desk. "How?"

"There is one thing I know that Veronique cannot resist."

"And that is?"

Roman would have liked to think that *he* was that one thing. But he knew what Vee loved above all else.

Chapter 32

VERONIQUE PAUSED AT the south tower.

There, floating on the chill of the evening, she thought she heard the faint sound of a piano. She turned, cocked her head to one side, and listened. It had to be Roman playing, but she was surprised that a piano existed in the castle.

She pulled the shawl around her shoulders and ran the tip of her tongue over the ridge of her teeth for the hundredth time—checking, always checking. Since waking up from what Roman had called her "restoration," she constantly assessed herself. She knew she had changed, but she couldn't qualify exactly how she *had* changed.

Sometimes her teeth felt longer and sharper. Sometimes she felt the urge to jump off the parapet—not to destroy herself, but simply to leap into the glorious space above the sea and enjoy the freedom she sensed she would find there. Sometimes, when Citizen Scott came to clean and leaned over to mop the floors, Veronique thought she could hear the woman's heart beating. Worse, the sound made her feel so uncomfortable and brought such unnatural inclinations to mind that Veronique had to leave the room.

She was going mad. She was conscious of blanks in her recent memory and haunted by the feeling that she had forgotten essential chunks of information about Roman and Ruby. She could remember escaping from the cell under the Central Compound. But everything after that was a blur.

Something was wrong with her, and she worried that her condition would only get worse.

But she couldn't tell anyone. If she were going mad, she would be taken away. She would be sent to the Norsea work camps, and never allowed to see anyone she cared about again. Even though she had lost part of her recent memory, she had a sense that there were people she cared about. Maybe even loved—if only she could remember.

Ruby and Roman had been so patient with her. She was grateful for their hospitality and concern, but the time had come to quit imposing on Roman. Invalids were not countenanced for long. Someone at the castle was surely keeping track of her idleness, ready to report her shortcomings to a commissioner. Every day that she wasn't in control of her faculties and didn't do her fair share of work was a day that she could be taken away by the Overseers. She had to get well. Or she had to leave.

The music of the piano swirled around her. Veronique closed her eyes and listened intently. There, that passage seemed familiar. Hope leapt inside her. She flowed toward the door that opened onto the tower staircase, hardly aware of her feet touching the flagstones. She was eager to hear more and focused all her senses on the tinkling notes coming from below. As she moved toward the door, her heart surged in her chest and her head swirled with color.

Overwhelmed by sensation, she had to brace herself for a moment with one hand on the wood panel of the door, while relief and joy washed over her. She knew this piece. It was a Chopin piano concerto called Romance Larghetto.

Maybe if she could recall the song in its entirety, she might remember everything about Roman. For the first time since she'd awakened, she felt a sense of hope.

Humming along with the melody, Veronique hurried down the stone steps, anxious to get closer to the music and the master hand that produced such perfection from the keys.

Veronique wound through the stairways and halls of the castle, following the music, until she came upon a room just off the great hall. She had never been in the chamber before, as the door had always been closed. But tonight, the portal stood partially open, beckoning to her. She stepped though the half-open door into the small chamber.

The walls were lined with books, and a red Persian carpet lay over the stone floor. Beneath the narrow window sat a settee and two chairs, and to the right, lit by a brace of candles as thick as her arm, was a tall brown piano, an upright grand. And sitting at the keyboard, intent on what he played, was Roman Brandt.

With the music spilling into her heart, Veronique paused in the doorway to listen. But as she stood there, she realized she was not so much listening to the melody as she was staring at the musician, entranced. There was something about him—something that drew her like a moth to lamplight.

She had fought the urge to reach out to him ever since she had awakened from her restoration sleep, as Roman made a point of keeping her at a distance. She could not recall what had happened to make him avoid her. Had she hurt him in some way? Offended him? She hoped she would remember soon, before she left, so she could make amends, as he had been nothing but kind to her.

She watched him play. His wide shoulders dwarfed the keyboard in front of him, and the ends of his dark brown hair trembled as he attacked the keys. He was so intent on what he played that she doubted he realized that she had come into the room.

The candlelight glinted off his glossy hair, danced along the planes of his rugged face and disappeared in the luxurious pile of his velvet evening coat. She stared at his muscular back and powerful arms—down to the snowy white cuffs of his shirt. And then she saw his hands.

Roman always wore gloves. But to play the piano, he had removed the fine leather gloves and placed them upon the piano bench beside him. Veronique glanced at the castoff articles for only a second and then turned her attention back to his hands—his poor, broken hands that could play so exquisitely. Something twisted in her breast. Not pity. Something much stronger: a memory that began as a sharp ache and then blossomed into a vivid recollection. She had kissed those fingers once.

The sight of his hands brought on a rush of visions. She remembered eating with Roman, playing music with him. She could remember kissing Roman's hands and kissing him as well, but most of all, aching to make love to him. Her heart swelled with longing so great that she gasped.

The music cut off. Roman turned to look over his shoulder.

"Roman?" she began, not knowing where to start. So many emotions tumbled inside her that she couldn't form a coherent sentence.

"Veronique." Roman stood up, his face dark with worry. "Are you unwell again?"

"No." She shot a trembling smile at him and leaned against the doorway for support. She thought she might collapse from the onslaught of memories surging through her. She remembered being in this man's arms, caressing him and pushing her fingers into his shining hair.

"The music." She raised a shaking hand and pointed at the piano. "It has helped me remember."

"As I hoped it would." Roman smiled and took a step toward her. "What are you remembering?"

"I remember you."

Slowly, his eyebrows rose. "And what do you remember about me?"

"That I—" She broke off. How fair would it be to Roman if there was something wrong with her, and she burdened him with her failing mental health? If he loved her, as she hoped he did, then he would be honor bound to take care of her. That was the type of man he was. She knew that much about him.

"I remember that you and I once played music together."

The light in his eyes flickered. Was he disappointed? Relieved? She couldn't read him. "Yes, we did."

"I remembered how I enjoyed it."

"Then come," he swept the air behind him. "Do so again. Sit."

She walked to the bench, conscious of each step she took upon the blood-red carpet and conscious of his regard on her back as she slipped onto the bench. His cologne, a mixture of sage and pine, hung in the air, haunting her. When he sat down beside her, she held her breath, unsure whether she would be able to bear the closeness of his body without breaking down and flinging her arms around him.

As he settled upon the piano bench, she closed her eyes and concentrated on subduing her racing heart. Now was not the time to succumb to schoolgirl fantasies. Now was the time to act like the woman she had become and do the best she could for the man she was certain she loved.

Veronique felt him take her left hand in both of his. "You're freezing," he remarked.

"Yes." She knew she was freezing. Since she had awakened, she had noticed how chilly her hands and feet were—but only on the surface. She didn't feel cold on the inside. It was if her madness kept her core warm while her outer self slowly turned to marble.

"And I—I—" she stammered, pulling at her hand even though she longed for Roman to hold her close. "I don't think I can play. I shouldn't be here."

"Why?" He squeezed her fingers. "What are you remembering, Veronique?"

"It's not so much what I remember." The black and white keys swam before her eyes. "It is what I know I must do."

"And what is that?"

"Leave."

His grip tightened. "What?"

"Leave." She raised her eyes to glance at him. "I have overstayed my welcome."

"Nonsense."

"You have been so kind to me, Roman. I will never be able to repay you."

"I don't expect to be paid. I don't *want* to be paid."

"This is a mistake!" She wrenched free of his grip and stood up. He followed with remarkable speed and stood in front of her, blocking her exit.

"I shouldn't have come down here."

"I wanted you to come down." His voice grated with emotion. "I want you to remember, Vee. Everything. Everything we were to each other. And you have, haven't you?"

She glanced up at his serious eyes. "Yes."

"Then how can you stand there like that, so cold, so aloof?"

"To protect you." She swallowed and turned to step away, but he caught her elbow.

"From what?" he demanded.

"From me."

For a long moment, he studied her face, his dark brows drawn together in a scowl. And then his expression eased. "What are you talking about?" His grip relaxed, but he did not let her go. Instead, he reached for her other elbow and urged her around until she was forced to face him. The nearness of his chest made her suck in her breath and overwhelmed her with desire. "How could you possibly hurt me?"

"I don't know!" she retorted, frustrated and confused. "There's something wrong with me. I don't know what it is."

"What are you talking about?" His clear gaze swept over her.

"I'm changing. And not for the better."

"Vee!" He squeezed the tops of her arms. "Look at me."

She looked at him, unable to refuse the command.

"Tell me. You can trust me. You know you can trust me." He leaned closer. "Whatever is wrong, just tell me. We can work it out. Together. I promise, I will not think any differently of you than I do right now."

She looked into his clear gray eyes—his serious and strangely compelling gray eyes, and her heart flopped in her chest. If she told him what she feared was true, he would realize she was stark raving mad.

"Whatever it is, Vee," he added. "We can deal with it."

"I don't think so." She shook her head and looked down, determined to pull out of his grip. But again,, he moved too quickly for her. Instead of breaking away from him, she found herself being drawn into a powerful embrace that she could not—and did not want to—resist.

"Veronique," he whispered into her hair. His large hands cupped her shoulder blades, urging her closer. "No matter who you are or what you are, I will never turn away from you. Never."

"No matter what I am?" She clung to him, overcome by the strength of his arms and the solidness of his chest. She buried her nose in his cravat and wrapped her arms around his neck, hoping that he would never let her go. His embrace was everything she needed to heal her soul completely and forever.

"No matter what," he said at last.

How could she live without the heaven of Roman's arms? And yet if she told him the truth about herself, she knew his embrace would fall away, no matter how vehemently he had vowed to stand by her. She would be a fool to admit to her suspicions and take the chance of losing him. And yet, she could not stand another minute locked in the private hell in which she'd been living the past few weeks. She had to tell someone.

"Trust me, Veronique." His breath fanned over her ear. "Come back to me."

His words sent a thrill through her. She longed to return to him. With all her heart and soul, she longed to fight her way back. But to come back, she had to confess her fears. Steeling herself for the biggest disappointment of her life, she took a deep breath. "Something has happened to me." She swallowed and broke off, not sure how to continue.

He stroked her hair and waited for her to find the words to express herself. His quiet patience gave her the strength to go on.

"When I was ill. Or before. I don't know."

She could feel his head tip against the side of her hair as he slowly nodded.

"It's going to sound crazy, what I'm going to say." She swallowed again and licked her lips, which had suddenly gone dry.

"Go on." His voice rumbled in his chest.

"You will probably turn me out when you hear what I have to say."

"I'm not going to turn you out."

She pressed her nose into the cloth at his neck and shut her eyes tight, wishing she could be anywhere else but here, struggling to explain herself to Roman—and yet there was nowhere else she would rather be than in his arms. She stood silent for a moment, drinking him in and branding the sensation of him onto her thoughts. She might never know such perfect closeness again.

"Roman, I..."

He kissed the lobe of her ear, and just like that, his lips released her confession.

"Roman, I think I'm turning into a vampire."

Roman froze.

Her worst fears were realized when he pulled back and stared at her.

"What?" he demanded.

"My teeth change sometimes," she blurted out, now that her madness had been revealed. "At night. And I have the strangest compulsions. I wear this shawl, but I'm not really cold. Ever." She might as well tell him everything. By the shocked expression on his face, she knew she had lost him, just as she had known she would. "Sometimes I want to jump off the ramparts, as if I could fly. Like I know I could fly. I've lost my appetite for food. And sometimes, I feel as if I will absolutely burst!"

Roman stared at her, his light eyes sparking with disbelief. His glance swept over her, from her hairline to her toes and back again. Then he reached for her hand and lifted her fingers toward the candles burning on the piano.

"Your nails," he said, holding them to the light.

"Yes. They're strange, aren't they?" She stared at the iridescent color glinting in the darkness. "What does it mean? Am I going crazy?"

"Oh, Vee!" He turned and drew both her hands to his mouth. He kissed the tips of her fingers and then gazed down at her.

To Veronique's immense relief, he didn't push her away. In fact, she thought she saw a sparkle of relief in his eyes.

"That is the best news I've heard in years," he remarked, grinning. "Centuries, even."

"You aren't shocked?"

"Not at all. Good God, I never expected this, at least not so soon!" He tipped his head back and laughed. The sound bounced off the stone walls and spiraled into Veronique's heart, lifting her spirits considerably.

"Aren't you concerned about my state of mind?" She searched his face for clues to explain why he found her confession so amusing. "I just told you that I think I'm turning into a vampire."

"Yes." His eyes danced as he grasped both sides of her face in his hands and planted a joyful kiss on her lips. "I heard you, Vee."

She pulled back. "And you aren't bothered by that?"

"Not in the least."

"You believe in such creatures?"

"In fact, I do."

Veronique stared at him, utterly perplexed, her brows knitted together. "You do?"

He nodded. "Your father was a vampire, your mother a human. I didn't think you would ever cross over."

She blinked, amazed at his blasé reaction. "You don't think I'm a freak then?"

"Not at all," he grinned. "On the contrary, I am relieved to hear that we now have much more in common than a love of music."

It took a moment for the meaning of his words to sink in. Veronique's jaw went slack with shock.

"Yes, Veronique." Roman stroked her cheekbones with the pads of his thumbs. "I am exactly what you are thinking."

"A vampire?"

"Yes. I am surprised you did not remember that about me."

"No." Her voice trailed off. "I didn't."

"As is Ruby."

"I guess after everything that went on in Londo, maybe my mind couldn't handle the shock."

"Can you handle it now?"

"Yes." She swallowed and gazed up at him, deciding to trust in the moment and trust this man.

"Because I am more than just a vampire." His voice lowered to a soft baritone. "I am the man who has waited lifetimes to find you,

Veronique. I am the man who claimed not to believe in soul mates but who actually does. And I am the man who loves you."

"You love me?" she repeated, dazed by the sound of the phrase. Though she had lost part of her memory, she was certain no one had ever said they loved her.

He loved her. She mattered to someone. She was not alone.

"All this time," she whispered. "Why didn't you tell me that we loved each other?"

"Because I had no idea how you felt about me."

"I never told you?" She couldn't believe she had been able to withhold the way she felt about Roman. Her love for him was like a ball of shimmering delight that threatened to leap out of her chest.

"No." His laughing eyes sobered. "And I wasn't going to make the same mistake."

"What mistake?"

"Of directing your life in the way I thought it should be lived."

"You did that?"

He nodded and frowned. "I thought I knew what was best for you. I didn't tell you everything—about your family or even about me. Don't you remember how upset you were with me for doing that?"

"I confess I don't."

"Good." He smiled, and his craggy face transformed with happiness. "I made the mistake of assuming you couldn't handle the truth. I didn't realize that you could handle anything. Anything that came your way."

She stared at him, struck mute by his praise.

"I will never be that foolish again, Veronique. You are Gabriel's daughter—unlike any woman on Earth. You will forge your own life your own way—and I, for one, am looking forward to seeing what you make of it."

He kissed her again, closing his glittering eyes as he bent to her lips. She kissed him back, as her world expanded beyond anything she had ever imagined. This strong, talented man loved her, respected her and obviously wanted her as much as she wanted him. She couldn't be more blessed. Tears of gratefulness and hope welled in her eyes.

After a long moment, Roman straightened and slowly disengaged from her mouth while still cradling her head in his hands. "I once thought that I had seen everything, done everything. I was so weary of life. But then you came along."

"And?" she looked up, consumed by his warm gaze. She felt herself melting into the clear depths of his eyes.

"And now it seems my life has just begun."

Epilogue

DECEMBER 18, 2525

Joanna woke up to the smell of stale wine breath wafting over her face.

"Wake up, citizen," the nurse slurred. "Time to clear out."

Joanna blinked the sleep from her eyes and sat up. The nurse flipped the coverlet halfway down Joanna's body and reached for her wrist. With a cruel tug, she ripped away the tape that secured a tube into the back of Joanna's hand. Then she pulled out the glass device that had been part of the medication line running into her hand.

"What are you doing?" Joanna gasped. "What's going on?"

"Seems my boss has been killed. I don't have a job."

"Killed?"

"That means no more cushy private nurse for you."

Cushy? Joanna fought to hide her disdain. Being held prisoner in a bed and force-fed with tubes was not her idea of cushy. But if the nurse was thinking of freeing her, she didn't want to antagonize the woman. She kept her mouth shut.

The woman untied Joanna's hospital gown with a couple of impatient yanks. "I only found out because I didn't get paid. The bastards."

She ripped away the feeding tube.

"They would have let me go on here, taking care of *you* forever, if I hadn't raised a fuss."

All sleepiness vanished as Joanna steeled her body for an assault by the nurse or the opportunity to attack the woman. Though her human body was weak because of her long illness, her vampire strength might kick in and be enough to overwhelm the nurse. She brought her knees together, ready to strike her a second time.

"You're leaving?" Joanna asked.

"You bet I am. There's a train at noon. I don't know why it comes to this dump anymore. But it still does. And I'm going to be on it." The nurse continued to unhook tubes. "I will miss the wine I found here, though. Tasty stuff."

"What about me?" Joanna inquired, hoping to keep the woman talking and distracted. She wiggled out of the coverlet, using her feet to pool the blankets at the bottom of the bed.

The nurse took a moment to glance at her face. "You?"

"Yes. Me."

"I couldn't care less what *you* do. If they don't pay me, I don't need to bother about their precious prisoner."

The nurse tossed the last tube to the floor and planted her fists on her large hips. "There. My work here is done."

"What about these?" Joanna held up her manacled wrists.

"What about them?" The woman glared at her. "You aren't in my good graces, citizen. Not after that kick the other day."

The nurse turned on her heel and headed for the door.

Alarm spiked through Joanna. If the nurse left her shackled to the bed, she would starve to death.

"Please!" Joanna cried. "At least leave the key."

"All right." The nurse fumbled in her apron, held up her keys and dropped them in the middle of the room. "There you go, Citizen Wilder. Have fun now."

Joanna watched the woman hobble away and slam the door. The nurse had left her to die. She sank back, defeated. She could never reach the keys. They were at least twenty feet away, glinting in the weak December sun. She fought back a sob of despair.

"Think, Joanna, think," she muttered. "Crying never helps. Thinking does."

She forced herself to calm down instead of succumbing to panic. She was strong. She knew she had more strength than a mortal man. A man could move a heavy piece of furniture, couldn't he? Easily. If she could get out of the bed, she could drag the hospital cot across the room *to* the keys.

She dropped her legs over the side of the mattress. Her feet landed on the cold planks of the bedroom. For a moment, she stood there, bent over the pillow, one arm extended to the far manacle. She allowed her trembling legs to grow accustomed to bearing her weight again. Then, with quaking muscles, she pulled one corner of the bed, rotating the frame until she stood on the other side of the headboard, like a carthorse.

"You've got this, Joanna Wilder," she said out loud. She took a step backward, tensed her trembling muscles, and dragged the cot across a plank. Her muscles shook so hard with the effort, she thought she would collapse. But she kept on. She had no alternative. She focused on the keys behind her, gleaming in the sun now, beaconing to her. Her only hope.

Picking up the keys with her toes was going to be tricky. Getting the keys from her toes to her mouth was going to be even trickier. But she would do it. Somehow, she would do it.

TWO HOURS LATER, JOANNA trudged across the sand of the hidden cove at Port Pennwood, dressed in clothes that no longer fit her emaciated body. A bitter wind raged through her cloak and hair. She clutched the garment at her throat and continued, head down, plodding through the sand. Her feet felt like blocks of stone and her heart pounded in her ears, warning her that she was overtaxing her physical reserves. But she pressed on.

Gabriel.

The recurring tunnel dream had to mean something. It just had to. The dream was now her lifeline—the only goal she had. Maybe Gabriel had contacted her from beyond the grave. She had to know if her dream was a real message or just a mirage. She had to know if he were dead.

If he were dead, she would lose her mind. But she couldn't allow her thoughts to venture down that dark path. She had to concentrate on putting one foot in front of the other and get to the smugglers' tunnel.

Darkness fell over the moor in a black flood while a band of orange sank ever lower into the sea. She turned up the beach and slogged toward the cliff where she and Tam had once huddled together after the fire at the inn.

As she approached, she scanned the base of the cliff. Her memory was razor sharp now. She could remember the rock formation that concealed the opening of the tunnel. She could remember spotting Gabriel galloping toward her on a horse so long ago.

Gabriel.

Tears clogged her throat at the memory of that day. That was the day he had told her he loved her. How she remembered that day. Each and every word. The sound of his voice. The kind lights in his eyes. His sincere, wonderful eyes.

And Veronique. Their little girl. What had become of her?

Ten years. She had lost ten whole years. Her daughter would be a young woman now—if she had survived.

Joanna's throat clenched. Gabriel and Veronique could not be dead. No. She would not accept the idea. She would find them. Both of them—if it was the last thing she did.

Not dead. Not dead. Alive!

The fervent chant echoed in her mind as she skirted the rocks and found the tunnel.

A dark shape lay prone inside the opening, unmoving, just like in her dream. Joanna sucked in a breath.

"Gabriel?"

Panting, she dashed into the tunnel and knelt in the sand beside the body. She put a hand on his shoulder. He was as emaciated as she was and hard as stone. He lay face down, his head to one side, with his burnished hair falling over his features.

"Gabriel?" She reached for the hand that lay outstretched on the sand. His flesh was brown, the color of polished walnut. Her heart sank at the sight. But she bent to the back of his hand and kissed it anyway. His flesh felt as hard as wood. Was he dead? Had he turned to stone here, like a piece of petrified wood?

"Oh, Gabriel!"

She brushed back his hair to inspect his face. His eyes were closed, and his mouth was slightly open. Though his face was the same brown color as his hand, his flesh was in perfect condition. If he had died, wouldn't he have decomposed in some way?

Yet, Gabriel was a vampire. She had no idea what happened to vampires when they died. She'd only seen them dissolving to ash or vanishing after having their hearts pierced.

"Oh, my love," she murmured. She caressed his cold, oddly solid cheek. "What happened to you?"

She sat back on her haunches and gazed at him, hanging on to the last shreds of hope while her heart wept for her ruined lover. He must have come looking for her. Moray or his henchmen must have attacked him and left him for dead. How long had Gabriel been lying here on the sand? And was he beyond help?

If he were dead, there was nothing she could do. But if, by chance, he still lived in some kind of fugue vampire state, she had to help him.

"Think, Joanna, think."

What had Gabriel done when she nearly died in the Londo City riot? He had given her blood. His blood. How had he done it?

"Think, Joanna, think. Remember."

She commanded her thoughts to return to the night Gabriel had changed her human life forever. The memory rushed at her in a blur of visions and sensations. He had brought her back from the brink of death by piercing his chest and urging her to drink. The taste of him had been the most exhilarating experience of her life, beyond anything she could dream. Love and awe at the memory swelled in her chest.

She knew what to do.

With shaking hands, she untied her cloak and let if fall. Then she unbuttoned her vest, shirtwaist and chemise.

Without a second thought, she dragged her index finger between her breasts. Her nail was surprisingly sharp, as if it had transformed at her mental command. A dark line appeared on her white chest, oozing with droplets of blood.

She nestled in the sand beside Gabriel, as if preparing to suckle a child, and gently pressed his head between her breasts.

"Take me into you," she whispered, recalling every word Gabriel had said to her so many years ago. "Take me into you, Gabriel. And live."

Love for him burst from her heart and up her throat in a surge of ecstasy so great, she thought she would turn inside out. A ball of golden light surrounded them, fired by the energy roaring from the center of her being.

After a few moments, she felt his mouth move against her, like the flutter of wings on her skin. Joy rocketed through her.

"Gabriel!" She embraced him and closed her eyes and melted with utter bliss as her spirit subsumed into his.

Gabriel would live. She was sure of it now. He would heal and come back to her. And together, when he was able to walk the earth again, they would find their daughter.

"Veronique," she whispered into Gabriel's hair. "We are coming, my dearest little one. We are coming, Nica. We will find you."

The End

If you liked this story,
please consider leaving a review.

Veronique's Music

Chopin: Number 1 in B Flat, Opus 9
Debussy: Arabesque I
Bartok: Piano Sonata
Chopin: Etude, Opus 10, Number 3 in E Major
Dvorak: New World Symphony
Mendelssohn: Heilig
Chopin: Piano Concerto No. 1 in E Minor, Op. 11: II. Romance
(Larghetto)

More Books

Whisper of Midnight
The Legacy
Raven in Amber
Lord of Forever
The Haunting of Brier Rose
Night Orchid
Black Panther Series | Lord of the Nile
Black Panther Series | Lost Goddess
Mystic Moon
Just Before Midnight
Jade
The Forbidden Tarot | The Dark Lord
The Forbidden Tarot | The Dark Horse
The Forbidden Tarot | The Last Oracle
Spellbound
Imposter Bride
Death in Amsterdam
The Londo Chronicles | Marriage Machine (Novella)
The Londo Chronicles | Apothecary
The Londo Chronicles | Phoenix
The Londo Chronicles | Prodigy

Visit Patricia Simpson's Website
www.patriciasimpson.com[1]

1. *http://www.patriciasimpson.com*

Don't miss out!

Visit the website below and you can sign up to receive emails whenever Patricia Simpson publishes a new book. There's no charge and no obligation.

https://books2read.com/r/B-A-EZJM-WTNJB

BOOKS 2 READ

Connecting independent readers to independent writers.

About the Author

Patricia Simpson is a bestselling writer from the Bay Area of California. She has won numerous awards, including multiple Reviewer's Choice Awards from Romantic Times as well as a Career Achievement Award. One of her more recent novels, SPELLBOUND, was nominated Best Indie Paranormal of the Year. After a long career with TOR, Silhouette and HarperMonogram, Patricia is now enjoying creative freedom as an indie author.

Read more at https://patriciasimpson.com.